He concentrated only on the steps. And on the woman in his arms.

This dance was more than slightly risqué in the eyes of society, he knew—and to perform it with an unmarried virgin of Lily's class was nothing short of scandalous.

He wanted to kiss her. In fact he could not remember ever wanting anything so clearly, so intensely, as he wanted this now.

He wanted to forget the vow he had made to protect her. He wanted to take her up to his room, pull the emeralds from their leather case, put them around her smooth white neck and undress her so she was wearing nothing else.

He wanted to lose himself in her. To forget what he was and be with her what he might have been had he never gone to war.

For a moment he stood, mouth inches from hers, and they swayed together as if dancing still, pulled in towards one another, her gaze locked with his. All he could hear was her breathing, somehow soft and harsh all at the same time, threaded raggedly within and around his, in time with the pulse that throbbed faintly, sensuously, in the hollow at the base of her throat.

Daniel took his hands off her before he did something he knew they would both regret...

Author Note

It's been a while since my last book, but I knew that I was not yet ready to say goodbye to the Westhaven family—so I was excited at the chance to revisit Oakridge.

A generation has passed since a highwayman met his match in THE ROGUE'S KISS, and now it is his son, Daniel, who lives alone within Oakridge's imposing walls, recently returned from war with his life and hopes for the future in pieces. This is his story, and that of Liliana, the woman he is honour-bound to protect—whether she likes it or not!

I hope you take as much pleasure in reading MAJOR WESTHAVEN'S UNWILLING WARD as I did in writing it!

Do e-mail me at emilybascom@live.co.uk—or come and visit me on Facebook—to let me know what you think!

MAJOR WESTHAVEN'S UNWILLING WARD

Emily Bascom

MILLS & BOON

First published in Great Britain 2010
Harlequin Mills & Boon Limited,
Eton House, 18-24 Paradise Road, Richmond, Surrey TW9 1SR

© Emily Bascom 2009

ISBN: 978 0 263 21453 6

are natural,
/ood grown in
process conform
/ of origin.

Printed and bound in Great Britain
by CPI Antony Rowe, Chippenham, Wiltshire

Emily Bascom lives in London with her boyfriend, a sunflower, and a dog named Giles. She has a degree in English and Drama from Royal Holloway University, London. In her quest to find a real job she has been a milk(wo)man, a charity fundraiser and a station assistant on the London Underground—all of which she loved. She craves olives, hates cricket, and dreams of retiring to Uganda.

A previous novel by Emily Bascom:

THE ROGUE'S KISS

*To Errol, who picked himself up
and learned to walk again.
I will love you all my life.*

Prologue

South Carolina, America—April 1781

Major Daniel Westhaven knew he was dying from the moment he opened his eyes.

He was lying on muddy grass, still on the battlefield, the air around him filled with smoke, the stench of burning flesh—and the cries of his men. As he blinked, he became aware of the pain coursing through his lower body, robbing him of breath, making him so dizzy he thought he would pass out again.

He took a deep breath and tried to take stock.

The ground beneath him was wet, his breeches similarly sodden. When he put out a hand to explore this wetness he found it was blood. His blood. Panic ran in quicksilver streams through his limbs.

Focus on something else...

His men.

Turning his head, he could see his second-in-command lying motionless beside him, face ashen, eyes tightly closed. 'Pevensey?'

There was a low groan and, slowly, Captain Robert Pevensey opened his eyes. 'Daniel?' A hand, caked in blood, reached out and, after fumbling in his direction, grabbed his arm.

'It's me, Robbie.'

Fear showed clear on the man's blanched white face. 'I can't see!'

There was a large wound in the younger man's chest and blood matted in the hair and long grass at the back of his head. From what Daniel could see, Robbie had not long to live, either.

Daniel was growing ever more dizzy, but he managed to disengage the hand that gripped him, taking the cold fingers of his friend tightly in his own.

'You'll be fine,' he said thickly. 'Try to sleep a little.'

'You're a damned dreadful liar.' The voice was weak, but there was a wry smile in it. 'What state are you in?'

'Not too bad.'

'I hope to God that's true, at least.' Robbie's eyes closed slowly.

Daniel squeezed his fingers, but he was no longer sure the younger man could feel him. 'Pevensey?'

'Wait.' Withdrawing his hand, Pevensey reached into his jacket and pulled something out—a miniature in an oval frame, Daniel realised, as it was handed across to him. 'Where are you?'

'I'm here.' Daniel, with some effort, took it and squinted at the tiny likeness, exquisitely detailed. Green eyes stared back at him, flowing honey-blonde hair and a sweetly smiling mouth. 'Who's this? Your sweetheart?'

'Lily. My sister, you remember.'

How could he have forgotten? Daniel cursed his befuddled brain. He had seen this painting before, six months ago, during the most serious conversation of his life—and he knew with a dreadful sinking feeling what was coming next.

'Daniel?' The other man's breath was coming in gasps now. 'I need to ask you…'

Alarmed by the way the colour was draining from his friend's face, Daniel touched his arm and attempted to sound authoritative. 'Save your strength, Captain. There'll be time enough later.'

With an effort, Robbie shook his head. 'Please. Listen to me.'

His friend knew he was dying, that much was obvious. Daniel frowned, trying to concentrate, though his own mind felt increasingly fuzzy. 'Go on.'

'Remember…what I asked you?'

'I remember.'

'You still have the…' Robbie groaned, eyes closing momentarily.

'I still have the papers, yes. Of course.'

'You…are the best man I know. She will need a guardian. Please, promise me you will do as you said and care for her—watch over her. Find her…a husband. It pains me to ask…but I am all she has, and without me…'

Daniel hesitated. He knew he would never make it back to London. This sister of Robbie's would be alone in the world regardless of what he had said six months ago, and it was no longer in his power to prevent it… However, the belief that she would be helped was important to this man, among the most loyal of his officers but—more importantly—among the best of his friends. And God knew he would do it if he was able.

'Daniel?' The face that turned towards him held all manner of pain, sightless eyes wide and panicked. 'Are you there?'

'I'm here,' he said again. 'I promised you, and I'll not go back on that promise. I'll see that your sister is provided for.'

A long sigh escaped Robbie's pale lips. 'God bless you.'

'She is fortunate to have such a brother.'

'And…' A grimace of pain crossed the young man's face. 'I am fortunate to have a friend such as you…to…' He bit down on a moan of agony. 'Just…tell her…I died well…will you?'

'I'll tell her.' He shoved the miniature into his jacket and found his captain's hand once more. 'You've served bravely and well. Better than most. She will hear of it, I promise.'

'Thank you, my friend. Now, just—'

'Robbie.' As his own pain gnawed more intensely, Daniel was struggling to maintain his focus. 'Rest.'

'Just…one more thing.'

'Name it.'

Green eyes turned to his face. 'It has been an honour fighting with you—but more so, knowing you. Your father will be…beside himself with pride.'

Daniel's throat closed. 'God go with you, my friend.'

Robbie's blood-caked lips parted in a radiant smile, even as his eyelids drifted shut. Then, where the space between them had been filled with his ragged breathing, there was nothing but silence.

The fingers in Daniel's grip went slack.

He closed his eyes and tried to force down the grief that welled up from within. He told himself it did not matter, this lie to a dying man. His soul was condemned at any rate, he was sure. But he would have liked to fulfil his promise…if only for the sake of this friendship, forged in a futile war.

A horrible cold was creeping over him now, seeping into his bones as the blood flowed from his body. He would be grateful to sleep a little, also… But just for a moment the image of a beautiful woman, all honeyed tresses and smiling green eyes, floated before him. Her full lips smiled at him, as soothing as they were sensuous, and Daniel thought they formed his name, just for a moment.

'Major!'

Very far above him, a voice penetrated the fog of exhaustion and pain. An Irish accent, urgent. His lieutenant was calling him.

Daniel knew as he slipped away from the pain, body slackening, that whatever it was, it was important no longer.

Chapter One

London, England—Spring 1782

'You call that kneadin', Miss Lily? We'll never make a kitchen hand out of you at this rate!'

Looking up from her work with strands of honey-blonde hair in her eyes, a smear of flour across her face, and laughter on her lips, Liliana Pevensey grimaced good-naturedly across the kitchen at her companion. Straightening her elbows, she pounded her fists into the dough anew.

'I found nothing to complain about in last week's loaf,' she retorted.

Josephine—ladies' maid, cook, housekeeper and, lately, companion to the lady of the house—rolled her eyes.

'Only because I rescued it at the last minute!'

Lily shook her head fondly at the younger girl. 'What would I do without you?'

It was said in jest, but true enough. It had been four years since her brother had been sent to fight for his country against the rebels in America. Four years since she had been taken in by her aged Aunt Hetty, and come to live here, in the middlemost of a row of cottages in Highgate. Yet it was only in these last three months—since the old lady had died—that Lily, alone in the world with a slowly dwindling income, had begun to know the maid who had laid out her clothes every morning.

Jo was resourceful and hard-working in equal measure, as well as ever ready to cheer up her young mistress. Lily, realising she would soon be unable to pay the household its wages, had gradually let the other servants go, expecting her maid to seek work in a more prestigious household. Yet Jo had stayed, uncomplainingly taking on further tasks as her wages ever dwindled, though Lily knew a ladies' maid of her talents could have found work anywhere.

She was also, Lily mused, her hands slowing on the dough as her carefree mood slipped away, about the only person in the world who knew her mistress's true circumstances.

Money had been tight since her brother Robbie had been killed in the war in America. He had always provided for them, ever since the death of their parents when Lily had been fifteen. The money they had been left had been enough to keep them going for a while, and Robbie had sent back most of his salary once he had joined the army. Lily had been provided for, indeed, and proud of her brother, in his smart red uniform, going off to quell the rebels.

Who could have known it would go so badly wrong—that he would be killed so shortly before Cornwallis surrendered, before the war was over and the British soldiers—those that were left—at last came home? Lily had been left reeling from a grief so all-encompassing that she did not remember with any clarity the weeks following the news of his death.

'Miss Lily?' Jo was at her elbow. 'I think that'll do.'

Lily smiled. 'I was dreaming.'

'Worrying, more like.' With a wry smile, Jo scooped up the dough and pressed it into a pan. 'Something will turn up, you'll see. It always does.' She brightened slightly. 'Just take your mysterious benefactor, fr'instance.'

'Hmm.' Lily crossed her arms, brow furrowing. 'I would feel more comfortable if I knew who he was.' The money had been coming regularly each month, since last summer. It was forwarded through her solicitor, and she could not for the life of her prevail upon the crusty old man to tell her who was behind it. 'A friend of your brother' was the only clue he professed himself 'at liberty' to give. In all honesty, the funds had been her lifeline these past few months, especially with the expenses for Aunt Hetty's funeral. But she hated being beholden to someone she had never met.

'Perhaps you could marry him,' Jo mused teasingly. 'He must be rich, surely.'

''T'would be hard, without first having met him,' Lily countered with a faint smile. 'Especially as—'

She broke off as the sound of the huge brass knocker against the front door echoed through the house.

Jo sighed dramatically. 'I'll just be a moment.'

She was back in no time, holding up a crisp white packet of paper. 'It was only a messenger, miss. With this for you.'

'A letter?' Lily held out her hand for it. 'How exciting—no one ever writes to me!' Her face fell somewhat upon seeing the seal. 'It's from Mr Morley.' Hastily, she wiped her hands on her apron and tore the packet open, revealing a single sheet of paper.

'The solicitor?' Jo made a face. 'Perhaps he's found some money hidden somewhere and he's sending it so we can all live happily ever… Miss Lily?'

Lily, face white, looked up from her hurried perusal. 'He says he regrets to inform me that Cousin Jack has returned from the Continent.'

'Your Aunt Hetty's boy?' Jo snorted. 'It never failed to confuddle me how such a sweet old lady could have such a gallivanting good-for-nothing for a son. God rest her soul,' Jo added belatedly, crossing herself.

Lily nodded dumbly, the kind but firm lines that her solicitor had written still burning in her mind.

Jo put her hands on her hips. 'Well—what of it? Are we expected to give him free board and welcome him with open arms?'

'Worse. She left the house to him,' Lily told her mournfully. 'Don't you remember, Jo? It was in her will. Now he is returned upon hearing of his mother's death, and he wants to sell it.'

'To fund more gadding about overseas, I don't doubt! His good mother—God rest her soul—has been in the grave these three months, and only now he comes?' Puffed up with outrage, Jo came closer. 'Miss Lily—what will you do?'

Lily shook her head, trying to calm the panic within her. 'I don't know.' She could cope with this as she had coped with everything else, surely. If she just thought a little, the solution would come to her... And yet her mind was a blank. There was no money, nothing to sell... There was no question of being able to afford to buy the house from her cousin.

'Your mystery benefactor? Could we ask him?'

Lily turned a worried face up to her maid. 'No—certainly not. Even if Mr Morley would tell me who he was, I cannot ask such a thing from a perfect stranger! It's bad enough that I must be reliant upon his charity as it is.' She bit her lip. 'Not that I'm not grateful... It's just...'

'I know, Miss Lily.' Jo pressed her hand. 'But don't you fret—there will be a solution. God never gives us more than we can take.'

Lily looked again at the letter, as if the answer was somehow hidden there. 'I am sure you are right.' But still she could not, for the life of her, think of anything.

'You'll have to ponder it later, miss,' Jo said tactfully. 'That is, if you're still going to the ball.'

With a gasp, Lily put a hand to her mouth. 'The ball—I'd quite forgot! What time is it?'

'Almost five.'

Lily's eyes widened. 'I shall never be ready by the time Lady Stanton's carriage calls!'

Untying her apron, she hurried from the room, leaving her maid, shaking her head indulgently, to follow.

'Does it truly look good enough, Jo?'

Examining herself in front of the mirror, Lily bit her lip for the hundredth time and frowned into her own deep green eyes.

She was wearing a gown she had made herself and that she was proud of, a far cry though it was from those in the windows of the fancy dressmakers of Bond Street. The cobalt-blue silk complemented her light colouring and its full sweeping skirts, gathered and padded at the back, served only to further emphasise her slender waist.

Her hair, the colour of honeycomb, was swept up on her head in an array of soft curls that cascaded downwards in ringlets, brushing her shoulders. She was pleased with the effect her maid had achieved, but still she worried. This ball, a week into her second Season, was important for her future. She needed to make an impression, now more than ever—and that meant hiding her true circumstances from the world.

'You look like any of them posh folks and more,' her maid told her with affection. ''Cept you've still got flour on your cheek.'

'Heavens—get it off!' Lily angled her head into the mirror. 'Where?'

'Let me.' Josephine deftly swept a hand over her mistress's smooth skin.

'Well, it is fashionable to be pale, I understand.' Lily met the maid's eye in the mirror and grinned. 'And I don't suppose any of the other ladies at Lady Langley's ball will have baked their own bread ready for tomorrow's breakfast.'

'That they won't.' Jo beamed back.

But the smile had already faded from her mistress's face as Lily turned her mind once more to the daunting task ahead of her. She must prepare herself, from today, for the action she had hoped never to take, reserved only for the direst circumstances.

Would that her brother were here to give her courage.

But then, Lily mused, if he was here she would be free to enjoy the Season like any other young woman, instead of living with the threat of bankruptcy and homelessness in her future. She pursed her lips. There was no use in wishing for what could not be—she had learned that lesson well, this last year in particular.

'You're thinking about Mr Robbie again, aren't you?' Jo said gently.

Thus prodded gently back into the present, Lily smiled at her. 'Is it so easy to tell?'

'He'd be proud to see how you've carried on, miss,' said the younger woman softly. 'How you're makin' a life for yourself.'

With a sigh, Lily looked at her glamorous reflection. 'Is that what I am doing? I thought I was going out to catch myself a husband.' She shook her head sadly. 'God knows I never thought I would find myself here, forced to seek a marriage for money.'

Since her parents had died in the fire that had destroyed their ancestral home six years ago, Robbie and Lily had been alone. Eight years her senior, he had seen her educated and provided for, whilst carving out a career for himself in the British Army, a career he loved second only to his younger sister. He had given her the freedom she craved, and, after his death, she had only been more determined to make her own decisions and remain self-sufficient.

All of which now made the thought of marriage to a stranger—especially marriage for financial reasons—repugnant to her. Lily had always hoped she would be able to marry for love, that she would be a wife to a man who respected her need to enjoy the independence her brother had always given her. But what choice was there, now that they no longer had a home to live in?

Jo echoed her thoughts. 'We must survive any way we have to, Miss Lily.'

'You did not have to stay with me, yet you have,' Lily corrected her.

'Who would do your hair, else?' Jo looked fondly at her mistress. 'You'll not find a husband to support you without a little help, my lady.'

Lily nodded. 'I will make it up to you, once my situation improves.'

She was determined that her life would be under her control again as soon as possible. Which was why this dress was so important— along with the charming, carefree persona she adopted for such occasions. She had been that girl once—without a care in the world—and she could play her again, for the sake of survival.

It was time to face up to the fact that she could not live on thin air.

It was time to find a husband.

Chapter Two

After four dances with four equally dull gentlemen, Lily was cursing her vow.

She was doing her best to be what they seemed to like best, effervescent and charming, simpering prettily at them between turns and promenades on the floor—but it was exhausting. She did not know how the other girls around her seemed to achieve such an effect so effortlessly—from the old hands to the veriest débutante.

Nevertheless, it seemed one man was particularly interested in her performance.

Looking up by chance at the end of an energetic country dance, flushed and smiling, she happened to glance across the room—and found a pair of smoky grey-blue eyes watching her.

He did not look away as their eyes met.

Tall, hair so dark as to almost be black, he stood upright at one end of the dance floor—despite his civilian dress an unmistakably military stance. He was immaculately turned out—dark navy jacket and matching waistcoat exquisitely embroidered about the sleeves and hem, close-fitting fawn breeches disappearing into boots, rather than the more fashionable buckled shoes that other men wore this evening. His shoulder-length hair, that unusually dark colour, was tied securely at the nape of his neck, and did not look like it would dare to attempt escape.

All this she took in as, for a moment of pure surprise, she stood fixed in the beam of his gaze across an expanse of laughing people. And, just for a moment, a single strand of awareness stretched between them, unbroken by the laughter, music and innumerable conversations happening around and between them. He did not look at her as the other gentlemen did: admiring her pretty dress, the way her hair curled about her shoulders in tendrils, her smile, even her much-praised eyes.

He looked at her as if he saw her.

It was not a comfortable feeling—and yet, even as she recognised her discomfort, Lily was aware of something else curling into life within her: a warm feathery longing, an unfamiliar but nonetheless unmistakable attraction to this handsome stranger. For handsome he was, she had to admit, even in this instant, held in his stare.

She wanted to smile, yet she could not. She felt the slightest of flushes creep across her cheekbones, and saw—did she imagine?—a response in his dark blue gaze, far though he was from her.

Who was he? Why did he look at her so, as though he could take all of her and more, see through her act and know her completely—all without moving from that spot. What did he want?

Because she did not know what else to do, she dropped her eyes and turned away, watching the dancers take to the floor again, needing a moment to compose herself.

When she looked back—simply because she could not do otherwise—he was talking to the gentleman next to him. In profile he was equally striking, slim about the hips yet broad shouldered, his strong features offset by a generous mouth that set Lily wondering, in a moment quite unlike her usual sensible self, what he looked like when he smiled.

Frowning slightly, she averted her gaze again before he caught her staring—what was she thinking, sizing him up so? Turning slightly away, she scolded herself for such foolishness—was this all it took— a handsome man to make eye-contact with her—for her to behave like a man-shy debutante?

She needed something to distract her and, luckily, something presented itself in the form of a young admirer, bowing prettily over her hand and asking most courteously for a dance. Gratefully, she accepted and allowed him to lead her to the floor.

And yet, even while dancing, she was aware of the other's eyes upon her, watching her every move, giving her a new feeling of self-consciousness. Telling herself she was imagining it, she smiled at her partner and applied herself to the dance.

But when she did glance back, just for a moment, it was to find those grey-blue eyes on her face once more. Lily looked down at her feet as she almost missed a step, the first glimmer of irritation growing in her.

Did he not know it was impolite to stare so? Was he trying to disconcert her? If he wished to make her acquaintance, why did he not simply seek an introduction? Must he stand there appraising her as if she was a horse he was minded to buy?

Even as annoyance flickered into life, Lily knew it was senseless to mind such attention. Was that not, after all, why she was here—to parade herself, an offering for the highest bidder? Was she not reliant upon one of these men being taken enough with her to ignore her lack of land and fortune and propose?

The dance eventually ended, to her relief and, thanking her young partner—it seemed increasingly that the men at such events were becoming ever younger—Lily slipped across to a refreshment table, picked up a drink, and cast her eyes about for Kitty Stanton, the friend who had accompanied her to the ball. She wished to ask about the stranger who still, she saw, glancing hastily across the room, stood where he had been throughout the last two dances, though his conversation partner had changed.

He was nursing a drink in one long-fingered hand, she noticed suddenly, making no effort to sip from the glass as he conversed idly with the older man now at his side. Though he listened and responded politely enough, nothing the gentleman said seemed to move him—or perhaps he was simply immovable. Lily, thinking of his inscrutable gaze, bit her lip in thought.

Who was he? Why did he stand there so, expecting people to come to him?

As she watched, another gentleman and a lady joined his small party, a girl that Lily vaguely knew, and her brother. Introductions were completed, with the stranger still polite but impassive. It was not, Lily mused, that there was anything lacking in his manners—there was just no warmth in anything he did; he held himself at a distance from proceedings, almost.

The lady was gesturing to the dance floor now, casting her large eyes up at the stranger, imploring. Lily could almost hear the exchange—it was very charmingly done—and she hid a wry smile.

But the stranger was shaking his head, looking detachedly regretful. He gestured to the girl's brother, then to the floor. The insinuation was obvious even to Lily, standing several metres away from them, out of earshot. He was refusing to dance, inviting them to continue without him.

Lily could not help a disapproving frown appearing between her brows. Why would he not dance, when asked so prettily? Could it be, she mused, taking in his flawless appearance, that he did not wish to rumple his clothes? She could not abide men who took themselves so seriously—why attend a ball if you had no intention of taking to the floor? Surely it was a gentleman's duty to stand up with the ladies?

The lady and her brother were leaving him now, proceeding to the dance floor. Lily thought it was a shame that the young girl had been forced to ask for her own dance and been refused—such an indignity, and all at the hands of this enigmatic stranger.

Almost as if he had heard, he glanced up.

Their eyes met, and she did not have time to replace the frown with a more benign expression. For a long moment he just looked at her. Then, slowly, he raised his glass in greeting, a silent toast across the room that no doubt looked innocent—and probably even charming—to those around. But Lily did not miss the sardonic tilt of his lips, a half-smile tempered by something else entirely in his eyes—something guarded, almost hostile.

Confused, blushing once more, she dropped her gaze.

Now he was mocking her! What gave him the right to look at her so, when they had not even been introduced? And then to make her feel ashamed for watching him? *Who was he?*

Gritting her teeth, she turned her back on the dance floor. She was not engaged for the next two dances—and she needed to take some air. Let him stare at some other poor fool while she was gone.

Daniel Westhaven could not quite believe his eyes.

Robbie Pevensey's sister was every bit as spoilt and feather-brained as every other simpering powder puff of a woman in this place. He had watched her for most of the evening: speaking to gentlemen, dipping her lashes and smiling winsomely, dancing, flirting and sparkling her way about the ballroom in a dress that told of indulgent expense in its deceptive simplicity of line.

It had taken her a long time to notice his interest, so absorbed in herself had she been. But once she had seen him looking, it was obvious she was trying to impress him.

And then, when he had caught her watching him, he had seen it— disapproval writ clearly on her face. She wondered, no doubt, at his seeming unwillingness to dance and make merry. Like all her kind, pleasure was all she lived for.

His fingers tightened around his glass. This was not what he had expected—he had heard that there was interest in her, that she was out in society again after the death of her brother... But somehow, he had expected the sister of his friend to be different. If not serious, exactly, then with a little intelligence at least.

He sighed inwardly. It did not matter. He was not looking for approval, and God knew he did not expect her to become fond of him. He had survived to keep his promise, against the odds, and now he had a duty to perform—that was all. He would do so, for Robbie.

He did not have to like it.

'Lily! I have been searching for you!'

Standing in a trance before the fish pond in Lady Langley's elegant garden, Lily looked round dazedly to see the sweet face and button nose of Lady Katherine Stanton peering out at her from behind a row of potted palms.

'Kitty.' She smiled fondly. 'I was dreaming.'

'Of a handsome gentleman to whisk you away?' Kitty, two years her junior and the liveliest of the little group of ladies Lily called her friends, came forward, eyes sparkling. 'There are many here tonight, for sure.'

'Have you seen anyone in particular?'

Kitty considered, head on one side. 'No one as handsome as my Tom, of course. But I have just made the acquaintance of a *very* dashing gentleman, or, should I say, he made mine. I had fancied him the perfect husband for you at first, but he's *ancient*—definitely over thirty. Nevertheless, he seems awfully eager to meet you, so I promised to facilitate the introductions—do come along!'

Lily hid a smile. 'Ancient indeed.' She frowned. 'Why does he wish to meet me?'

Kitty rolled her eyes. 'Because he is enraptured by your beauty, of course!'

'He said that?'

'He had no need to!'

'Kitty, really.' Lily ran her hands over her gown, knowing it could not hope to approach the cutting-edge fashion displayed within by the confident, wealthy daughters of the *ton*.

The younger girl flashed her a wide smile. 'Forgive me—I am just so excited that the Season is begun at last! Surely this year we shall find you a husband!'

Lily shook her head indulgently. What would Kitty say if she knew the resolutions she had made earlier tonight? And yet, could she not allow herself to hope, surrounded by all this glitter and style, that she would find love along with her much-needed husband?

Such dreams were foolish, she knew. Yet, though she was older than many of her similarly unmarried peers, she could still feel, occasionally, the girlish thrill of a handsome man paying her attention. This year she had looked forward, despite herself, to the round of balls and parties. There was peace to be found in trivial things: chatting with her friends, discussing which gentleman was most handsome, and dancing her way through the long summer nights helped her forget the darker thoughts she experienced, and her fears for the future. These past few years had not been easy ones, the last in particular heavy with sadness.

Kitty, who had been snapped up by the dashing Lord Stanton almost as soon as she had made her début last Season, always tried her best to cheer her, however. Despite her married status, Lily increasingly thought of her as a younger sister—and the girl was regarding her now with approval. 'You do look lovely tonight, Lily. I am quite jealous.'

Lily looked down at herself, touched at the compliment. 'You are kind to say so.' She smiled. 'But you know you have nothing to be jealous of.' Small and girlishly lovely, with abundant shining dark hair and huge brown eyes, Kitty had a dramatic effect on men, who seemed to want to sweep her up and protect her. Her husband had faced stiff competition before he had at last carried away his prize.

Kitty grinned impishly. 'Come, let us go in so you can flirt with Major Westhaven. He looks like he could do with cheering up.'

Lily sighed. 'Honestly, Kitty!'

'I will go and fetch him. Count to ten, then follow me.'

'Very well.' Lily could not help smiling at her friend's flair for the dramatic.

She lingered on the steps up to the terrace, patting her hair to make sure it was in place and pinching some colour into her cheeks. If this man was as attractive as Kitty said, she wished to make a good impression, ancient or not.

Then, carrying herself with all the grace she could muster, she stepped inside the ballroom.

'Ah, Miss Pevensey, there you are!' Kitty was on her at once, with a naughty wink, laying a hand on her arm. 'I was just telling the Major you could not have gone far.'

Lily smiled. 'I was just outside, Lady Stanton, taking some…air…'

She faltered as her eyes fell on the man who stood beside and slightly behind her friend. She should have been prepared—it was obvious, thinking about it now, who the man who so wished to meet her would be.

It was the mysterious stranger whose eyes had followed her so insistently all night.

Close up, his looks were just as striking, the contrast between his dark hair and lighter eyes only highlighting the fact. Ancient he was certainly not, but Kitty had been right—he must be at least a decade older than Lily's own twenty-one years; his face bore the look of a man who had seen much, experienced life.

Taking all this in, she realised that his eyes—somewhere between blue and grey—were watching her with an odd expression in them once more, almost as if he knew her. And yet Lily was sure she had never beheld this almost indecently handsome man before tonight. Surely she would have remembered?

What she did remember, however, was the mocking salute with his glass, and his dismissive attitude to the merrymaking about him.

She forced herself to smile, though he was still staring.

'Liliana, may I introduce you to Major Daniel Westhaven?' There was a girlish excitement in Kitty's eyes that amused Lily, even as she smiled politely. 'Major, my good friend, Liliana Pevensey.'

'Major.' Lily held out her hand. He took it in strong, warm fingers and bowed over it, eyes still on her face.

All at once her hand was suffused with an odd, tingling warmth that spread up her arm and deep into her belly. There again was that curling attraction, reaching across the space between them, making her feel most peculiar inside. Exasperated with herself for her reaction—let alone the knowledge that she was flushing an alluring shade of pink—Lily hastily withdrew her hand, chastising herself inwardly. Just because he was the best-looking man she had seen in a long time did not mean she should behave like she was still in petticoats! Looks, as she had seen earlier this evening, could cover all manner of other vices, and she hated rudeness and snobbery above all things.

Where had he sprung from, all of a sudden, to torment her so?

'The Major is back with us after the war in America,' Kitty informed her, as if sensing the unspoken question.

Lily's eyes widened even as she captured and buried, through long practice, the stab of painful misery the very mention of those words awoke in her. She half-frowned at her friend, wishing Kitty had thought to warn her, even as she nodded carefully, composing herself invisibly, talking herself back into the persona of the carefree, effervescent lady she must be tonight.

She smiled up at the man before her. 'The fighting was finished a year ago, my lord,' she said lightly. She looked at him through her lashes, ever so slightly flirtatious, the way she had practised endless times in front of the mirror, thinking of Kitty and quashing her pride. 'Where have you been hiding yourself?'

'I have a house in the country,' he said, voice deep and rich, yet measured somehow, as if he was careful with his words. 'I have found little occasion to come to town these few years.'

'Yet now you join us.' She allowed the corners of her mouth to tilt up alluringly, while her eyes told him how she really felt. 'We are fortunate, my lord.'

She knew he had not missed the sarcasm under her cool exterior. Something crossed his face that looked very much like displeasure, but was hidden again so fast that Lily could not be sure.

'Oakridge is very beautiful, so I hear,' said Kitty helpfully. 'My mother has never forgotten the balls your parents used to give, my lord.'

'Yes,' he said shortly. 'Well, it has been some time since I had visitors.'

'We could redress that for you,' Kitty told him, touching his arm conspiratorially. 'You should have a ball—would that not be delightful, Miss Pevensey?'

Lily, swiftly stifling a grin at her friend's daring, nodded. 'It would indeed be most enjoyable, my lord.'

He smiled tightly. 'I would be honoured to have so beautiful a guest in my home, Miss Pevensey.'

Lily gave him her usual sparkling smile. And yet, there was something not quite right. It was exactly the sort of thing she had expected him to say, in truth, yet she could not escape the feeling that he had said it precisely for this reason. There was, she realised, looking up into his closed expression, nothing sincere in his manner at all.

She was distracted by Kitty laying a hand on her arm.

'I must go and find my husband—I fear he has escaped home while my back has been turned—do excuse me, Miss Pevensey, my lord!'

With this she headed hastily into the throng, leaving them alone.

Lily, resisting the urge to roll her eyes at such an obvious *exeunt*, turned back to Major Westhaven and—just for a moment—there fell an awkward silence the like of which was unfamiliar for her in such a situation. She refreshed her smile.

'Tell me, my lord, have you recently become acquainted with Lady Stanton, or are you old friends from when last you were in society? She said her mother knew your parents?'

'Indeed. And her husband is a member of my club.' His tone was dismissive, his manner somewhat changed now, darker, more subdued. 'Miss Pevensey, I wonder if I could call upon you tomorrow?'

'Oh!' Surprised, Lily blinked. 'I thought you wished us to visit you, my lord?'

'In time,' he said shortly. 'But I have something I need to discuss with you. Would that be acceptable?'

Taken by surprise, she was unable to think quickly enough to fabricate a reason why she would not be at home, so she could only nod dumbly. 'Why, of course… Well…shall we say mid-day, then?'

He nodded, expressionless.

'I…shall look forward to it.' Lily could not entirely mask her bewilderment. What could he possibly have to say to her? For such a handsome man, he was disconcertingly lacking in social graces. Perhaps all he needed was to relax a little. If she was to entertain him tomorrow she supposed she should give him another chance.

'I must confess to noticing you earlier tonight, my lord,' she told him, wondering if she could broach the subject of his blatant staring.

'Indeed?'

She nodded. 'You did not look as if you were enjoying yourself.'

He threw her a measured look. 'How could I not, in such company?' His ironic tone caused her teeth to grit instinctively. Carefully rearranging her features into one of polite disinterest, she smiled coolly. 'You do not care for Lord Langley's brandy? I am told it is of the finest quality.'

For an instant confusion clouded his face, then he followed her gaze to his glass, still half-full. He raised an eyebrow. 'I see you have taken careful note, Miss Pevensey.'

'As you appeared to be doing with me, my lord,' she replied sweetly.

'You are not used to gentlemen watching you?' It was said low, almost a growl, and it reached Lily deep in her stomach. Startled by the sudden hot lurch within, she raised her eyes to his. What she saw in their stormy depths was uncharted, dangerous—and suddenly she knew that this cool exterior, this frosty disdain, was not the real man at all. He was capable of much more than this…much more passion, hinted at in the curve of that generous mouth. The mouth that was, in truth, not so far from hers…

Lily dragged her gaze away from his lips, unaware that her own were parted sensuously. Everything seemed very far away suddenly, everything but him—he stood close enough to touch, looking at her so differently all of a sudden.

What was happening to her?

Lily stepped back slightly. 'People usually seek an introduction if they wish to speak to someone,' was all she could think of to say, lashes covering her confusion.

'As did I.'

'You did.' She looked away for a moment, gathering her wits about her. 'Eventually. I suppose manners recovered are better than manners lost for good.'

There was a short, surprised pause. Then he drew himself up. 'Miss Pevensey, I am not sure—'

But she was too far along to care for politeness now. 'You do not dance, either, it appears, Major?'

He did not reply.

Looking up at him, Lily was surprised to see that his expression had become stony, as if she had taken some unimaginable liberty. She raised her eyebrows and smiled pleasantly, encouraging an answer. He regarded her for a long moment, jaw tight, as though he did not know quite what to make of this performance.

'Regrettably not,' he said curtly. 'But I am sure there are plentiful supplies of younger men available to assist you.'

She blinked. 'You think this is my way of asking you to stand up with me?'

'Is it not?'

'Why would I ask you when you have made it clear you find such things distasteful? Although,' she added, because she could not resist seeing his response, 'I will never refuse a dance if asked nicely.'

'I can only offer my apologies.' He did not sound remotely regretful.

'My lord!' Lily said, an acidly teasing tone in her voice. 'Surely you are not suggesting that your years are too advanced to allow you to dance? Why, there is old Mr Georgestone on the dance floor now, sixty if he is a day! See how he can still turn a pretty step, even with his old bones? I think you would have little trouble, if you did decide to—'

'I have given you my answer.'

His tone was so cold that it stopped Lily immediately, her eyes widening and darting to his. Again she felt her colour rise as she realised he did not take kindly to being baited, however lightly. This man had no intention of dancing with her—worse, he looked at her as if he could think of nothing more repugnant. She lowered her gaze again.

'Forgive me, my lord,' she managed, 'I had not intended—'

'Miss Pevensey.'

She turned as a handsome blond-haired man came up beside them and bowed deeply, looking absurdly young in his fashionably striped waist-coat and formal jacket. 'Can it be that you are becoming more lovely?'

'Lord Denham!' Lily smiled with all the pleasure she could feign under such straitened circumstances. First the cold Major Westhaven, and now this popinjay also?

A dandy and a flirt, with a reputation for his love of gambling and frivolous attitude to the opposite sex, Lord Denham often sought her out to flatter and tease. She knew he could have no interest in her, penniless as she was—but that did not prevent him playing with her, amusing himself, she suspected, until a more serious prospect presented itself. He was everything she disliked in a man: bored, spoilt and idle. Perhaps, she thought caustically, she could introduce him to Lord Westhaven; they would probably become firm friends. At least then they would leave her alone.

'Can it be that you are becoming more insincere, my lord?' she said, a teasing note in her voice, because she knew that was what he expected. It would not do to get a reputation for churlishness—and she knew Lord Denham could scupper her prospects with barely a word to his fashionable friends if she fell out of favour with him.

Sighing inwardly, she turned back to her sullen companion. 'Major Westhaven, I trust you know Charles Denham? His father is Lord Ashburton.'

'We are acquainted.' Major Westhaven bowed slightly to the newcomer, still stony faced.

Lily gritted her teeth. Why was he so unpleasant? Stung, she turned to Lord Denham and beamed at him, slipping back into the role she was supposed to be playing, that of carefree socialite. This was, at the very least, her chance of escape.

'Lord Denham—I wonder if you would do me a favour?'

He bowed extravagantly.

'Certainly. Whatever I can do to be of service.'

'You are so kind.' She dropped her lashes in the time-honoured way and, out of the corner of her eye, she was sure she saw the Major clench his jaw in obvious displeasure. Spurred on by an unexpected delight in annoying him, she simpered, 'You see, I have the most delightful new dancing shoes…' Withdrawing her gown just enough to allow the pointed tip of one shoe to peek out—blue to match her dress, embroidered with dark pink roses—she tipped her face up to his. 'So pretty, do you not agree?' She looked over at Major Westhaven, including him in the moment.

He was watching her, trying hard to conceal an irritation that showed clearly in his eyes, while Charlie, conversely, looked enchanted.

'Very pretty indeed. And how may I help, Miss Pevensey?' the younger man asked smoothly, clearly gratified by her attentions.

She pouted in mock admonishment. 'Why, sir, the Major will not deign to dance with me, and you are almost as neglectful! You have been here all night and you have not yet asked me!' Blushing prettily, she swept her luxurious lashes down until they touched her cheeks. 'I know you will forgive me, my lord—though it should be your place to ask. But I am so excited by my new shoes—I cannot wait another minute to try them out.' She smiled winningly at him. 'You could assist me greatly by asking me to stand up with you.'

'Well, I had indeed come over with the intention to see if you would do me the honour,' the young man said, smiling at Lily. 'If the Major does not object.'

'On the contrary. Miss Pevensey was just looking for a dance partner and, as I cannot oblige…' Major Westhaven inclined his head to Lily. 'A pleasure to have met you, Miss Pevensey,' he said softly, in tones so sardonic Lily felt her blood rise.

'The pleasure was all mine, my lord,' she said, voice every bit as chilling as his. 'You will be the darling of the whole town in no time with such manners.'

His eyes met hers, and she saw a flash of tightly controlled anger in their stony depths. Lily raised her chin. She was not some pup of a soldier, his to discipline on the field. She was a lady who had been treated very shoddily by a stranger who seemed to think his looks alone were enough to get by in the drawing rooms of the *ton*.

He said nothing, only bowed and turned away.

He was not quite out of earshot when she turned to Denham, furious. 'What an awful man!' She cared not whether he heard—and, sure enough, her heated retort must have reached his ears, for she saw his shoulders stiffen almost imperceptibly. Triumphant, she fixed the amused-looking dandy before her with a dazzling smile.

'Come, Lord Denham, let us dance.'

* * *

Lily danced until her annoyance at Major Westhaven faded, swept away on a tide of smiling faces and soothing music. At last, feet aching but temper much improved, she sought refuge on a well-padded *chaise longue*, placed beside the open French windows where a gentle breeze from the terrace cooled her wonderfully.

The smell of cigar smoke reached her as she reclined, mingling with low male voices outside. Glancing out past the gently blowing lace curtains that hid her from their view, Lily saw the boyishly good-looking face of Charlie Denham, hair ruffled from dancing, looking pleased with himself as he always did at such events and—in fact—in general. His companions, a group of five or so men, were similarly dishevelled. All but one—tall, devilishly handsome and still immaculately turned out, Major Westhaven was leaning nonchalantly against the stone balustrade. With a twist of annoyance at the sight of him, Lily was about to rise to her feet and seek rest elsewhere when she heard her name. Instinctively, she drew further back behind the curtain, its sheer folds allowing her to see the men while shielding her from their view. Not that they were concerned with anything but their conversation—of which she was the topic, it seemed.

'Miss Pevensey is lovely tonight,' Denham was saying, in tones of appreciation that made Lily's flesh creep. 'As always.'

There were several murmurs of agreement, but nothing from the Major, gazing out across the gardens as if such a topic did not interest him. Denham smiled. 'You were unimpressed by the beautiful Liliana, Major?'

Laconically, the older man turned his attention back to the group. 'Not at all. She is indeed lovely.' Blue plumes rose from his cigar into the night air as Daniel Westhaven arched a wry eyebrow. 'Have your eye on her, do you, Denham?'

Charlie laughed, and to Lily's ears he sounded a little uncomfortable. Surely the Major must know that he would never seriously court any but a rich woman? 'Would not any man? She's penniless, of course, but she's from good stock.'

Something must have been betrayed in the Major's face at closer quarters than Lily could see for, sounding amused, Charles asked, 'Not your type, eh? You want a woman who'll what—converse with you? Is that what you learned fighting the rebels, Major? Personally, I'd thank the Lord for a wife like Liliana Pevensey to keep my house, warm my bed and host my parties. When I want conversation I'll go to my club.'

Major Westhaven smiled tightly, irritation sketched in the clean lines of his stance. He did not take kindly, it seemed, to the subtle mockery of his peers. 'It appears I am in the minority. Apparently beautiful and vacant is what the men of the *ton* want these days, for she seems to have all of you enthralled.'

Lily, frozen to the spot, felt the colour rise in her cheeks. She could see only his profile now, looking out towards the garden.

Beautiful and vacant.

Had she imagined that? A little shudder passed through her. Beautiful she had been called before—men said it to her all the time— Major Westhaven himself had said it not two hours ago! But it was usually accompanied by *sparkling*, or *gay*, or even *effervescent...*

But *vacant*?

Humiliation burned up her spine, making her shiver all over again, bringing tears to her eyes. Vacant could not be flattering, not by anyone's standards. And the other men had hardly tripped over themselves to defend her there.

She tried hard to swallow and found she could not quite manage it.

Desperately she tried to talk some sense into herself, to redress the damage those words had done, sinking into her flesh like so many barbs.

After her parents died, her life had been filled with misery and loneliness, especially when Robbie had left for his faraway war, and she had never felt at home anywhere since. She had wanted nothing more than to hide from the world, immersed in the comforting routines of running her aunt's house—keeping her mind off the uncertainty of her future, trusting always that her brother would return. But he had not— and she had come to realise that no one would take care of her if she did not take care of herself.

She had been unable—and unwilling—to make her début when planned, due to the mourning that followed Robbie's death. But she had finally come out last Season, at her aunt's urging. As a débutante last year, she had assumed that other girls received more attention than herself because she was somewhat older; but she had soon come to see that the others made themselves alluring to men by dampening their own wits—by simpering, giggling and flirting their way into the affections of men like Charles Denham.

So at the start of this Season, by now quite alone in the world but determined not to be beaten, she had made a choice.

She needed to marry or become destitute, so she had determined that she, too, could find a husband this way. She had transformed herself—become lovely, carefree Liliana Pevensey, her slender waist, golden curls, graceful carriage and elegant neck the subject of many a compliment by various gentlemen who barely remembered making her acquaintance the year before. She had laughed and danced as if she lived for nothing else, and tried desperately to forget how her heart bled beneath her homemade gowns.

A year ago the very idea of playing such a role would have been abhorrent to her; she knew that her brother would not recognise her if he saw her this way—would very likely despise what she had become.

But he was dead, and this was how she must survive. She was careful to always be chatty at parties, eager to flirt and converse—and, true enough, more attention was paid to her. She had survived by telling herself that, once they were married, her husband would not want her to remain for ever the living doll he had married. They could, in time, become equals.

But now…was she not fooling herself? In her mind she heard Denham's words once more: *'When I want conversation I'll go to my club.'* There had been murmurs of agreement from his friends. Was this what she had to look forward to in marriage? He had defended her beauty staunchly enough—but not her wits. How could he— when he had no idea she could do anything other than sparkle like an expensive bauble? When he did not care, and neither did his peers?

Lily clasped her hands together tightly in her lap, trying to hold in the despair that gripped her. She knew she was not vacant. Was she to care what this…this…war-embittered *hermit* said? And yet she knew precisely why such damage had been done by mere words from a self-righteous stranger.

Because deep within her, Lily knew that Major Westhaven was right.

She knew, in her heart, that many thought what he did of women who behaved as she had. This flippant, frivolous character she portrayed was what men wanted—but must she play this role for the rest of her life when the consequences were to be called…*vacant*?

Lily rose to her feet, a tear spilling down her cheek before she could stop it. Wiping it away, she frowned defiantly. Who was this man, who seemed to think he could say what he pleased with no repercussions?

She did not want a husband—necessity required that she find one. She had a mind, and knew how to use it—and mere words could not make it otherwise! She must hold fast to that, believe against her mounting doubts that she could still marry one of these men without losing herself.

Daniel Westhaven was nothing to her—she would not let him spoil her evening or her plans. He had money, after all—he did not know what it was to fear bankruptcy!

Lifting her chin, she stood up to rejoin the party.

She would sparkle, be vibrant and lovely, without a care, as if it was true of her wounded soul. And no one would ever know otherwise.

Chapter Three

Lily was amazed when the sound of the heavy brass front door-knocker echoed through the house the next afternoon. Hastening to the window, she saw the upright figure of Major Westhaven on Jo's immaculately polished steps.

'He has come!'

'Good thing I made some scones, then.' Jo grinned at her surprise. 'He did say he would come, did he not? You said so last night.'

'Well…yes…but…' In truth, awakening this morning with her mind full of all there was to be done, she had quite forgotten all about the promised visit. She had not told her maid about what had passed between herself and the Major, or the things she had overheard—it was too humiliating. She was truly surprised to see that he had actually come, after he had clearly found her so distasteful.

But he was here, so she supposed she must entertain him.

'Very well. Please show him in.' She looked around her at the shabby sitting room. 'On second thoughts, show him into the garden. I don't want him looking down his nose at everything.'

With Jo dispatched to the door, Lily hastily smoothed down her hair and dress, seized the first book she saw and fled through the house and out into the sunny walled garden that she tended so diligently. Vines trailed up the walls, flowers stood in tubs, perfuming the air with their heady fragrance, and there was an apple tree at the end of the garden. The sight of her haven immediately served to relax her, and Lily was able to take a couple of deep breaths and calm herself.

Whatever this arrogant boor of a man wanted, all she had to do was sit, be polite, and eventually he would leave. She could manage that.

She seated herself at the wrought-iron table and chairs that stood on the carefully tended grass, and attempted to look as if she had been there, absorbed in her novel, for some time.

Almost immediately, footsteps heralded his arrival, and when she looked up Major Westhaven was filling the doorway.

She rose, laying her book aside. She had forgotten quite how tall he was. His looks were just as arresting here, in daylight, as under the twinkling lights of the ball. But he looked, if possible, even more serious, with not the barest hint of a smile to soften his finely wrought features.

'Good morning, Miss Pevensey.'

'My lord.' Automatically, she held out her hand. He took it, his own much larger palm enveloping hers. At his touch she felt again the uncertainty of last night, the tension like an invisible rope, stretched between them. She stepped away. 'Please, be seated.' As they sat, she attempted a smile for both of them. 'Will you take tea?'

'No, thank you.'

Jo, just appearing in the doorway with the tea tray, grimaced at her mistress behind their visitor's back and took it away again.

Lily smoothed her hair. 'I trust I find you well?'

He inclined his head. 'Very. Thank you. Yourself?'

'Of course. As always.'

He nodded. He looked slightly quizzical, she thought, and wondered if he was asking himself why she was not fluttering her eyelashes at him as she had last night. Lily did not care. She did not have the energy this morning, and goodness knew there was nothing about this man that she wanted to impress.

She sat, composed, through the brief silence that followed. He looked down at his hands, then back at her. 'Miss Pevensey, I regret this is not a social call.'

Lily pursed her lips. 'Evidently.' She knew he had seen her exasperation at his formal manner, but she did not care. 'Might I ask then, my lord, what brings you here?' She smiled tightly, trying to soften her initial reaction.

Just for a moment, he hesitated. 'It is a topic of some… delicacy. There is a matter of great import that I must discuss with you.'

He looked at her so seriously that Lily felt her smile dying. 'Concerning myself, my lord?'

'Concerning your brother,' he said quietly.

Lily felt herself stiffen. Whatever she had expected, it had not been this. 'Robbie?' she said faintly, voice not quite steady.

He nodded. 'We were in the 63rd Regiment together. He served under me.'

'I see.' Forcing herself to remain still, Lily fought back the wave of grief that broke over her.

It was this way whenever, without warning, she was made to think of her brother: golden, smiling, heading bravely off to war with ideals of heroism and victory for king and country. Instead the war had been for nothing, the colony lost and Robbie with it, his body buried far from home, broken like his hopes for the future—and those of his sister.

Pushing her emotions deep within her, she raised her chin and hoped the pallor she knew had taken her over was not too evident.

The Major's eyes were on her face. 'I must tell you, Miss Pevensey, he was among the best—'

'How well did you know my brother, Major Westhaven?' she interrupted desperately, hands buried in her skirts and balled into fists, her nails digging into her palms as she willed her eyes not to fill with the tears that came whenever she allowed herself to think of Robbie.

Grey-blue eyes met hers. 'He was my second-in-command. And my friend. I was with him when he died.'

Lily, shocked, nodded stiltedly. She had expected to be generically told what a good man her brother had been by someone who vaguely knew him…not this. She could not think about it, could not speak of it with this tall, forbidding stranger who had seen her beloved brother at the very moment of his death. She did not want to hear about Robbie's last hours—not now. Perhaps not ever. But she must not weep—she must retain her composure before this man, who seemed so unlike someone her brother would call his friend.

'So you have come to describe his death to me?' she said stiffly. 'You feel it is something I should hear?'

'That is not why I am here.' Major Westhaven was watching her closely. 'You have been receiving money every month, have you not?'

'Money?' Thrown by his change of tack, she was momentarily nonplussed. 'Well, yes, but I do not see…' Trailing off, she blinked. 'It was…from you?'

He nodded.

'Oh!' This was so far from what she had been expecting that it took Lily several seconds to compose her face into a look of graceful gratitude. 'I have often longed to meet my benefactor, sir. I must thank you…but…' Unable to stop herself, she continued, 'May I ask…why you have done this for me?'

'Because he asked me to look after you.'

'He asked *you*?'

His jaw tightened—he had not missed the disbelief in her voice. 'Perhaps you should read what he has to say for yourself.' He handed her an envelope of thick, white paper. 'He gave me this to deliver to you some months before he died, when he first asked if I would be responsible for your well-being in the event of his death.'

She stared at it. Her name was written on the front in a scrawl she knew as well as her own, neater script. 'This is from Robbie?'

He nodded.

Dropping her eyes to her lap so he would not see the sudden tears that threatened, she took a couple of deep breaths. 'Thank you. I will read it later.'

He frowned. 'I really think—'

'If that is all…' She rose to her feet. 'I am sorry, I feel a headache coming on…I think I should lie down for a while.'

'That is not all.' He pushed himself up off the chair and stood, looking down at her from his much greater height. 'Miss Pevensey, your brother has seen fit to make me your guardian.'

For a long moment, she stared at him. 'My...what?'

'It was planned out in advance—but was also his last wish,' he said quietly, voice betraying no emotion. 'He wanted you to be provided for. I visited your solicitor this morning and I have taken charge of your financial affairs. You will come to live with me, or you may live in my house in Richmond, whichever you choose. I will provide for you until you are married.'

Lily, openmouthed, was shaking her head. Truly, the man was insane. He had taken charge of her affairs? He wanted her to *live* with him? He had planned her future, just like that, without so much as informing her in advance?

'By what authority have you done this, sir?' she demanded, stunned almost into laughter by the ridiculousness of such a situation.

'Captain Pevensey put everything in place before he died, as I have said.' He handed her another piece of paper. 'This was what he gave me to make it official, and he instructed his lawyers also. I am assured it is legal—I am your guardian.'

Hand shaking, Lily took the paper, and her knees gave way when she saw her brother's unmistakable handwriting on this unbelievable document. She sat down with a thud, eyes fixed on the words. Robbie's signature. Major Westhaven's signature. It was official.

It was true.

Her brother had signed her over to this cold, cheerless man, as if she was no more than a favourite horse. And he had done it without so much as hinting to her that one day she would be sitting in her garden, trying desperately not to weep before the stranger who was to be responsible for her well-being. How could he do such a thing?

Very slowly, she looked up, willing all trace of emotion from her voice. 'I thank you for your interest, my lord,' she said carefully. 'But it is not needed. I have no need of your...*guardianship*. I have a home, and sufficient money.'

He took the paper as she handed it back, but did not put it away.

'Forgive me, but I know that is not true. You are almost penniless, and your home is about to be sold.'

'How do you know that?' She stared at him, incredulous. 'When I myself found out only yesterday?'

'Your solicitor entrusted me with the knowledge, knowing I would use it in your best interest.' He left her a moment to digest this in stunned silence, then added, 'Even if your home were not to be sold, you cannot live here as a young woman alone. It is not appropriate.'

'Appropriate?' Lily was amazed. 'And living with you would be *appropriate*?'

'As I have said,' he told her, with maddening patience, 'you need not live with me if you do not choose. I have a home in Richmond.'

'So you will closet me away in the country, to rot?'

Major Westhaven got to his feet. 'I can see you will need a little time to get used to the idea, Miss Pevensey. I will leave you to think on it.'

'I do not need to think on it! I know I will not leave my home to live with a stranger!'

'Visit me in Richmond,' he said. 'You will like Oakridge.'

'Do not tell me what I will like!' Lily was dangerously close to tears now. 'I do not need you, sir, or your platitudes!'

He stood for a moment, just looking at her. Then, quietly, but with great authority, he said, 'Miss Pevensey, you do not have a choice. This is what your brother has decided for you, and it is for the best.'

'Then why do you look as if you go to the gallows?' she spat at him. 'You are all too obviously less than thrilled at having to fulfil such a task! Why do we not just agree to forget the matter?'

A muscle ticked in his jaw. Drawing himself up, he bowed stiffly. 'I shall leave you to read your letter.'

Helpless, Lily turned away as he left, unable to protest lest she lose what little control she had left. Hastily, she tore open the letter in her hand, desperate for an explanation. A single sheet of paper lay inside, the writing achingly familiar.

Taking a deep breath, she focused on the words.

Lily,

If you are reading this then I am glad I wrote it, for it seems I have left you alone in the world. Forgive me—all I wanted was to come back to you.

I thought long about what to do in the event of my death, and this was the solution I found. Daniel Westhaven is a good friend, the best man I have ever met. He is a man of honour and integrity, and if I had to entrust you into anyone's keeping, it would be his. If you are reading this—and it seems you are, dear sister—then it means I have plucked up the courage to ask him this greatest of all favours, and that he has agreed, and kept his word by finding you. Trust him, as I do—he will not fail us.

All that remains is to say goodbye, my beloved Lily. I will see you when we meet again. Until then, be happy.

Robbie

By the time Lily had finished reading, tears were coursing down her cheeks. It was as if she had heard him speaking to her, so typical was this letter of her brother's cheerful rhetoric. And yet, how could he have so misjudged his commanding officer?

Major Westhaven was a man grudgingly fulfilling a promise he obviously regretted making, involving himself with a woman he appeared not to like in the slightest. He had not pretended otherwise, or attempted to consider Lily's feelings.

How could Robbie have done such a thing?

Weeping now, Lily dropped the letter and buried her head in her hands. This message from her brother was precious, but in such circumstances…

'Miss Lily?' Jo was standing before her. 'Major Westhaven's just bolted out of the house like the devil was after him. He said I should go to you.'

'Did he now?' Lily raised a tear-streaked face to her maid. 'He has started fulfilling his duties already, then! And as to the devil being after him, I dare say it is no more than the truth!'

'I'm not sure I follow…' Jo picked up the letter and frowned at it. 'May I?' When Lily nodded she read its contents, slowly, brow furrowed to ensure she was making sense of things.

'But, miss, he's saved you.'

Lily shook her head. 'He thought he had. But apparently he has no grasp of what manner of man Major Westhaven is!'

'What makes you say that?'

Lily stared at her maid in disbelief. 'Did you see him? The man can barely exchange pleasantries—and Robbie says that is honour and integrity?' And he had spoken of her at the ball so rudely—as if she was his to judge. Perhaps he considered that he was.

Jo bit her lip. 'True, he is a little rough around the edges. But he has been out of society a long time, Miss Lily. Perhaps he has forgotten how to deal with ladies.'

Lily was wiping her eyes in a vain attempt to stop crying. 'He wants me to visit his home in Richmond. He says I can live there if I do not wish to live with him. But how can I go—it will look as if I am agreeing!'

Jo took her hands. 'Miss Lily. May I give you some advice?'

Lily nodded, helpless.

'Trust your brother. You need not trust the Major, you don't know him from Adam, after all. But give Robbie a chance, at least.'

Very still, Lily stared at her. 'I have always trusted Robbie.'

'Then don't stop now.' Jo smiled wryly. 'Besides, this house is to be sold out from under you, and you've no money. What choice do you have, really?'

Lily frowned.

'Just visit him, at least.'

'But then I am as good as accepting his ridiculous proposal!'

'It is not his ridiculous proposal,' said Jo gently. 'It's Robbie's. What was that you were just saying about trust?'

Lily took the letter from Jo and read her brother's bold scrawl again. This was the last wish he had, Major Westhaven said, that she would be looked after. The last thoughts he had on earth had been regarding her, and her safety. Did that not merit something?

She sighed. 'Very well. I will visit him, and see if he can at least be civil. But that is all.'

Jo smiled, and squeezed her arm. 'It's a start, Miss Lily. It's a start.'

Chapter Four

It was overcast on Wednesday afternoon, the flinty grey of the sky matching Lily's mood as she climbed into the carriage Major Westhaven had sent for her.

'Do move over—there is no room for me!'

She looked over her shoulder as Kitty clambered in beside her, burnished ringlets springing everywhere.

'I do not know how anyone would ever consider you a suitable chaperon, Lady Stanton,' Lily said, smiling despite herself.

'How dare you? I am an old married woman now—I have the moral fibre required!' Kitty gave a wicked smile. 'Besides, you have no need of one anyway—Major Westhaven is your legal guardian!'

'I still want you with me.' The mere mention of his name dampened Lily's spirits anew. 'He is the most conceited and unfeeling of men, Kitty. The sooner we can conclude our visit and come home, the happier I will be!'

'I still do not understand why you say such things,' her friend protested. 'He seemed perfectly lovely at the ball. And he is so handsome.'

'He was different when you left—I have told you. And when he visited me at home he was awfully high handed.'

'Do not despair.' Kitty leaned into her friend, and gave her a little nudge. 'He may yet be the perfect host!'

'Nothing would surprise me more,' Lily muttered.

* * *

She tried not to dwell on her dread of meeting him again as the streets of London gave way to country and the carriage drew ever closer to Richmond. Perhaps he would be more bearable in his own home.

And she had to admit, as they eventually turned into an almost hidden entrance and the trees fell away from the long driveway, revealing Oakridge in all its white-stoned, columned glory, that his home was beautiful. The house was set in a large park, sitting before an oval lake on which swans glided. There was a wood off to one side, and a chapel was visible in the distance. Lily bit her lip. He was clearly very wealthy. Perhaps that accounted for some of his arrogance.

The carriage drew up on a sweeping circular drive, and Lily and Kitty were greeted by an ancient but distinguished-looking silver-haired servant, who gestured them up the imposing stone steps and into the hall and took their things.

'Welcome to Oakridge Park. His lordship will be with you shortly.'

His lordship? Lily frowned a little. If he had a title, why did he call himself merely Major Westhaven? She was given little time to ponder this before there were footsteps behind her, and he said, 'Miss Pevensey.'

Lily turned. He was, again, immaculately turned out, in a dusky red jacket and fawn breeches, the boots he favoured over less militaristic footwear polished to a high sheen. He looked every inch the haughty landowner.

She reminded herself to smile, though he barely had. 'My lord. Thank you again for the invitation.'

'Thank you for accepting.'

She ignored the trace of irony in his voice and held her smile. 'I could not have done otherwise.' It was, after all, perfectly true. He himself had told her that she was responsible to him under the law.

He looked like he doubted this, but made no further comment.

'You know Lady Stanton, of course,' she said belatedly, remembering Kitty, uncharacteristically quiet beside her.

He bowed. 'Of course. Welcome to Oakridge, Lady Stanton.'

Kitty, who had been watching them both with a look of calculating fascination, roused herself to smile dazzlingly at him. 'Thank you, my lord. How lovely to finally be here—and how beautiful your home is. I was quite enraptured coming up the drive. My parents did not exaggerate, it seems.'

He nodded slightly, his smile a little distracted.

Kitty, clearly expecting him to have something to say to this mouthful of compliments, looked a little taken aback by his lack of response. Lily wanted to elbow her and mouth *I told you*, but he was watching her too intently.

'I have ordered afternoon tea,' he told them. 'But first, would you care to walk in the long gallery?'

She nodded. 'Very much.' At least looking at paintings would give her something to say to him. 'Kitty?'

'Oh!' Her friend was lost in contemplation again. 'Yes, lovely. Do not mind me, I shall follow on behind.'

'Excellent. This way.' He gestured for Lily to walk before him. Reluctantly leaving Kitty's side, she did so.

The gallery was bathed in the full sun of the afternoon, slanting through the huge windows that ran from the wooden floor to the high, vaulted ceiling. Stretching out before them were dozens of paintings of Westhaven ancestors—mostly long dead, Lily imagined. They went forward slowly, footsteps echoing on the floorboards, the air between them palpably awkward. Out of the corner of her eye Lily could see Kitty hanging back, apparently deeply enthralled with a vase that stood by the wall.

After a few moments, when it seemed Major Westhaven would make no attempt to start a conversation, Lily cleared her throat discreetly.

'Has Oakridge been in your family long?'

'Several generations.'

She waited to see if he was going to elaborate, but he did not.

'You live alone?'

He shot her a hard look. 'Yes.'

'You have no family in the area?'

'I have two older sisters—both married with children, one in

Bristol, the other in Hertfordshire—and two younger brothers. One lives on the family estate in Ireland, and the youngest is at Oxford.'

'Are they often in London?'

'Practically never.'

There seemed little to say to so succinct a summary, so Lily merely nodded, racking her brains for something else to say. Her eye fell upon a portrait, somewhat badly placed in a shadowy corner—a younger version of the man at her side. He was in full military regalia, slim in his red dress coat, dark good looks and somewhat brooding expression captured perfectly, she thought.

'Were you long in the army, my lord?' she asked lightly.

His eyes moved to the painting, and a furrow appeared between his brows. 'Eleven years, until my discharge last year.'

'You were in the war in America for its duration?'

'I was.' Angling his body away from her, he gestured to the opposite wall. 'My parents.'

Grateful to be diverted from a subject she was never comfortable with, Lily turned to feign admiration at yet another painting—and found herself transfixed.

Large and in pride of place, mid-gallery, in an ornate gilt frame, it was a likeness of a handsome raven-haired gentleman and his wife, slender and beautiful, her reddish-brown hair curling in tendrils about her face.

'They look so happy,' she murmured, smiling up at the work as she forgot to feel awkward for a moment; it was so well done, and the people in it looked so lively and yet at ease, as if they needed nothing but each other.

He followed her gaze. 'It was done shortly after they were married.'

'And this one?'

The next painting along was the same man as before, she was sure, years older, hair grey now, but with the same kind expression and distinguished good looks. 'Your father again?'

'Yes,' he said shortly.

There was something in his voice that made her turn, but his countenance was as smooth as ever, giving no clue as to what lay beneath.

'You're like him,' she said, without thinking. For though the dark eyes in the picture were very different to the blue-grey ones watching her now, there was a likeness around the mouth, and the same inscrutability of expression.

He gave a derisive grunt. 'The similarities between us were slight, I assure you.'

Lily hid a smile. 'I meant merely to suggest you resemble him *physically*, my lord.' For, in truth, there was precious little of his surly son in the face of the man in the painting before her.

Major Westhaven glanced at her, seemed to guess her meaning, and frowned.

'Obviously, I can never hope to be the man he was.'

Lily raised her eyebrows. 'Well. We all have our faults, Major.'

His jaw tightened. 'Indeed we do, Miss Pevensey.' There was a brief, loaded silence. Then he said, 'Tea, I think.'

She smiled, equally tightly. 'Lovely.'

They continued their progress, slowly, Lily feigning absorption in the many works of art displayed on his walls—the Major giving her time to admire his ancestors, but commenting on no other paintings.

By the time they had passed through the large double doors into a well-appointed sitting room adjoining the gallery, another uncomfortable silence had descended. Kitty, bringing up the rear, looked quizzically at Lily when the Major's back was turned and received a frown for her trouble.

The ancient butler entered with the tea as Major Westhaven ushered them to their seats, courteous but still silent. Remembering with an inward sigh that she was supposed to be making an effort to like him, Lily determined to try lightening the atmosphere. 'Your home is beautiful,' she said, turning once more to look into the long gallery behind them.

His gaze was dispassionate. 'Lately I have come to prefer the convenience of my house in town.'

'And where is that?' she asked, hearing the obvious forced cheer in her own attempts at polite small talk.

He shot her a look, as if he had heard this thought also. 'Brook Street.'

'Oh. Lovely.'

'It's convenient for my club,' he said.

'Mmm.' Lily, usually so engaging in any social situation, could think of nothing else to say. Kitty, at her side with her hands demurely in her lap, appeared to have been struck dumb for the first time in her life, providing no assistance at all. Gratefully, Lily smiled at the butler as he placed a teapot, cups and a plate of dainty cakes on the table between them, welcoming the distraction.

'Shall I pour, my lord?' she asked.

He inclined his head.

Not allowing herself to be irritated, she forced a smile, pouring tea for all of them. Carefully, she picked up his teacup, proffering it at the same time as he put out a hand to take it; the collision rocked the dainty cup and tea slopped into the saucer.

Immediately his hands were under it, steadying the saucer, his long fingers against and between hers, his thumb grazing her knuckles.

An odd jolt went through Lily at his touch, both a heat where his flesh brushed hers, and another shot of warmer, tingling *something* deep inside—so that for a moment she could do nothing but stare at him, as they held up the teacup together.

'I'm sorry,' she said, feeling herself flush, lost in his smoky blue-grey gaze.

'Allow me,' he said, smoothly enough. He took the cup and placed it at his elbow, adding a lump of sugar and stirring his tea as though nothing had transpired, but she did not miss the slight hint of an undercurrent in his tone, nor the small sardonic lift at the corner of his mouth.

Lily gritted her teeth—now he would think she was so mindless that she could not do a simple thing like pouring tea! Immediately, her brow furrowed at this unexpected inner lament. She did not care what he thought. That was why she was here, making small talk, was it not? To prove that he could be as unpleasant as he liked and it would not stir her?

She passed Kitty a cup of tea and, thoroughly disconcerted, tried to remember where they had been in the conversation. He lived in Brook Street…it was convenient for his club…

'Do you truly prefer town?' she asked, trying to sound nonchalant. 'It must be so nice to get away from the noise and smoke every now and then. To shoot…and such like.'

He looked at her impassively. 'I am not fond of shooting.'

'Well…' She resisted the urge to ask him if he was always so difficult. 'To relax, then. The countryside has a wonderful tonic effect, I find.'

Now he just looked bored. 'To be honest, Miss Pevensey,' he drawled, 'I am in half a mind to sell the place.'

There was a clatter from the doorway behind them as the butler all but dropped the tray of sandwiches he was bearing.

Major Westhaven looked up, brows drawing together in irritation. 'For God's sake, man, have a care!' He turned back to Lily, stony faced.

She, further taken aback by the aggressive way he spoke to his servant, tried all the harder to smooth things over. 'I had understood you spent almost all your time here this last year, my lord.'

He nodded tersely. 'Precisely why I am starting to tire of the place. Perhaps it is time for change.'

The butler, unloading his tray, was shaking his head. 'If your father could hear you now,' he muttered.

Lily, astonished, turned to look at him. Though still upright and slim of build, the man must be approaching seventy. In the grand houses she had visited before, the servants would never have dreamed of interrupting in such a fashion.

'When I am in need of a lesson on family history, John, I will ask for one.' The Major's voice was low-pitched and even, but Lily sensed a clear undercurrent of carefully suppressed anger.

'I very much doubt that.'

She saw the Major's eyes flick from his butler to her, and saw his jaw clench further. 'Excuse me a moment,' he said tightly and rose, ushering the old man before him into the long gallery. The double doors did not close fully behind them, however, and from where they sat it was possible to both see and hear all that was said. Lily, eyes averted, tried nevertheless to appear engrossed in stirring her tea as the Major, upright with indignation, confronted his servant.

'How dare you show me so little respect in front of my guests?'

The butler was not quelled. 'You know how he worked to save Oakridge when he inherited it—and how he guarded it for you in turn. If he could hear you talk so, as if the place means nothing to you—'

'That's enough!' Major Westhaven's voice rose. 'You forget who is master here!'

'I could not forget if I tried, I assure you.'

There was a moment of silence, in which neither man moved.

Then, his voice a little lower but just as dangerous, the Major said, 'Oakridge is mine now, however much you may wish otherwise. And I will speak as I please in my own home.' Lily exchanged a look of alarm with Kitty, all pretence of deafness forgotten. Through the two inches or so between the doors she could see him, glaring down from his superior height upon the other man, who faced him bravely. 'Have a care, old man, or you shall find yourself swiftly unemployed.'

This did cause John to falter, his grey brows drawing together. 'How can you say such a thing? This was my home long before you were born!'

'No.' His master's gaze was icy cold. 'It was my father's home. And now it is mine. Take care to remember that.'

He drew himself up as the old man shuffled away, then returned to the two women. Kitty hastily busied herself with refilling her cup, a look of deaf ignorance on her face, but Lily could not look away. Something in the way they had spoken to each other told of a bond deeper than the usual master-servant relationship; yet this only made the way the Major had spoken to the old man more appalling. Lily felt hurt and insulted on his behalf: she could not imagine serving a family for decades and being spoken to so! She wondered only that John did not leave.

The Major, seeing the accusation in her gaze, returned it defiantly none the less.

'I apologise for my staff,' was all he said, and the arrogant nonchalance in his tone almost undid her. She pressed her lips tightly together for fear of speaking her thoughts aloud and concentrated on not flinging her teacup at him.

'Now. Where were we?' he asked.

But Lily could pretend no longer. 'If you do not mind, I think I would like to go home now,' she said at last, stiffly.

'We have not yet discussed your living arrangements, Miss Pevensey.'

'We can do so at a later date.'

'You have not finished your tea, and you have eaten nothing.' His tone was dangerous.

She tipped up her chin, teeth clenched. 'I cannot speak for Lady Stanton, my lord—but I have quite lost my appetite.'

He did not even glance at Kitty, but stared straight back at her, eyes stormy in a face that could have been carved from stone. A muscle ticked in his jaw, and for a moment she thought he was going to argue.

'Very well,' he said eventually. 'If you will wait here, I will arrange for my carriage to be readied.'

'My thanks.' She watched as he strode off, then, turning to Kitty, hissed, 'Did I not tell you? He has not the manners of a…well—he has no manners at all!'

Kitty looked thoroughly taken aback. 'It was most odd,' she conceded, eyes wide. 'Yet perhaps he has reason to—'

'Reason? What reason could he have to behave so?' Rising to her feet, Lily went to the double doors and peeped back into the long gallery.

There, as she suspected he would be, stood the old man, a slight, miserable figure before the huge painting of the previous Lord and Lady Westhaven.

'Wait here a moment,' she said softly. Then, without waiting for an answer from her friend, she slipped through the doors and went forward, feet light on the floorboards, down the long room towards him.

'John?'

He turned slightly as she drew near. Her heart twisted as she saw there were tears in his eyes.

'I'm sorry,' she said, because she did not know what else to say.

The old man was shaking his head, eyes sad. 'If Kit Westhaven could see his son now… He cherished this place…would have given all to preserve his family home.'

'You served him?'

He nodded. 'Almost my whole life.'

'How long has he been gone?'

John shook his head. 'Not quite a year,' he said desolately, shaking his head again. 'I never thought I would survive to see my master dead and his beloved Oakridge home to a man who no longer cares for anything. It is not right.'

'He should not have spoken to you so,' she said. 'I will ensure he will not throw you out, you have my word on that.'

John's rheumy eyes seemed to alight properly on her face for the first time. 'He'll not throw me out.' He looked past her to where Major Westhaven had stood. 'He is a good man, under it all. But he has changed, my lady. He was not always as you saw him, not before he went to fight in the war.'

'Many men go to war,' she said firmly. 'They do not all come back monsters.' With a painful twist in her heart she added, 'Some do not come back at all.'

His eyes softened, as if in recollection. 'Of course—you are Robert Pevensey's sister. Forgive my thoughtlessness.'

She was surprised. 'Major Westhaven has spoken of my brother?'

'He used to, often. These days he speaks little.'

'I wonder that you can put up with such behaviour,' she said with feeling.

He looked at her sharply. 'Of the ones who did return, Miss Pevensey, few lost what he did.'

She frowned at the sorrow in his eyes. 'What do you—?'

'Miss Pevensey.'

She turned. Major Westhaven was standing practically to attention at the end of the gallery. 'I have ordered the carriage.'

She nodded curtly. 'I am coming.' Turning to John, she smiled. 'It was lovely to meet you.'

His eyes filled with tears once more. 'You are kind, my lady.'

'Goodbye, John.'

'You'll not be back?'

'I do not think so.'

He nodded. 'I see.'

On an impulse, she put out a hand and squeezed his arm. Then, because he looked as if he was about to cry at any moment, she walked away, to where Major Westhaven stood waiting for her with a look of abject scorn in his blue-grey eyes.

'If you are quite finished, Miss Pevensey…'

Something in his tone tugged at her, so that the irritation she had suppressed flared into anger as he shut the doors to the long gallery behind her with a firmness that suggested the subject was also closed. 'No. I have not finished, Major. Not quite.'

She looked past him to where her friend stood, looking acutely uncomfortable at the tension crackling between them. 'If you wish to go and ready yourself to leave, Lady Stanton, I will be with you in a moment.'

Kitty hesitated. 'I'm not sure I ought to—'

'I'll only be a moment.'

Kitty shot her a telling look, but Lily, too angry to care, gestured pleadingly with her eyes to the door.

'Very well.' With a frown that told her friend she was not happy, Kitty left them alone, looking back uncertainly as she closed the door behind herself.

Lily, fuming, turned to face the Major, who was watching her with sardonic amusement.

'You go to great lengths to get me alone, Miss Pevensey.'

Lily's lip curled at his arrogance. 'I assure you, Major, this will be the first and last time.' She faced him, hands on hips, unladylike but furious. 'How could you speak so to an old man?'

'I am sure he will recover,' he said mildly.

'But you were so cruel! He has served you your whole life and this is how you repay him?'

He regarded her coolly. 'Do not let John fool you, my lady. He is tougher than most men a third of his age.'

'He would have to be,' she retorted, 'if he is treated so!'

His jaw clenched. 'I do not believe it is any of your business how I treat my servants.'

'Indeed not.' She was making no impression—she had been a fool to think she could get through to him when, evidently, remorse was completely alien to his character. 'Indeed, I think any business we may have had has been concluded, my lord. I will never move in under any roof of yours, regardless of whether I share it with you or not. Thank you for your sparkling hospitality. Good day!'

She spun on her heel and stalked towards the front hall, where Kitty waited.

'Lily?' Her friend came forward, concerned to see the look of fury on her face. 'What happened? I should not have left you!'

'Nothing happened. We are leaving.' Lily located her bonnet, waiting for her on the table, and jammed it on to her head, fastening the ribbons haphazardly. Then, throwing open the door, she started down the stone steps. 'Come, Kitty.'

'But, Lily—wait, we cannot—'

Ignoring Kitty's protests, Lily strode out of the door. She was halfway down the steps when she realised that not only was there no carriage waiting for them, but that it was raining.

'Miss Pevensey.' Now Major Westhaven was in the doorway above her. 'At least have the sense to wait inside.'

'Sense?' She turned her face, wet with raindrops, up to him. 'If I had sense, I would have known that to come here at all was a fool's errand, sir!'

With that, she headed off down the driveway, thinking only to put as much distance as she could between them. Behind her she heard Kitty crying her name, and vaguely registered the Major say something to the younger woman, but she was too angry to wonder what passed between them. 'You may tell your driver to catch me up!' she cried over her shoulder.

Her words, however, were drowned out by a huge clap of thunder. Out of nowhere, the steady rain became heavier, intensifying in moments until it was veritably pouring.

Lily, temper undampened, kept walking.

It was only when someone grabbed her arm that she realised Major Westhaven was behind her. Looking up at the streaming sky, he muttered something that she suspected may have been a profanity, and promptly dragged her off to one side. She fought him with a shriek, but she was no match for his iron grip and superior strength.

'You are frightening your friend,' he ground at her, jaw clenched.

'I am sure she will survive—let me *go!*'

Despite her protests, however, Lily found herself pulled relentlessly across already sodden grass until she was under the protective cover of a large oak tree, its canopy of foliage stretching out above them for several feet.

'How *dare* you?' Jerking her arm free, Lily braced herself against the thick bark of its trunk and tried to ignore him and catch her breath simultaneously.

She pulled off her dripping bonnet, turning her back upon the man at her side as she surveyed the sheets of rain that now surrounded them, dripping through the leaves above. It did not look as if it would ever stop, and the promised carriage was still nowhere to be seen. In the distance the house stood, impassive, as if it had witnessed such scenes before. Of Kitty there was no sign. Lily felt a stab of guilt.

'Where is Lady Stanton?' she snapped.

'Inside,' he said, sounding thoroughly out of sorts. 'And a damned sight drier than we are, I'll warrant.'

She rounded on him. 'Kindly moderate your language! You are not on the battlefield now, *Major.*'

'Evidently,' he muttered. 'My men never surrendered themselves to such histrionics.'

Lily glared at him, but shut her mouth tight, desperately trying not to give him the satisfaction of a response, as he seemed so determined to bait her. She crossed her arms and attempted to pretend once more that he was not there.

It was not as easy as she had hoped—plus she was beginning to be cold, now that the energy of scrambling for shelter was no longer required.

Beside her, Major Westhaven shrugged off his coat.

'Here.' He draped it roughly about her shoulders where, though damp, it did afford some warmth. Anger overcoming an absurd flash of gratefulness, Lily drew it wordlessly about her, trying not to let him see that she was shivering.

A stillness descended, broken only by the relentless patter of rain through leaves above them. Lily took a deep breath and attempted to regain some semblance of dignity.

'You need not wait with me,' she said at length, when the silence was becoming oppressive. 'Just tell your driver to stop here and pick me up.'

He made no reply, as she was beginning to see was usual for him. Exasperated, she turned to him. 'If you would be good enough to perhaps go and see what is keeping them? Lady Stanton will be worried, and I do not wish to stand here all afternoon and be soaked to the skin!'

His face grew distant as he looked down at her. 'I had not thought you the sort of woman to be overly upset by a little rain, Miss Pevensey. Especially as you yourself brought us here.'

'It is not the *rain* that has upset me!' she retorted. The slight stung her, as she remembered afresh his words at Lady Langley's ball and the original reason she was so annoyed with him. 'But I find it odd indeed that you had formed any opinion of me as any sort of woman at all, in light of the fact that you barely know me! Although, no doubt, you think otherwise.'

His eyes narrowed. He was looking increasingly out of sorts. 'Can it be that I have done something else to upset you, Miss Pevensey, other than discipline my own servant?'

She shook her head, amazed at his gall. 'Odd as it may seem to you, my lord, I do not take kindly to having my character assassinated in public.'

He raised an eyebrow. 'Your character?'

She nodded. 'I am perfectly able to hold a conversation. That I do not choose to do so with *you* says more about your character than mine. And just because a lady is cheerful it does not mean she is *vacant*, my lord.'

Realisation dawned in his face. 'Lady Langley's ball.'

'Yes!' she spat. 'Lady Langley's ball, where you seemed so eager to hold forth on the subject of my personality—or lack of one, if I remember rightly!'

'You were not supposed to hear that,' he told her, almost accusingly. 'And, if you remember, most of it was not said by me.'

'You began it!' she snapped.

'They do say, my lady, that eavesdroppers never hear well of themselves.'

'Eavesdroppers?' Lily gasped. 'How—?'

'Is that not exactly what you were?'

Unable to answer this without incriminating herself, Lily merely glared at him. 'I am only surprised, sir, that, after such an appraisal of me, you did not retract your magnanimous offer to take me into your home. Or were you hoping to educate me once I was under your roof—make me a little less empty-headed?'

He was silent for a moment, watching the way she stood, eyebrows raised, waiting for his answer. None was forthcoming.

Infuriated, Lily gritted her teeth. 'I am not usually contrary by nature, sir. There are many who would find me the perfect companion, I assure you, and none of them would presume to speak of me— or *to* me, for that matter—as you have done. It is no failing in myself that I find you so extremely…'

'Provoking?' he suggested helpfully.

She resisted the urge to stamp her foot for fear it would send her up to her ankles in mud. 'Now you are *laughing* at me?'

'I assure you, I would not dare.'

'Then explain to me why you make such judgements about women you do not know!'

He raised a sardonic eyebrow. 'Perhaps you should explain why you are so eager to hear my explanation.'

'Because… Ugh!' Lily threw up her hands. 'We are going around in circles. I bid you good day, sir. I will walk from here.'

With that she set off, out from under the tree and across the soaked grass, furious, humiliated and all the while wondering at the strength of the emotions that coursed through her. It had been true, what she told him of her character. She was mild, courteous Liliana Pevensey: unassuming, quiet living and, of late, tastefully coquettish in polite company. How had she turned into the type of woman who shrieked at men in the rain?

It was all his fault—and she would have no more of it! He was an uncivilised boor and about as far from a gentleman as she had ever encountered.

The ground squelched under her shoes, and the rain still had not let up, but Lily gave little thought to these trivial matters—she wanted simply to be as far from Major Westhaven as possible.

Unfortunately, he seemed to be following her.

'Miss Pevensey.'

Those long legs apparently allowed him to cover ground much faster than she—he was gaining on her.

She swung around, narrowly avoiding losing her balance.

'Leave me be, sir!'

'Where are you going?'

'To the gates to flag down a cab, of course!'

'I have a perfectly good carriage.' He sounded as if he was trying to pacify a child, and it infuriated her. 'And, even if I was willing to explain your unchaperoned departure to your friend, you are unlikely to find a cab out here, I assure you.'

She scowled as he drew level with her. 'I cannot wait another moment if you are to wait with me!'

He took her arm again as she turned away.

'Stay.'

It was said with such calmness that she actually paused. She looked at him, his hair plastered to his head with rain—and all of a sudden she felt more wretched than she had in a long time.

'I just want to go home,' she said, shoulders drooping as the anger drained from her body. 'You are quite right, my lord. I have not the character for running about the country with mud in my shoes. If that is what gentlemen wish for these days, then I shall happily remain an old maid.'

A frown crossed his face as she met his eyes but fleetingly.

'I have truly upset you, haven't I?'

Something in his expression stung her straight back into fury. She wiped rain from her face and scowled at him. 'Upset me? Why ever would you think that I have enough substance of character to feel upset?'

'Perhaps if you would—'

'You must forgive me,' she interrupted, 'but it is not easy to learn that your temperament is out of fashion, sir. Even the most vacuous— the most *vacant*—of us have feelings!'

She stalked past him, tears stinging her eyes. Must she endure such comments from such a man? Not, she reminded herself firmly, that she cared a fig what this particular man thought.

'*Plenty* of your peers find my conversation perfectly satisfactory,' she snapped over her shoulder. 'Perhaps you should consider that it is yourself who is wanting, not those of us who are merely trying to make things *pleasant* for others, so we may *all*—'

'It seems I was wrong,' he said from behind her.

Lily stopped. 'What?' She turned to face him as he reached her side once more, mud sucking at his boots.

'It seems you can carry on a conversation. With or without a partner, it would seem.'

She frowned, disarmed and ruffled. 'Now suddenly you wish to agree with me?'

'It seems so.' Was that *amusement* in his eyes? Was he laughing at her, again?

'Well—how terribly convenient!' She glared up at him, eyes blazing.

'What about my mindless chatter, sir? Does it not grate on your nerves how I can speak of nothing but dancing, and cannot comment on foreign policy in the Colonies, the role of the British Army or the state of the economy? Do you not wish there was a fishwife somewhere to divert your attention with her witty banter? Or perhaps you find my banality soothing, as you yourself are so very—'

Her tirade turned abruptly into a startled squeak as, taking her chin none too gently in an iron grip, he stepped forward and covered her mouth with his.

His kiss was almost fierce in its intensity, his lips warm and firm against hers. It was a sensation quite unlike anything she had ever experienced.

Lily, jolted out of her temper by the oddest feeling of awakening, felt with wonder the way her mouth moulded to his, the way her body was filled with an unexplained and tingly longing that started in her belly and spread rapidly outwards. Her lips were tender beneath his, and she felt her eyes closing, unspoken reservations swept away on a tide of arousal.

As if feeling her response, he pulled her closer, his kiss hard, insistent, leaving her in no doubt as to the passion that lay just beneath the surface of his cool manner. She found herself pressed against him, surrendering to the depths of his mouth, allowing his long fingers to brush the rain from her face.

She clung to his lapels, his arm around her back the only thing keeping her upright. Her mouth actively sought his now—and she felt no shame, only an odd sense of completeness, as though their quarrel had in some way been leading to this point all along.

At last he broke away, still holding her to him, eyes smoky with suppressed desire. He was very close, rain glistening on his skin, and Lily, too shocked to speak, could not take her eyes from his mouth. Her knees were threatening to deposit her on the ground at any moment, yet all her brain could focus on was the woody scent of cigar smoke that clung to him.

Then he released her and, abruptly, she came to her senses.

She wished to scream at him, but she could not quite catch her breath. So instead she drew back her arm to slap him as hard as he could.

He stopped it inches from his face, pulled her hard up against him and looked down into her face.

'Try that a second time,' he said silkily, 'and I will show you what it is like to be really kissed.'

'Let me go,' she ground out between her teeth, almost sobbing with frustration, humiliation and desire. For she knew, pressed against him, that if he was to keep his promise and kiss her again her body would respond just as ardently. She was disgusted with herself.

He let her go.

Dropping her eyes, she stepped away from him, trembling now not only from the chill rain that still poured upon them, her anger dissolved. Her teeth were beginning to chatter as, utterly wretched, she wrapped her arms about herself for warmth.

'Is *that* what I can expect if I am to live under your roof, sir?'

A frown creased Major Westhaven's smooth features. 'No,' he said gruffly. 'No, of course not.'

'Then why—?'

'Come.' He took her arm firmly. 'The carriage is here.'

Too overcome to protest much, and puzzled by the expression he now wore—a kind of fierce, guilty regret—Lily allowed herself to be led back to the house, where the carriage had just drawn up.

'Lily!' It was Kitty, hurrying down the steps, an expression of bewildered terror on her pale face. 'Where were you?'

Lily took one look at her and, absurdly, tears came to her eyes. 'I'm sorry, Kitty. I didn't mean to frighten you. I am fine, truly.'

Speechless, Kitty could only shake her head in confusion.

'If you will allow me, Lady Stanton.' Major Westhaven held out a hand, for all the world as though he was not dripping wet, and helped her solemnly into the carriage.

Then, turning to Lily, he took her cold fingers in his, even as she attempted to evade him. Heat flooded her at his touch, and—just for a moment—she was lost once more in his gaze, oddly fascinated by the way the raindrops clung to his eyelashes. He supported her as she climbed into the welcome dryness of the carriage, her skirts clinging to her. Then, coming to herself, she snatched her hand away.

'I will call tomorrow to discuss arrangements,' he said.

Brushing aside the hair plastered to her face, Lily made a valiant attempt to pull herself together. 'Do not trouble yourself, sir. I will not be moving under your roof.'

The ghost of a smile tugged at the corner of his mouth. 'Keep the jacket. It suits you.'

He slammed the door before she could get it off to fling it at him. Stifling a scream of pure frustration as the carriage began to move, Lily balled her hands into fists and struck the padded seats as hard as she could.

Never in all her life had she met such a thoughtless, arrogant— He had kissed her, as no man had ever before, as if it was his right to do so! And, *most infuriating of all*, she had let him!

What had possessed her?

'Lily!'

Realising her friend was staring at her as if she had run mad, Lily froze. 'Kitty…'

'What on *earth*…? Why would you run out into the rain like that?'

Lily dropped her eyes. 'I thought the carriage would be there. I was so angry…'

'What happened out there? You were gone for an age!'

She had not seen. Relief tinged with shame suffused Lily—she could not tell Kitty the truth: that she had, in a moment of what had to be pure insanity, allowed a man who was little more than a stranger—a man who purported to have a duty of guardianship towards her, no less—to kiss her as only a husband should. She would be shocked—Lily was shocked at herself.

'Nothing happened,' she said softly. 'I was furious at Major Westhaven for the way he spoke to John, that is all. I ran off and became lost in the trees. I know I should not have behaved so. Truly, I do not know what came over me.'

'But *look* at you! You are soaked to your underthings!'

'Do not worry, Kitty, please. I will be fine after a few moments by the fire.'

Kitty was still looking at her almost warily. 'I truly thought you had gone mad. I should not have left you alone.'

'I left you with no choice. Forgive me.'

Kitty sighed, some of the dismay leaving her expressive eyes. 'Of course. As long as you are recovered now.'

'I am. I promise.'

Flopping back against the seat, Lily tried to catch her breath and gain some perspective.

He had kissed her.

Well, she had let him—she had been too shocked not to. True, she had made a fool of herself in front of her best friend—and he had taken a shocking liberty as a result. But no one had seen. Her reputation was intact.

Lily sighed aloud. Let him try to send money to her if it assuaged his conscience. Now that she had regained her senses, she would make sure she *never* had to see him again.

John came up behind his master, watching the carriage depart through the window and dripping steadily on the carpet.

'Lord Westhaven?'

'John.' Turning, Daniel regarded his servant with an icy gaze. 'Do you remember me instructing you to address me as Lord Westhaven? Or could it be that I have expressly asked you *not* to refer to me by my father's title?'

There was a silence. John regarded the man he had known as a babe in arms with tightly closed lips. 'You have,' he said at last.

'Then never call me that again.'

Sighing, John turned to leave. 'You'd best get out of those wet clothes.'

There was no reply.

John shut the door behind him and went about his business.

Chapter Five

'Miss Lily!' Josephine, calling up the stairs for the second time, was beginning to sound impatient. 'Lady Stanton's carriage is outside for you, miss!'

'I am coming!' Descending carefully, so as not to trip on her gown of embroidered rose damask, Lily reflected once again on how lucky she had been. Upon returning from Oakridge Park, soaked and shivering, she had been grateful to find that Jo, by some divine providence, was out. She had escaped to her room, removed her wet gown, and attempted to pretend—especially to herself—that nothing untoward had taken place.

'How pretty you look, Miss Liliana. That colour is delightful.'

Lily smiled her thanks, gratefully accepting the wrap the girl held out. Having left the highly stoked fire in her room, she was beginning to feel a chill on her shoulders. Her feet, encased in their snug satin dancing slippers, felt as if they were immersed in iced water. And suddenly she felt as if she were going to…

'You are ready?'

Lily nodded, unable to reply because of the eye-watering tickle that had begun in her nose. Before she could even try to stop herself, she sneezed.

'Bless you!'

'Thank you.' With a watery smile, Lily fished a handkerchief from her sleeve.

Jo was frowning. 'You do look flushed, miss—could it be you're catching a cold?'

'No, of course not! I feel...perfectly...' She stopped, breath hitching, and hastily buried her face in her handkerchief as another huge sneeze gave the lie to her words. The dull pounding in her head intensified.

'Goodness!' Jo was looking on with concern. 'Shall I run out and tell her ladyship that you're ill and will stay home?'

For a moment Lily was tempted to do as her maid suggested and seek the warm solace of her bed. Lord knew it would be preferable to parading herself at another ball like a market trader laying out her goods. But Kitty was expecting her—had driven out of her way across London to pick her up...it would not be fair.

'Truly, I feel fine—I am only flushed because I was sitting too close to the fire, that is all.'

Josephine sighed. 'If you say so, miss. But do come home if you feel ill.'

Lily smiled fondly. 'I promise.'

Her maid nodded, then made a shooing gesture. 'Well. Come on then, or you'll be late, and it's me her ladyship will blame!'

The ball was crowded, as Lady Asterley's events always were, and Lily, ensconced on a *chaise longue* beside Kitty, found herself chatting to friends in quite her normal manner. Feeling better, she allowed herself to accept invitations to dance, hoping that her earlier malady had been a passing thing.

The first dance was a minuet, slow and elegant enough to enjoy, even feeling somewhat fragile as she was. Lily danced it with Charlie Denham, who, as usual, was all smiles and extravagant compliments. No doubt, she thought as they promenaded, he assumed her heightened colour was a response to his charm.

However, following a sedate first few pieces, the band struck up into a more energetic country dance, and Lily, keeping up rather less easily than she usually did, began to find herself short of breath. By the time she was delivered back to her seat by her partner, another dashing young dandy, she was beginning to feel dizzy.

Fanning herself, she waited for the feeling to pass, looking about the room as if engrossed in proceedings. No one seemed to have noticed that she was not quite herself, and for this she was grateful. Everyone else certainly seemed to be having a lovely time, laughing, chatting and—

Lily stifled a sneeze against the back of her hand, and, cheeks flushed, looked up furtively to check if anyone had seen.

A pair of piercing blue-grey eyes met hers across the ballroom.

Major Westhaven was watching her. *Again.*

Immediately, Lily dropped her gaze, feeling herself turn even more red. She had not expected him to be here tonight—she was not ready to face him after all that had transpired at his home. She should, surely, have told someone of the fierce way he had kissed her—did it not amount to a shocking impropriety? Yet she had stood there and allowed it, even if only for a moment.

He was still watching her, his eyes almost predatory.

'Miss Pevensey?'

Lily snapped to attention, jerking her gaze away and turning to where Lord Denham stood, proffering a refreshment of some kind.

'I wondered if you would like a drink.'

'Oh! How kind.' Lily wondered if it was ungrateful to be surprised at such a gesture—after all, Lord Denham rarely sought her company more than once in an evening, and never for long. However, her relief at having something to soothe her sore throat overtook any misgivings, and rendered her almost glad to see him. Rising to her feet, Lily took the glass, smiling through the haze of dizziness that suddenly assailed her. 'Thank you.'

Unexpectedly, he did not leave, but stood by her side and talked to her of trivial things as they watched the dancers. The temperature in the room seemed to have risen considerably, however, and for some reason she was having difficulty hearing him. At last, fearing she might faint at his very feet, she laid a hand on his arm.

'Do excuse me for just a moment, my lord.'

He bowed, taking her glass and smiling into her eyes as she left him. 'I shall be waiting for you.'

Lily managed a smile back. She made her way out of the ballroom, trying to walk as smoothly as she could, in search of fresh air, turning this way and that, not knowing where she went, only desperate to be away from people before she disgraced herself.

It was darker here, in a corridor of some sort. She had quite lost her bearings, but it was infinitely cooler. Paintings watched her from the walls, curious, it seemed to her, as to whether she could remain on her feet.

Lily was wondering the same thing herself.

She blinked, vision blurring for a moment, even as she tried to locate a place to sit down. Her dress was laced far too tight—she could not breathe—her face, when she put up a hand to wipe her brow, was clammy. Lily gripped a table as the world spun around her.

'Miss Pevensey?'

Footsteps were coming towards her. Lily tried to focus, frowning as she recognised the voice. Of all people, why Daniel Westhaven? She opened her mouth to repel him in the strongest terms, only to find herself unable to remember what it was she was going to say.

His voice sounded very far away, his words oddly jumbled and disjointed. She could not understand him, and was too weary to try.

It was then that she realised he was supporting her, that her body sagged against his, and his firmly muscled arm was around her waist.

'Forgive me…I don't feel well,' she murmured, mortified but unable to move.

'That much is evident,' he said wryly, his free hand brushing damp strands of hair from her forehead. 'You've a fever.'

'I'm just a little warm,' she told him.

'As you wish. Still, I shall escort you home.'

'Please,' she murmured, remembering she was angry at him, 'no—my lord….'

Ignoring her protest, he half-carried her through the house and into the large entrance hall, speaking authoritatively to the maid there, sending someone to inform Kitty, collecting her wrap and his coat, and leaving a message for their hostess.

Before she knew it they were in the blessedly fresh night breeze, going jerkily down the steps, and a strange carriage—his? Assuredly not hers—was being brought round.

'Liliana?' Kitty was suddenly peering at her, brow wrinkled in concern at both her semi-recumbent state and—no doubt—her proximity to the tall man who supported her.

'Miss Pevensey has been taken ill,' he said, the quiet authority still there in his voice. 'I'm escorting her home.'

'Oh, please, do not trouble yourself.' Kitty sounded unsure. 'I can take her home with me for the night.'

'My carriage is already here.'

Kitty still seemed to hesitate, but then, with a shrug of her shoulders, acquiesced. 'You are her guardian, Lord Westhaven.'

'*Major* Westhaven,' he said, voice abrasive in Lily's ear.

'Oh, of course. I quite forgot you don't use your title. Such a pity— it's so distinguished!'

The arm around her tensed noticeably and she heard his irritated intake of breath. Mortified, Lily opened her eyes. 'Kitty!'

'Hush, now. You're in good hands,' was all Kitty said, having switched allegiance rather too abruptly when faced with Major Westhaven's domineering insistence, Lily thought with annoyance. 'Come, my lord, you'd best get her inside.'

There was a slight pause while he seemed to be considering his options. Then, to her surprise and horror, Lily felt herself being lifted off her feet as he scooped her up and lifted her into the carriage, lowering her to the well-upholstered seat.

Through half-open eyes she was aware of his closeness, his breath warm on her face as he settled her, the tang of his cologne and the warm, masculine smell of his skin. He perched himself across from her, bade Kitty good night and swung the door shut.

He was silent for the short journey, with the single crease between his dark brows giving no clue to where his thoughts lay.

* * *

Lily only realised she was dozing when the carriage drew to an abrupt halt and she was jolted awake. By the time she was helped out and up a number of stone steps the front door was open, and it was only the sheer number of concerned faces all around her in the much grander front hall that alerted her to the fact that this was not her house.

'Major?'

'Hmm?'

Major Westhaven, still supporting her lacklustre form, was helping her up an unfamiliar staircase now.

'Where am I?'

'Brook Street. My town house.'

Her eyes snapped fully open. 'What? But...no, I cannot—'

'We will discuss it in the morning.'

He was releasing her, allowing her to sink down on to an unfamiliar bed. A maid hovered in the background.

'But...' She blinked, dizzy and heavy-headed.

'Tomorrow. For now, I will bid you good night,' he said, deep voice reaching her through her stupor.

Raising her head, she met his eyes properly for the first time since the ballroom, and gave in. 'Thank you,' she said softly.

He inclined his head. 'You should rest.'

She nodded, wondering vaguely why he still stood there before her with that odd look in his eyes. Until, looking down, she realised she was still holding tight to his hand.

Mortified, she dropped it. 'Forgive me.'

He merely bowed, straightened up and turned away.

Dazedly, Lily watched him cross the large room to the door—and noticed for the first time that he walked with a pronounced limp.

She had felt it as he walked with her through Lady Asterley's hall and down the steps, she realised, but had not understood—and she had never observed his walk at a distance. He had always been behind or beside her before and she had not noticed.

How could she not have noticed?

Now she saw all too clearly the stiffness in his left leg, the way it did not move as freely as the right.

And she realised, with a rush of shame, why it was that he did not dance.

'You're hurt,' she said hoarsely, her heated brain unable to form the sentiment more cogently.

He turned in the doorway, just bidding the maid good night, a frown marring his smooth features. His eyes were darker than usual in the lamplight. He saw where her gaze lit and followed it briefly, then snapped upright, jaw tight.

'An old war wound.'

Something in his face made her regret mentioning it—he looked so forbidding all of a sudden. Yet she could not help asking, 'Does it pain you?'

A slight pause, his expression unfathomable. 'No.'

She nodded. 'I'm glad to—'

'Good night, Miss Pevensey.'

Chastened, she dropped her eyes. 'Good night, my lord.'

She barely heard the door shut behind him as the maid, helping her out of her clothes and into a nightgown—blessedly cool against her heated skin—looked worriedly into her flushed face.

'Shall I send one of the boys for a doctor, ma'am?'

'No, truly, I need only to sleep.' Lily waved her away, eyelids already drooping. 'I will be fine…in the morning.'

She knew no more, for exhaustion sucked her down into its black depths and held her there.

Exhausted and in a foul mood, Daniel headed straight to his room, leaning on his good thigh as he climbed the steps that seemed only to get steeper when he was tired. His leg ached with a dull pain from thigh to knee, the result of standing all night and his endeavours with Miss Pevensey.

Shutting the door to his chamber behind him, he poured a generous slug of whisky into one of his father's crystal tumblers and downed it immediately. He did not want to think about Liliana Pevensey. True, the memory of her soft curves pressed against his body heated his blood, distracting him from the throbbing in his left leg…yet the pain was preferable, less complicated.

He stripped off his waistcoat and shirt and, bare-chested, poured himself another generous measure. Glass in hand, he crossed the room to where his huge, claw-footed bath stood permanently in front of the fire, filled, as always, by his staff with lightly steaming water in readiness for his homecoming.

He lowered himself to the stool beside it, grimacing slightly now he was alone. Some nights the pain was worse than others—some it did not trouble him at all. Sipping at his second glass of whisky, he placed the glass on the floor beside him and, with a grunt of effort, pulled the knee-length leather boot from his good foot. This, too, he let fall to the floor, then rolled his breeches as far up his left leg as possible, revealing the straps tightly buckled above his knee and higher. With relief he unfastened them, unfurling the leather flaps from about his muscular thigh.

Then he lifted the wooden leg, still encased in its boot, clear from the stump which was all that remained of his lower leg.

He dropped it with a thud to the carpet, bending his knee and examining the scarred, uneven stub just beneath it where once his calf and foot had been.

He had been lucky, he knew—he had been told a hundred times—that the surgeons had been able to preserve the knee joint. As it was, he could walk without a stick most of the time, he could ride almost as if nothing had happened, he could bend his leg naturally when sitting. But his wooden prosthesis, carved to resemble a foot so that it fooled casual onlookers into thinking he was merely lame, sometimes rubbed uncomfortably on a stump that could still be tender, a year after cannon grapeshot had destroyed the leg that had once been there.

The wooden limb had been specially made; its deep leather bowl, lined with sheepskin, cupped the three inches or so that remained of his leg below the knee, held securely on with the straps he had just unbuckled. Daniel prided himself that few knew his secret—but it was a relief to take it off in the evening, nonetheless.

Realising that he was letting his bath go cold, he slid off his breeches, swung himself up off the stool, on to the edge of the bath and into the water. Warm, scented with sandalwood oil, it soothed both his ragged mood and the throb of his old injury.

He lay back, trying to ignore the small nibbling pain in the left toes that were no longer there. He often experienced this, so often that it now no longer alarmed him—it was as if his body remembered the leg it now lacked. At times he welcomed it for, closing his eyes, he could feel his missing limb acutely.

Daniel slid down until his head disappeared beneath the water, only breaking the surface once more when gasping for breath. He groped for the glass by the side of the bath and drained it, wishing he had left his decanter within reach.

It had been a strange night.

Once he had relished the thought of attending a ball, loved to dance and flirt with the loveliest creatures the *ton* had to offer. Now they had only this effect on him—making him want to drink until he forgot the man he had once been, and the women that man had known.

Unbidden, a picture of Liliana Pevensey in her pink ballgown rose up before his eyes. Daniel muttered a curse. Just the memory of those full lips and he was tasting them again, in the rain, all her fire and fury enclosed in his arms. Even tonight, though flushed and feverish, he had been unable to ignore the softness of her, the scent of rosewater and femininity that rose from her skin…

He swore again between gritted teeth, feeling himself growing hard at the very thought, as he had that day beneath the tree. He closed his eyes and pressed his damp head back against the cool porcelain of his bath.

He was utterly undeserving of the trust that Robert Pevensey had placed in him. He had promised to see her safe, to wed her to a decent man, not to kiss her at the first opportunity like a hot-blooded youth.

And now she was under his roof, and the very thought was tormenting him so exquisitely…

He did not even like the woman—that was the strangest part of it all!

After serving with her brother, the best of men—level-headed, intelligent and loyal—and carrying her portrait with him all these months, meeting the lady herself had been a bitter disappointment. Her beauty was an accurate likeness, that was true—the abundant hair and captivating eyes that had haunted him in the feverish dreams that followed his injury were even more so in the flesh.

But she had *changed the subject* when he had tried to talk about her brother, and shown minimal interest in the letter he had presented at her home…as if Robert represented some past distastefulness that she had no wish to think about. As if his wishes meant nothing to her.

She cared more for shoes, it seemed, than the memory of her own brother.

It was not what he had expected.

She was completely unlike the other women who attracted him. Granted, she was not quite as shallow as he had first assumed, but she was frivolous and frilly, given to idle chatter and flirtation—all the things he despised.

Yet attracted he was, in spite of it all—the evidence of that was plain, even to his stubborn mind. And his body—more stubborn still—refused to listen to reason.

Daniel gritted his teeth hard.

Had he died on the battlefield with her brother, he could have been no less use to this woman, not as he suddenly wished to be. He was half a man, scarred by the war he had thought would make the boy he had been into something more, not the broken wreck he had become. His career in the army was over, his men under the command of another. His body was damaged beyond repair. He had inherited a home he did not want and a title that did not fit.

She was not for him, with her love of dancing and her delight in the stifling crush of parties that bored and irritated him, especially now. He knew this. And he should know better than to toy with her.

And yet, he would rather bait her, if it would ensure that those arresting eyes continued to blaze contempt at him, rather than radiate pity.

Daniel hated pity, and he had seen enough of it in this last year to last him a lifetime.

It was what he had seen tonight, as she looked at him, eyes bright with fever but soft with compassion as she saw his damned limp—and this without knowing the full extent of it. He had not asked for her sympathy and he did not want it.

What he did want was to possess her, all of her, contradictions be damned—with all of himself, not the broken, lame shadow of the man he had become.

As his fingers tightened around the glass, he realised any hope of escaping his black mood tonight was fast disappearing, and this only served to increase his building frustration.

Swearing aloud, he flung the tumbler as hard as he could, watching as it shattered against the far wall, shards arching in a waterfall of glass to the floor.

Daniel felt little satisfaction in the gesture. He was still painfully hard beneath the water, the rigid ache adding to the throbbing of his leg.

It seemed he was to get no release from either this night.

Jaw clenched, he hauled himself from his bath, grabbed the crutch that was always to hand in his rooms, mocking him as a symbol of the cripple he had become, and went in search of his whisky decanter.

Chapter Six

When next Lily opened her eyes the morning sun was streaming through a crack in the curtains and her maid was at the dressing table, artfully arranging a bouquet of cream-and-yellow cut flowers into a vase.

'What are they?' Blinking, Lily propped herself up on an elbow. She felt a little better, though still weak—and her head felt as if it was filled with wool.

'Roses from Major Westhaven.' Josephine smiled at her over her shoulder. 'Fresh, and lovely smelling, too.'

'Why on earth has he sent me flowers?' *He hates me*, she added silently to herself.

'Why indeed?' Jo's smile was teasing.

Lily frowned at her, feeling a slight flush heat her cheeks still further. 'When was he here?'

There was a slight, awkward pause. Jo frowned. 'Why, this is his house, miss.'

'His…what?'

Lily cast her eyes about the room and realised that her maid was right. This grand, if somewhat impersonal, room was most certainly not her home. The ceiling was far too high, to begin with, and edged all around with elaborate cornicing.

Memories from last night began to filter back—humiliating recollections of being unable to walk, of having to have him support her…of him ignoring her protests as he brought her here.

Asking herself crossly why she was admiring his plasterwork, Lily shook her head, her brow furrowing anew as she met Jo's eyes.

'Wait. If this is his house, why are you here?'

'He sent for me, miss. First thing.'

'Did he now?'

Jo nodded, looking quite disloyally impressed with the Major, in Lily's opinion.

'Hmph,' said Lily. 'Well, you should not have come. We will be returning home directly.'

Jo shrugged. 'As you wish.'

'Why should I not?'

'Perhaps you should see the rest of the house before you decide.' Jo looked momentarily wistful. 'I doubt he ever has any trouble with his chimneys.'

Lily frowned. 'Chimneys or not, we have a home! It was wrong of him to bring me here when I was in no state to protest.'

Jo, eyes twinkling, made a face that clearly showed her difficulty in imagining her mistress unable to protest to anything.

Flinging back the covers with a scowl, Lily went unsteadily to the window. Brook Street looked very clean and correct in the sunlight, all spotless white stone and imposing iron railings. Even the traffic passing by represented a better class of carriage, Lily thought wryly. As a residence, it suited him.

Even as she thought this she heard the front door opening directly beneath her window. Major Westhaven, as if summoned, appeared on the steps below.

He looked very handsome today, in a black moleskin coat and tan breeches—disconcertingly so, when she was trying so hard to stay angry with him for bringing her here against her will, to not picture his lips upon hers or his unexpected kindness the previous evening. She watched him go down the steps to his carriage, noticing again the unevenness in his step. An old war wound, he had said. Well, old it certainly could not be, unless he had seen war before the fighting on American soil. But it did not, in truth, seem to cause him any pain, and certainly did not seem to affect his strength. She could hazily remember him supporting her, lifting her, when she was ill…

Lily came to herself with a jolt as she realised he was looking up at her.

For a moment she saw again that dark longing in his grey-blue gaze—the same expression she had glimpsed before he had kissed her, a fiercely nameless force that made her mouth feel dry. She swallowed, trying to smile, feeling the heat rise in her face.

Then, with a nod, he tipped his hat and turned back to his carriage, swinging himself inside. She watched as he was driven off, then retreated from the window. She did not know what to make of his manner at all.

She would just forget all that had happened at Oakridge, she told herself sternly. After all, look where it had brought her! She must convince him that she didn't need a guardian, and concentrate on getting home. The sooner the better.

'I do not need to live here! I *have* a home!'

Lily was standing before the fireplace in the drawing room, remonstrating with the man who insisted upon referring to himself as her guardian.

The Major, unmoving, leaned nonchalantly against the shoulder-high marble mantel and regarded her without emotion. Afternoon was swiftly slipping into evening; she had waited for him all day until he saw fit to return from whatever errand he had been on, then come immediately to confront him. Now—after a day of frustration and circling thought—to have him look at her so dispassionately, as if *she* was the one being ridiculous, heated her blood.

'How are you feeling?' he asked, for all the world as if he had not been listening for the last five minutes.

She sighed, exasperated. 'Perfectly well, I assure you. Well enough to return home!'

'We both know it is not your home,' he muttered.

She frowned. 'If I speak to him, perhaps my cousin will agree to let me remain there—perhaps if I pay him rent—'

He was shaking his head. 'Even if he is willing—and it seems unlikely, from what I have heard—you cannot remain there.'

'Why can I not?'

'I took the liberty of visiting the place today, to examine what state it was in,' he was saying, but she could listen no more.

'It was a liberty indeed, sir! You were not invited to perform such a duty!'

He raised an arrogant eyebrow. 'It falls to me, as your guardian, to ensure your living situation is adequate.'

Lily closed her eyes, holding on to her temper by the tiniest of margins. There was nothing of the attentive, almost gentle, manner of the previous night in the man who stood before her now.

'That may be true,' she said eventually, mourning for the hundredth time Robbie's error of judgement in entrusting her life to this unfeeling creature, 'but I have made a life for myself there.'

'As you will do here,' he assured her.

'You cannot keep me here against my will!'

He sighed. 'I wish you would not speak to me like I am your gaoler. You know very well you are not a prisoner—this is your home now. And, if you allow yourself, you may even find you like living here.'

'But I can find a way around this, I—'

He held up a long-fingered hand. 'We are going around in circles. Your cousin intends to sell. Not that the house is suitable for anyone to live in, least of all you, alone and with no servants.'

'And yet we lived there happily enough!' *Including Robbie*, was what she did not add. But the thought stabbed her heart with a shard of pure misery just the same.

'It has rot, Miss Pevensey,' he said, maddeningly reasonable. 'And the chimney has not seen a sweep this side of the war.'

She dropped her eyes, feeling the shame of his judgement sweep over her. 'Money has been...lacking...somewhat recently.'

For just a moment, she thought his face softened. 'Not a concern that will trouble you again. I will make sure of that.'

It was enough for her to suppress her anger. 'My lord...could you not simply give me a modest allowance every month, if you insist on playing this role? Then I could find lodgings elsewhere, and your conscience would be clear.'

If he felt this barb, he let it go with only a clench of his jaw. 'Lady Stanton seemed to approve of you staying here. And your maid has no complaints.'

'If they knew what manner of man you were, they would not consider pressing me to accept your guardianship.'

That hit home. He stepped closer, taking her elbow in a firm hand and staring down into her face, his eyes flinty. 'And exactly what manner of man *am* I, Miss Pevensey?'

She glared back, eyes spitting sparks at him even as her heartbeat accelerated. She did not know why his closeness stirred her so, only that she did not like it.

Fiercely, she shrugged him off. 'Unhand me!'

He let go of her, but made no attempt to put any distance between them. 'You have not thanked me for the flowers.'

She tossed her head. 'Did you steal them from someone's grave?'

He seemed almost amused by this. 'Not the usual response I receive when I send flowers to a lady.'

She tossed her head. 'Nor how I usually react when I receive them, I assure you.'

Now a smile did quirk one corner of his mouth. 'Apparently it is my unique touch, then.'

Lily frowned slightly. Why the simple turning-up of this man's lips made her stomach flutter so she was unsure. She averted her eyes, confusion giving barbs to her tongue. 'It seems you gain great pleasure from mocking me, sir. I do not know what I have done to deserve such treatment, but I do know that I have no intention of remaining here with you!'

His eyes were darkening as he looked at her, and the smile had disappeared. 'I do not doubt that. And yet, as I believe I have already pointed out, it does not seem to me as if you have much of a choice.' He sighed. 'But we are circling again. And, delightful as your company is, Miss Pevensey, I do have other matters to attend to.'

'So the subject is closed?'

'It appears so.'

She regarded him desperately, eyes wide. 'Why are you doing this?'

'Have you ever tried to refuse a dying man his last wish?' Did she imagine the haunted look in his eyes as he spoke these words? 'I do what your brother wished me to do—and I would appreciate it if we could at least try doing things my way.'

Lily pursed her lips. 'It appears you are used to getting your way in most things, my lord.'

'Something we have in common, I think.'

'And what do you mean by that?' she snapped. 'Do you mean to suggest that I am spoilt as well as foolish?'

He looked down at her, face as unmoving as ever, but now she could see the barely suppressed anger in his gaze, and the set line of his jaw. 'I mean that it is evident your brother denied you nothing. Yet you cannot acquiesce to him even in this.'

The mention of Robbie was like a slap in the face. Lily, feeling all colour drain from her, could only stare at him.

'How *dare* you presume to know anything about our relationship?' she managed at last, voice shaking. 'He wanted nothing but the best for me—and I for him! Is that so wrong?' Already she could feel her throat thickening with threatened tears.

'As do I,' he ground out, 'though you are so determined to convince yourself otherwise!'

Furious, Lily curled her lip. 'You? How can you compare yourself to him? You do not even come close to *resembling* the calibre of man he was!' she said bitterly.

His jaw clenched. 'Then we have something else in common, for God knows I see little of his character in you.'

She heard herself gasp in the sudden silence.

For a moment she thought she might faint, so quickly did the blood rush to her head. All she knew was that she was gripped with the most terrible rage—she wanted to fly at him, to strike him, or…do *something* to make him understand how cruel his last remark had been…how…

She only realised she had turned away from him when he said her name, and she could hear in his voice that he knew something was very wrong.

He took a step towards her, but Lily held out a palm to prevent him from coming near. Shaking with anger, she faced him. 'No! Don't touch me. And don't you ever—*ever*—speak to me of my brother again—not for any reason!'

Then, without waiting for his reaction, she flung herself at the door in a whirl of skirts and fled, blinded by white-hot tears, finding her way to her room more by luck than anything else.

Jo was there, tidying her things, and when she saw the state of her mistress she straightened, face anxious.

'Miss Lily?'

'I'm fine,' Lily told her, barely getting the words out. She sank on to her bed, and tried to smile at her maid. 'Please, leave me a while.'

'What has he done to you? What did he say?'

'It's nothing, really.' Lily waved her away desperately. 'Go on.'

'Very well.' Though clearly not happy, Jo left, shutting the door behind her, just as the first anguished sob broke free from Lily's lips. She pressed her hands over her face and leaned into her pillows, chest aching, fingers gripping the linen. How could he speak to her so—as if he truly believed those horrible things he had suggested? That she was spoilt, that she did not respect her brother, the person whom she had loved most in the world… It was as if he thought she only mourned Robbie's passing because it meant she could no longer subvert him to her will.

Could that truly be what he thought of her? And, if so, why did he look at her so in unguarded moments, as if he was thinking of a rain-soaked afternoon at Oakridge Park?

Banishing the thought of his lips on hers, Lily vowed to think of it no more. He was heartless and cruel—and she would not stay here another minute! She would call Jo back, they would pack up her things this very moment, and—

Just as the decision propelled her to her feet, there was a firm knock at her door. 'Miss Pevensey?'

Lily sat back down abruptly. What was he doing here?

'Go away,' she called, trying not to sound as if she had been crying.

'I am coming in.'

Again, she leapt to her feet—apparently he was unfamiliar with the term 'go away'—or perhaps he was so sure of himself that he did not care what her wishes were. It crossed her mind that she should find a place to hide—but that was ridiculous, he knew she was here.

It was only then that she realised she had not protested, and that he would surely take this as permission to enter. By the time she had opened her mouth, however, his tall frame was filling the doorway and there was no escape.

Lily turned away and sat on her bed once more, staring at the wall. Perhaps if she showed no interest in him he would leave.

His steps came towards her, however, and then, unbelievably, the bed dipped beside her as he sat, legs outstretched, regarding her.

Too shocked to care that he would see the moisture on her cheeks, Lily swung round to stare at him, eyes wide.

The sight of her tearstained face drew his brows together. 'Forgive me,' he said, very gently. 'That was unkind, and uncalled for.'

She turned away from the concern in his eyes. 'Much of what you do seems to be uncalled for, my lord.'

'I am trying to apologise, Miss Pevensey.'

'Why?'

'Because I have behaved appallingly,' he said simply.

Surprise brought her face back round to his and she saw that, for once, there was no mockery in his tone. She tried to answer, but only got as far as opening her mouth before two more tears escaped.

Mortified, she closed her eyes. 'I will do whatever you want,' she said softly. 'You are right, I have no other choice. I will live here, or at Oakridge, whichever you decide best. Please just go away.'

He stayed where he was.

'Please,' she said shakily. 'Can you not see that—?'

'Will you permit me to speak to you on a personal matter? Then I will leave you to your thoughts.'

She frowned slightly. He still looked so earnest. 'I doubt I could stop you,' she murmured.

He nodded. 'Thank you. I have something for you. Something I should have given you last year.'

'You did not know me last year, my lord.'

'No.' He reached inside his jacket and withdrew something round and flat, wrapped in a clean linen handkerchief. Handing it to her, he let his hand linger over hers for just a moment longer than necessary. 'But I knew Robbie.'

'Rob…?' Lily's voice gave out as she recognised the shape she held. With fingers that trembled suddenly she unwrapped it, and looked, with a ragged gasp, down into her own face. 'Where did you get this?'

'He gave it to me.'

She raised tear-filled eyes. 'Before he died?'

He nodded, and she could not fail to see the compassion in his face, though her vision was blurred. 'I was there, as I said. At his side. I have fulfilled part of his promise to you, Liliana, but there is still one more thing. He wanted me to tell you the manner of his death.'

'I know how he died.' Tears were running down her cheeks anew. She pressed a hand flat to her chest, under her left breast. 'A wound, here. Was it not, Major?'

He inclined his head, frowning. 'Grapeshot.'

Lily nodded.

'How did you know?'

'I felt it.' She closed her eyes for a moment, remembering. 'I was in the garden and I felt such a pain, as though I had been shot. I knew he was dead.' She looked away, wiping her cheeks ineffectively. 'We did not hear for another two weeks. Aunt Hetty was almost driven mad with wondering. But I knew.' She looked at him. 'You were there, truly?'

He nodded. 'I held his hand.'

She looked down at the portrait in her lap. 'Thank you.'

'He died well,' he said gently. 'He was among the bravest of my men.' He paused, as if uncertain whether he should speak further.

'Go on,' she urged weakly.

'We were with Lord Rawdon at Hobkirk's Hill,' he said, 'I was commanding my company and Robbie was by my side. It was not an easy battle.' He stopped, and something in his face told her she did not want to know the details. 'When I was wounded he took over command—I have heard nothing since but how brave he was, how concerned for his men. I passed out soon after I was shot—and when I awoke he was lying next to me on the battlefield. We had little time to speak before he died, but all his talk was of you.'

'What time was it?' she asked dazedly.

'Around midday, I suppose. T'would have been around five in the afternoon here.'

Lily nodded, lips trembling.

'Many good men died that day, though the victory was ours.'

'But we lost the war,' she said dully. 'So it was all for nothing.'

He shook his head, grimly vehement. 'My men did not die for nothing. Your brother fought loyally for king and country and such a debt will not be forgotten. He asked me to make sure you knew that.'

'I knew it regardless.' Lily covered her face with her hands as, despite her best efforts, the emotion overcame her.

He put a hand on her arm. 'Liliana…'

'Please…' She pulled away slightly. 'I am fine.' She took a deep breath, face turned towards the window. 'It's just…I have been thinking about him these past few days…how he tried to provide for me…' Shaking her head, she tried again to dry her tears.

'Here.'

She took the handkerchief he offered and dabbed at her eyes. 'Thank you.' Looking down at the portrait she held, she sighed. 'I have one of him, at home.' She shook her head, desolate. 'It has been more than a year since he died and still I cannot believe he is gone.'

'This is why you would not speak of him to me before?' he asked quietly.

She nodded. 'I try never to speak of him at all.'

'He would not want that.'

She raised a tearstained face to his. 'Then what should I do? I cannot speak of him without weeping, even now!'

'It will not always be so. One day the good memories will outweigh the pain.'

'I hope you are right.'

In the silence he took her hand, very gently, and held it between his much larger, rougher palms. Lily, inordinately comforted by the gesture, was suddenly suffused with an odd longing to lean into his body, to rest her head against his broad chest. But, uncertain as to how he would react, she stayed upright.

'He wrote of his Major in letters, though he never mentioned your name,' she said softly, because she wanted to tell him something to repay him for this unexpected kindness. 'He said you were a great soldier, a leader of men—those were his words, I believe.'

Beside her, he made a sound that was halfway between a sigh and a laugh. 'He was always a great one for rhetoric.'

'He was.' Fondly now, she smiled. 'But he was a good judge of character.'

'Characters change,' was all he said to this, and it brought to mind something John had told her, at Oakridge. About the change the war had wrought in this man.

Softly, she asked, 'You were honourably discharged from the army after the war, were you not?'

His hands tensed around hers. 'I was,' he said shortly. 'Though God knows it was not of my choosing.'

'Do you miss it?'

He looked at her for a long moment, as if he did not quite know how to answer. 'I had planned to do nothing else with my life.'

It was not quite an admission, but Lily thought she was beginning to see the way he said things without saying them. And a man did not spend a year alone in the countryside if he had nothing to mourn.

A question furrowed her brow as something occurred to her. 'You said you should have brought this to me a long time ago?'

He nodded.

'Why did you not?'

It was as if a cloud had passed over his face. 'I was unable to.'

'Your injury?'

At the very word, his whole manner changed. He slipped his hands away from hers smoothly enough—but she sensed his withdrawal in more than this simple gesture.

'John said the war was hard on you,' she ventured. 'Is it very—?'

His jaw tightened. 'John had no right to speak of matters that do not concern either of you.'

Lily blinked, taken aback. 'I was merely—'

'Your brother was my friend,' he cut in. 'I spoke to you of the war because he asked it of me. Now that I have kept my word, I do not wish to speak of it further.'

'I did not mean to—'

'I will leave you in peace,' he said abruptly, pushing himself to his feet.

Lily sat, frozen, as the warmth that had hovered briefly between them evaporated, leaving only the dimming light and a stranger who did not believe his injury concerned her. 'My lord...'

'Good night, Liliana.' His voice was firm, but gentle. He opened the door and left without looking back.

Chapter Seven

Charles Denham threw down his losing hand in disgust and drained the glass of port before him. 'I'll pay you next week,' he told the gentleman seated opposite, causing a general ripple of amusement.

'Do you ever sit down to cards with actual blunt in your pocket, Denham?' asked one of his friends, availing himself liberally from the decanter that stood close at hand. 'I have so many credit notes from you that I shall have no need for firewood for at least a fortnight.'

Irritated at the laughter this elicited, Denham scowled at him. 'Unlike you, Hastings, I do not have a wealthy wife to keep me.'

More laughter, and much nudging of Hastings, who, unable to deny the accusation, shrugged good-naturedly.

Denham, unmollified, stood and walked away a little from the boisterous group, brows drawing together. White's was considered by many to be the most exclusive gentleman's club in London, and it cost him dearly to spend the time he did here. Already the meagre sum his father had allotted him for the month was long gone.

He had, in fact, applied to the old goat for an extension on his allowance this very morning, and been rejected in the harshest terms. His frown deepened as he thought about it. How did Lord Ashburton expect his heir to experience life on such a tight rein? Charlie was the future Earl; it heated his blood when he considered how he was made to live—without sufficient means for the fine clothing and leisure activities that befitted a man of his rank, forced to beg for funds from a senile old man—and all the while mocked by his peers.

Well, not for much longer.

Denham leaned against the window frame and stared unseeingly down into the street below, pondering the news which had come to him recently.

It seemed Liliana Pevensey had found herself a rich guardian.

Of course, he had noticed her before—for who could not notice such a swan among the lamentably duck-like young ladies of the *ton*? But he had not previously been able to consider her as marriage material. Until now, for word was that she had been taken to ward by Daniel Westhaven.

Although the Major was also a member at White's, Denham was not more than casually acquainted with him, but he knew—along with everyone else in London—the wealth he had recently inherited. Such knowledge made his new ward a very attractive package indeed. Liliana's dowry would be exactly what Charlie needed—no longer would he be reliant on whatever small change his father deigned to throw his way. He would be rich in his own right—and he would spend his money as he pleased without having to endure the old man's endless carping about prudence. Such a lifestyle would only be enhanced, of course, when his sire eventually decided to die and surrender up the whole estate.

Added to this, Charlie's new wife would be the envy of all his peers—so long as he bought her a pair of shoes or a pretty reticule every now and then, she would not have the wit to concern herself about where her husband spent his evenings. Or with whom.

Overall, it was a highly satisfactory plan, and one that should not take very much effort to bear fruit. She was not exactly a complex person, after all—and he was certainly not new to the art of seducing women. In fact, he had already started to pay her more attention—at Lady Asterley's ball the night before last, for example—and she was, he could sense, ripe for the plucking. It should only be a matter of time.

Denham, mood much improved, turned back into the room and returned to the card table. As he was soon to be a wealthy man, a few more games would not hurt.

Let his friends mock him when he bagged the catch of the Season.

* * *

Daniel returned from dining at his club to find no staff awaiting him in his house. Frowning, he left his hat and cloak on the hall table, and went to explore, following the sound of voices that drifted up to him from below stairs.

He did not have far to go before he found everyone.

Both maids were in the well-appointed kitchen—and his town butler, Thomlins, too—watching goings-on with interest. They leapt to their feet as Daniel entered and nodded a greeting. But it was beyond them that his interest lay, for, standing in the middle of the kitchen, cheeks flushed, talking animatedly to the cook, was his ward.

For a moment he stood, just watching.

She wore a simple light-blue day dress, but the unfussiness of the style and cut only served to emphasise her natural attributes: the curves beneath the fabric, the creamy skin at her throat, the way her hair curled in tendrils down her neck from where it was lightly dressed up on her head. Daniel was seized with an irrational urge to bury his fingers in it, to tease it out until it fell down her back in honeyed rivulets…

He swallowed. He had sworn not to do this—not to think of her in such terms. She was under his protection and—besides that—as far from the type of woman who attracted him as any could be.

And yet…seeing her here, gesturing to the table and the stove, talking quietly but earnestly to the woman before her, there was no trace of the silly, simpering flirt he had determined to become accustomed to. She looked like a woman who could be left in control of things, not a girl who would not know where to start.

The change was most disconcerting.

As he stood musing, she looked round and, relaxed as she was, gave him a wide, open smile that reached her eyes, her guard down, almost as if she was not thinking where she was.

'Major.'

It had been a long time, Daniel thought despite himself, since anyone had looked pleased to see him. He went forward. 'What on earth are you doing?'

He had not intended the question as an accusation, though it came out sounding brusque—but to his relief she seemed to sense this.

'Organising. Your staff are very capable, but they've no direction. I'm surprised you've had a decent meal since you returned from America.'

Daniel frowned. 'I haven't, in this house. Most of the staff are at Oakridge.'

'Well, what use is that when you are here?'

He opened his mouth to protest at her summing up of his domestic circumstances, then realised she was quite right, so he just shrugged instead. 'None, I suppose.'

'Exactly.' She gestured to the woman next to her, engaged at very short notice when he had realised he would need to bring his ward to live with him. 'Anna doesn't have much experience as a cook, but she's willing to learn. It won't take long at all—we've been through some meal ideas.'

Examining the sheets of paper on the table, Daniel discovered that they were menus. He cleared his throat. 'I dine at my club most evenings, Miss Pevensey.'

To his amazement, she actually looked crestfallen. 'I had thought that, if decent fare was provided at home, perhaps you would not need to.'

Meeting her eyes, still that mesmerising green but now sparkling with energy, he understood that she was offering him an olive branch.

Daniel nodded slowly. 'Perhaps you are right.'

'Besides,' she went on, 'I must dine here, must I not, if this is to be my home? I have no club to go to, so until the unthinkable becomes possible and yours admits women, I have no choice.'

He raised his eyebrows at his own thoughtlessness. 'Of course. Forgive me.'

'Good.' She nodded at the cook. 'Thank you, Anna. You know where I am if you have any questions.' Turning, she gifted the butler with a smile every bit as charming as those Daniel had seen her bestow upon gentlemen of the *ton* in its most exclusive ballrooms. 'I am sure the Major would welcome a drink, Thomlins.'

He assured her that it would be seen to and she thanked him graciously, then turned to a bemused Daniel.

'Shall we go back above stairs, Major?'

He nodded and gestured to her to precede him. Going up stairs was the activity he found most challenging, and he did not want her to see the effort it took.

But she saw it, none the less, in his face as he joined her in the hall. And there, just for a flash, was that pity in her eyes that caused him to knot up inside.

Before she could say anything, he said, 'I didn't ask you to live here because I needed a housekeeper, Liliana.'

Her chin came up at his brusque tone. 'I know that. I simply thought—'

'You do not have to work for your living.'

He spoke more softly this time, and saw in her face that she realised now he was not finding fault.

'I understand that.'

He nodded. 'Just as long as you do.' About to leave her, he hesitated. 'But…how…?'

'How do I know how to do something useful?'

He smothered a smile. 'Not quite how I would have put it.'

The twinkle in her eye almost suggested she was teasing him. 'Dancing and picking flowers all day can become dull after a while, Major.' Any sting her words might have held was neutralised by the smile that accompanied them. 'I'll leave you to your drink.'

Turning to leave him, Lily suppressed a triumphant smile. He had been surprised, that much was obvious—perhaps enough to revise his opinion of her. Not that it mattered what he thought, of course—what was important was that the kitchen would run more smoothly and she would no longer have to force herself to eat what had passed for food in this house before now.

As she walked through the hall, her eye fell upon a tall but neatly stacked pile of white cards, left disregarded on the hall table.

'You will miss engagements, my lord, if you do not keep your invitations somewhere you can see them,' she said lightly, without thinking.

He was still behind her. 'So you do wish to be my housekeeper, after all?'

'I have told you I do not.' Smiling at his wry tone, she went to examine the cards further, then checked herself. 'May I?'

He shrugged. 'Be my guest.'

She picked up the pile, shuffling quickly through invitations to balls, dinners and musicales. 'You see—many of these have already passed. How many did you remember to attend?'

'None,' he said shortly, after the briefest of pauses.

Lily shook her head. 'Then you should take more care, sir! Perhaps if you were to keep them along the mantel, or ask Thomlins to remind you—'

'Thomlins has his instructions,' he cut in. 'Which are to leave them there as they arrive.'

'But then you will never see them.' Lily, raising her eyes to his face, saw his closed expression and realised she was being dense. 'Do you never go out, Major?'

'I go to my club. That is sufficient excitement for me. I do not need to gallivant about the town like a man half my age.'

'But you attended Lady Langley's ball—and Lady Asterley's, too!' she protested, ignoring the sardonic thread in his tone.

'Purely to spy on yourself, I assure you. It may have escaped your attention, Liliana, but I do not enjoy such events.'

'It had not.' Lily sighed, leafing through the substantial pile once more. 'Yet—many of these are highly sought-after occasions!'

'All the better that I do not add to the squeeze, then.'

'But look—here is one to a picnic in Hyde Park—and for tomorrow!' She looked up at him. 'How pleasant it sounds—and in such a large space you cannot possibly feel crowded.'

He frowned at her persistence. 'I have never been enamoured of picnics. Now, if you will excuse me...'

Lily frowned as he turned and walked away from her, in the direction of the drawing room and his refreshment. He had moved back into London, therefore she had assumed he was moving back into society—but clearly she had been mistaken.

How long had he closeted himself away like this? To hear him speak, anyone would imagine him to be in his dotage, not a handsome, eligible man in the prime of his life. What effect had the war had, to make him so reclusive?

'I would like to go,' she told his back.

He turned. 'As you wish. I am sure Lady Stanton would be a willing chaperon.'

'I have not been invited.' It was a lie—the invitation lay on her desk at home. What had been home, that is, and if her desk still stood where it had. But he would not know that, she was sure. 'I could, however, go as your guest.'

His lips thinned. 'You wish to put me in order, as you have my staff?'

'I would not dare, my lord, I assure you.'

'Then why would you want me to go with you?'

She shrugged. 'I wish to see if we can be civil to one another. Just for an afternoon.'

Amusement twitched at the corners of his mouth. He looked down at the carpet for a moment, then up at her. She smiled back, and for a moment there was real warmth, just a fragile flicker, between them.

'Well,' he said eventually, 'I suppose we can try, at least.'

Hyde Park was bathed in sunlight the next day as a number of fashionable people descended upon it with picnic hampers, rugs and cries of excitement to see friends they had not beheld for several hours.

Lily, overseeing the unpacking of their picnic basket by the banks of the Serpentine, looked up to see Kitty Stanton approaching at speed.

'Lily!' Kitty held out both hands and took those of her friend. 'What is this I hear about you moving into Brook Street permanently?'

Lily stared at her, agape. 'How did you know?'

Kitty waved this away as if it was obvious that she would be party to everything of import in the city. 'Everyone knows.' Leaning in conspiratorially, she whispered, 'How are you finding it? Has he cheered up?'

Lily hid a smile. 'A little.'

'He's certainly handsome.' Kitty said, looking over her friend's shoulder to where the Major was exchanging pleasantries with an elderly couple on a bench. 'Perhaps he would have made a good husband after all.'

'Kitty!'

'What?' Kitty threw her an innocent look. 'I am always on the lookout for someone for you, you know. I think constantly of your well-being. Which reminds me—how are you feeling after you fainted in Lady Asterley's ballroom? Was the Major awful about it?'

'He was very kind,' Lily said firmly. There was no point in pointing out that she had not been in the ballroom at the time she was taken ill, nor had she truly fainted. Her friend had a habit of remembering events in an overly theatrical and often fanciful fashion, and no doubt this was the tale the *ton* had heard. 'Really, Kitty, he is not at all as bad as I first thought—I believe I may have judged him unfairly.'

'He *was* most solicitous at the carriage...' Kitty stared dreamily into space for a moment. 'You are lucky, Lily. A handsome guardian and an eligible young suitor to pay you attention.'

'I beg your pardon?' Lily frowned. 'Suitor?'

'Oh! Did I not say?' Kitty looked around them dramatically and leaned in. 'I saw Charles Denham at the opera not two nights after Lady Asterley's ball and he was asking after you. He spoke of you in the fondest terms and seemed quite disappointed that you were not there! When I told him you had been taken ill at the ball he was most troubled. Of course, I told him you were safely with your guardian and that seemed to put his mind at rest somewhat.' She nodded, the feathers in her hat waving elaborately. 'There. What do you think of that?'

'He is concerned as a friend,' Lily told her.

Her friend snorted in a most unladylike fashion. 'Lord Denham has never been friends with a woman in his life. If he was concerned— and let me assure you, he was—it *must* be because he favours you!'

She tapped Lily excitedly with her fan. 'And what a distinguished husband he would make—he will be an Earl when he succeeds his father, you know!'

Lily sighed. 'Really, Kitty, you should not read so much into everything!'

'We shall sèe,' Kitty said knowingly, then threw a dazzling smile over her friend's shoulder. 'Why, good afternoon, Major—how lovely to see you again!'

'Lady Stanton.' He bowed over her hand. 'I trust you are well?'

'Very.' She smiled winningly. 'Miss Pevensey tells me you are taking awfully good care of her, my lord.'

Lily mustered a smile as sea-coloured eyes sought hers. Would he think she had been gossiping and become irritated? But, no, he looked amused. 'It is all lies, I assure you. I set her to work in the kitchens immediately.'

Kitty giggled flirtatiously. 'How wicked you must be, my lord.'

'Perhaps I can improve your opinion of me.' The Major looked from one girl to the other. 'I have been thinking about your suggestion that I invite guests to Oakridge, Lady Stanton. I thought I might have a ball.'

'A ball?' they said together, and Kitty clapped her hands together in excitement.

'Oh, would that not be splendid, Lily?'

'Indeed.' Briefly, Lily looked at the Major, and found him watching her. From what she had seen so far—indeed, by his own admission—he did not enjoy such occasions. He was unable to dance, and seemed to find the endless talk dull. Why then would he wish to take on the expense and inconvenience of entertaining people he showed no sign of liking?

She saw the answer in his eyes. It was for her.

The knowledge so touched her that, for a long moment, she could say nothing more. Luckily Kitty felt no such compunction, chattering on about how wonderful it would be, and how very excited everyone would be when she told them.

'You do not mind if I mention it to a few people, do you, my lord?'

He shook his head. 'It will save on the cost of invitations.'

'Oh, but you must still send out invitations!' Kitty protested, missing the irony in his tone completely.

'Very well, if you think it best.' He gave her a tight smile. 'Now, Lady Stanton, if you will allow it, I have come to claim my ward.'

'Oh—of course—and I must find my husband before he eats our whole hamper and leaves nothing for me.' Kitty beamed at them both. 'Enjoy your lunch!'

When she was gone, Major Westhaven raised a quizzical eyebrow at Lily.

'I know,' she told him, trying to suppress a smile. 'I have no idea where she gets her energy.' Looking sideways at him, she said, 'When will your ball be?'

'Perhaps two weeks,' he said. 'I happened upon the idea last night and thought you would enjoy it.' He paused, eyes unreadable. 'Plus, the more events you attend, the more suitors you will attract.'

'Suitors?'

'Mmm.' He nodded. 'You know your brother's dearest wish was for you to be permanently provided for.'

'Of course.' Lily dropped her eyes from his, feeling suddenly foolish. Of course the ball was to find her a husband. What had she been thinking—that he wanted to please her? That he wished them to become closer? He was doing his duty—and she must become used to the idea that he was to determine her fate.

'I will decide nothing without consulting you,' he said gently, as if he could read her thoughts. 'You may depend upon that.'

Looking into his face, she believed him, as improbable as such a thing seemed. Robbie would never have agreed a match for her without asking her opinion first, she knew that instinctively. And she must rely on the fact that this man—to whom her brother had entrusted her security—would hold true to his word. What other choice was there?

She forced herself to smile. 'It is very good of you, my lord, to put yourself to such trouble.'

'It will be no trouble. And now, if I am to continue taking awfully good care of you,' he said, repeating Kitty's phrase in tones laced with irony, 'I must insist that you have something to eat.'

'That would be lovely.' Automatically, she began to move with him back towards the area where they had laid out their blanket.

They did not get far, for almost immediately the tall, customarily overdressed figure of Charlie Denham presented itself in their path.

'Major Westhaven, Miss Pevensey.' He bowed low.

'Denham.' The Major sounded ever so slightly displeased at the sight of him, but Lily did not think the younger man had noticed, so concerned did he seem to be in smiling at her. Her brows drew together, just for a moment. He was looking at her differently. The usual self-important air was still there, of course…but today he seemed much more earnest…almost sincere.

'How lovely to see you, Lord Denham,' she said, no more pleased to see him but wishing to make amends for her guardian's cool greeting. 'I trust you are well?'

'Very.' He turned to the Major. 'I wonder, may I walk a little way with Miss Pevensey?' he asked respectfully. 'I promise I shall not tire her out.'

The Major nodded, somewhat stiffly, Lily thought. 'Certainly. I shall see you back at the hamper, Liliana.'

'I shall not be long,' she said—she did not really wish to walk with Denham and would soon be seeking an excuse to escape—but he had already turned away.

'Shall we?' Lord Denham gestured to the path before them.

'Certainly.' Mustering her usual sparkling smile, Lily fell into step beside him.

'I was most distressed to hear you had been taken ill at Lady Asterley's ball,' he said, as they strolled.

'Oh—you must forgive me for never coming back,' she said, looking up at him. 'You must have thought me awfully rude.'

'Not at all.' He shook his head self-deprecatingly. 'I merely assumed you had found someone more worthy to speak to. It was not until Lady Stanton told me what had happened that I realised the truth.' He looked down at her solemnly. 'You should have confided in me that you felt unwell. I would have been honoured to be of assistance.'

'You are very kind,' Lily told him, masking her scepticism. She could not imagine him being of the slightest use in such a situation— he would worry about his fine clothes becoming soiled if he touched her. 'But, really, it was nothing. I am quite recovered.'

'I am glad,' he said vehemently.

They strolled in silence for a moment, taking pleasure in the lovely weather and the scenery. At least, Lily assumed that was what he must be doing. Her own mind was replaying Major Westhaven's words and expression as he talked of the ball that was, it seemed, to be in her honour.

She was pulled back to the present by Lord Denham clearing his throat gently.

'Forgive me.' She smiled up at him. 'I was so enjoying the sun. What was it you said?'

'I asked if it is true that you reside with Major Westhaven now? That he is your guardian?'

She nodded. 'He was a dear friend of my brother and Robbie asked him to be guardian to me when he died. Now he is back in town, he has taken responsibility for me.'

'I trust he is taking good care of you?'

'Very.'

He paused for a moment, then said, 'You know, we have been friends since childhood.'

'I didn't know.' Puzzled, she looked up at him. The Major had not mentioned such a connection—but as he never spoke of his past she supposed the news should come as no surprise.

'Mmm.' He was nodding solemnly. 'It pains me to see the recluse he has become.'

Lily narrowed her eyes. She was not sure it was appropriate of him to speak so, but perhaps he was merely concerned. 'Is he never in society, then?'

He shook his head. 'I have only seen him twice this year, at the balls you yourself attended. I wonder even that he took you in, for I hear he shuns the company of others.'

'I do not think that is entirely true—' she began, but he was not listening.

'In fact, I have heard it said that he is eager to marry you off so he may live as a hermit once more. It is most concerning.'

Irritated now, Lily bit back the urge to advise him not to listen to gossip, and instead forced a tight smile. 'My brother trusted his judgement,' was all she said. 'I am convinced that Major Westhaven wants nothing but the best for me.'

'Oh, I did not intend to imply otherwise.' Denham smiled down at her in a way she found distinctly patronising. 'I meant only that is a shame that he cannot integrate back into society. I am sure he cares deeply for your well-being, as do we all.'

Lily, eyes wide, regarded him with surprise. There was definitely something in his face that, through countless meaningless conversations and dances in drawing rooms and ballrooms all over town, had never been there before. He had teased her for his own amusement and never shown the least interest in her well-being. Where had all these earnest glances come from?

'It must be comforting to have such a wealthy protector,' he was saying now.

Lily frowned. 'I thank God that my brother saw fit to provide for me.'

'The Major has no plans, then, to marry you himself?'

'My lord!' Lily stopped short, taken aback. 'I really do not think—'

'Forgive me—I spoke out of turn.' He smiled beguilingly down at her. 'It is just that I have been so enjoying your company of late that I cannot imagine it being taken away.' He turned towards her and, before she was able to resist, took her hand in both of his. 'Your happiness is of the utmost importance to me.'

'Lord Denham…' she began, dismayed, then stopped, not knowing quite what it was that she wanted to say.

'Miss Pevensey,' he pressed on, 'lately I have realised just how very fond of you I am becoming. It would make me unutterably happy if you would give me permission to court you. I believe you could grow to care for me were we to spend a little more time together, getting to know one another. What do you think?'

Speechless, Lily stared up at him. He had never shown the slightest inclination to court her before. It could not be coincidence that now, just as she found herself living with Lord Westhaven, he had suddenly discovered feelings long buried. Did he think her so foolishly brainless that she would be charmed by such a speech?

And yet…could they not assist each other? She frowned as sense overtook instinct.

Even if he did want her for her dowry alone, was this not the answer to her problem? She had known Charlie for a year or more and—although there was more than a little of the rake about him, and he seemed a trifle too fond of superficial things—he was not, she was sure, a bad man.

This could be a way to the secure future that she so badly needed. Charlie would be very rich indeed when he succeeded his father. She would want for nothing, it was true. Major Westhaven would no longer be saddled with her, he would approve of the match as it met Robbie's requirements perfectly—and she need not feel a burden on him any longer… It was an ideal solution, in theory.

But the very thought of marrying Denham filled her with aversion, and not merely her usual distaste at the thought of marrying for money. There was no excitement in his company, no thrill if his hand happened to brush hers… And she did not like the way he looked at her—as if he owned her—or intended to.

'Miss Pevensey?' He actually looked worried. 'May I call on you?'

'I…' Lily could not bring herself to accept. She could not be this man's wife—apart from anything else, he would take longer to dress in the morning than she did—but for the life of her she could not think of a valid excuse to avoid his company. She could not simply say she did not wish to receive him—it would be unbearably rude. Besides, he would sulk, she was sure of it, and spoil her prospects with any others who happened to glance her way.

Perhaps she could ask the Major to refuse on her behalf. They were friends, apparently; perhaps offence would not be taken if the news was to come from him.

'Lord Denham,' she said, because he was still watching her eagerly, 'I will have to insist that you ask permission from Major Westhaven. I cannot receive suitors without consent from my guardian.'

'Of course.' There was triumph on Lord Denham's face as he raised her hand to his lips, eyes shining. 'I shall visit him at the earliest opportunity.'

Gently, Lily took back her hand. 'I shall look forward to receiving you, my lord. But now, I think, the Major is waiting for me.'

It was the only excuse she could think of to be away, to gain herself a little space to think about everything he had said without him watching everything she did. And yet, as he escorted her back to where the Major waited, back against a tree, long legs stretched out before him, she found herself wondering how she would sit still with her mind in such a whirl.

Denham had said that her guardian wished to marry her off. She knew this, of course, for he had told her—albeit in kinder language. But where had Denham heard such a thing? Had her guardian been seeking prospective husbands from among his friends? Begging them, perhaps, to take his ward off his hands, offering a handsome dowry as an incentive?

She fervently hoped he would not do such a thing. She had spoken truthfully of her feelings when she had defended his intentions to Lord Denham—and she wanted to believe him when he said he would decide nothing without consulting her.

But it still felt humiliatingly as if her future was being decided for her, despite her efforts to the contrary—and she could think of nothing she could do to change matters.

'Have you had a pleasant day?'

Walking beside the Major on their way back to the carriage, followed by two servants carrying the hamper and blankets, Lily turned to look up at him.

'Yes. It was most delightful to be out of doors.'

In truth, she had barely said three words to him all day, so busy had she been speaking to everyone who had heard about her fainting dead away—in some stories in the middle of dancing a minuet—into the arms of her guardian, or Lord Denham, or simply into a heap on to the floor, depending on who had heard which version.

Everyone was very interested to hear how the Major had come to be her guardian, but apparently no one had felt they could approach his forbidding person directly to ask for themselves. So for Lily, exchanging pleasantries with what seemed to be most of society, there had been no chance to talk to him of what Charlie had said to her, or ask him to refuse on her behalf.

Which was probably for the best—if he was to ask her why exactly she did not wish to become Lady Denham, she did not know what she would say. She had been trying to phrase a kind but firm rejection of his friend in her mind all day, so much so that now a headache throbbed persistently at her temples.

'You're quiet,' he said. 'Did someone say something to upset you?'

Surprised, she looked across at him. 'Whatever would anyone say?'

'I've no idea. I simply wondered.' After a pause, he added, 'People seem interested in our situation.'

She raised her eyebrows. 'Indeed. And they are very curious about you.'

He shot her a guarded look. 'What did you tell them?'

'Just that you and Robbie were friends.' She shrugged. 'It is none of their business, really.'

'Have you told that to Lady Stanton?'

She frowned at the disparaging tone in his voice. 'She means well.'

'I have no time for gossips, Liliana.'

'I am well aware of your opinion on chattering women, my lord,' she said, because she could not help it. Then, because she immediately felt guilty for bringing up an argument long settled, she said, 'Forgive me. I'm…just tired, I think.'

He stopped, turning to face her, and the anger she had expected was nowhere to be seen. 'You're not tired. You're brooding on something. What did Denham say to you?'

Startled at his perception, Lily looked down at her hands, clasped before her. 'I...I had meant to speak with you, in truth. He wanted to know if—'

'Major Westhaven?'

Before her, Daniel's entire body went rigid at the voice. Turning with him, she saw a stocky brown-haired man approaching at pace, all tanned skin and unruly brown curls, his open features wreathed in smiles. 'Jesus, Mary and Joseph—it is you!'

Her guardian was staring at him as though he was a ghost. 'Connor?'

Then he was upon them, and he and Daniel were embracing, holding tight to one another. Lily, watching her guardian slap this stranger on the back, did not think she had ever seen him show such emotion before, and certainly not in public.

He was shaking his head, eyes alight. 'It's good to see a friendly face.'

'Aye—tell me about it,' the other said in his lilting Irish accent, grinning hugely. 'You look well. How's the—?'

'Good.' Daniel put a hand on his shoulder. 'But I must introduce you.'

Connor, transferring his gaze, looked Lily up and down. 'Indeed you must! Have you gone and got married while my back was turned?'

Lily, meeting Daniel's eyes, blushed and looked away.

'Liliana,' he said, unabashed, 'this is an old friend, Lieutenant Connor O'Flaherty.'

'*Captain* Connor O'Flaherty.'

'Captain?' Major Westhaven raised his eyebrows. 'You've been busy.' Connor grinned. 'Always.'

'Well, *Captain*, this is my ward, Miss Liliana Pevensey.'

The grin faded slowly. Curious but kind brown eyes looked at her anew. 'Is it, now?' He took her hand and pressed it warmly. 'Your brother was a fine man and a grand soldier, Miss Pevensey. He's greatly missed among us.'

Lily, about to reply, felt the Major's hand rest between her shoulder blades, just for a moment, as if in reassurance. She smiled at Connor, bolstered. She could do this—could speak of Robbie as he deserved to be spoken of—with only pride and without tears.

'Thank you, Captain. He often wrote to me with affection of the men in his unit.'

'And he never stopped talkin' of you,' he replied. 'Boasting about his beautiful little sister so half the regiment was dying to get back to London just to catch a glimpse of you. He wasn't exaggerating.'

Now Lily's eyes filled with tears despite herself. 'I am glad he had such friends,' she said softly.

'But what on earth are you doing here? I thought the regiment was in the West Indies?' the Major asked, taking the focus off her.

Connor nodded. 'So they are.' He grimaced. 'Consumption. I fell ill a few days before the ship sailed and, sure, they couldn't get rid of me fast enough. I'm right as rain now, though,' he interjected at their looks of concern. 'Escaped from the hospital just this morning—and straight out I went to buy my passage to join them. I leave in three weeks—should be fighting fit by then.' He grinned. 'I had planned to look you up in the meantime, but that's one job the good Lord's solved for me.'

'You must dine with me at my club tomorrow.'

Lily watched as they arranged to meet, wondering once more at the transformation in her guardian. Was this what John had meant when he had spoken of the change in him wrought by war? Was this the man he had been before—good-humoured, almost carefree? Could he ever be like this with her?

Connor was taking his leave now, bowing to her, grinning at Daniel one last time, before he strode off, leaving the Major smiling to himself.

'He is a good friend?' she asked, trying to ignore the irrational little stab of envy that pricked at her.

He nodded, eyes still warm as he looked at her, previous conversation forgotten. 'I owe him my life.'

She wanted to ask what had happened, but she knew he would only change the subject. He did not welcome her asking questions about his past—and it seemed increasingly unlikely that he would ever let her into that part of his life of his own accord. She should learn to accept it, she told herself sternly, and stop wishing otherwise.

So she pushed the frustration down within herself, smiled as if she understood, and led the way back to the carriage.

Chapter Eight

'You can hardly see it in your walk,' Connor commented the next day, as they reclined over glasses of port after a lunch of roast beef at White's. 'Sure, you're lopsided, right enough, but I wouldn't be able to tell.'

Daniel smiled faintly, remembering his return to Oakridge on crutches just over a year ago, his lower leg missing and his thigh bone broken in two places. He would never forget the look of shock and hastily concealed horror on John's face as he stepped from the carriage—nor how long it had taken him to get up those impressive but exhausting stone steps that led up to the door. He had been unable to walk for months and when he had eventually trained himself to balance on the piece of wood with a fixed 'foot' that was his prosthesis, it had been very, very slow going. Until, finally, he had dispensed with his walking stick a couple of months ago, unwilling to draw attention to his injury when he returned to London life.

'I'll never be an acrobat, but I manage,' was all he said, appreciating the fact that Connor knew him well enough to read between the lines. 'How are the men?'

'Same as always, those who lived.' His friend took a sip of his drink. 'But you're missed. The new man's not a patch on you.'

Daniel smiled wryly. 'Thank you for saying so.'

'It was hard, losing so many. Good men. Good officers. But at least you lived—they'll be pleased to hear how you've recovered.'

'I've you to thank for that.'

Connor snorted. 'Me? All I did was apply a tourniquet and keep you liquored up.'

'You sat with me for days,' Daniel countered. 'I remember.'

'Aye, and I had not had a word of conversation out of you for all that time—at least, not one that could be heard by polite company.'

'You broke my fever.'

The Irishman shrugged. 'You saved my life.'

Daniel sighed. 'It's the one good thing that came out of that afternoon.'

They sat in a contemplative silence for a while.

Then Connor said, 'What's she like, Captain Pevensey's sister?'

'When we first met I thought she was the most ridiculous, spoilt, air-headed little girl I'd ever met. I don't think I've ever misjudged anyone so much.'

'Unlike you.'

'Hmph,' said Daniel into his glass.

'And now?'

Daniel considered. 'She's very like her brother.'

Connor raised his eyebrows. 'Praise indeed.' He looked, from the twinkle in his eye, as if he was going to say something else—until someone stepped up to their table.

'Major?'

Daniel looked up to discover Charles Denham looking down at him. 'Ah, Lord Denham,' he said, affecting a joviality he did not feel. 'This is an old army friend, Captain Connor O'Flaherty—Connor, Charles Denham.' He gestured to a spare seat. 'Will you join us?'

'The gaming tables are not being kind to me,' said the younger man with a wry grin, 'so perhaps I shall, just for a moment.'

Secretly disappointed that his offer had been accepted, Daniel exchanged a look that said as much with Connor. He knew Denham very little, their paths occasionally crossing here at the club—but try as he might, he could not help but disapprove of this young man. He told himself it was entirely due to Denham's reputation for squandering his allowance—and whatever additional funds he could solicit—on drink and gambling; but deep within he knew there was another, baser reason for his dislike—and it had to do with the way his ward smiled at the boy before him.

Now, as neither he nor the Captain were fashionable enough to be of any real interest to this young macaroni, he assumed Denham had an ulterior motive in stopping by, and he was certain he knew what it was.

Sure enough, after the obligatory pleasantries and comments on the weather, Denham came to the point.

'Major, I wonder if I could call on you at some point to speak to you regarding Miss Pevensey.'

Connor, picking up his glass, got to his feet. 'I have to be getting along, gentlemen—why not do it now?'

'Oh, I don't mean to interrupt,' said Denham hastily, in a manner that struck Daniel as decidedly false. 'Don't leave on my account.'

'Sure, I was leaving anyway.' Connor laid a hand on Daniel's shoulder. 'I'll see you soon, my friend.'

'I'll hold you to that.' Daniel raised his glass. Then, once the Captain was gone, he turned to the man beside him. 'Now, what can I do for you, my boy?'

The epithet, stressing the ten or so years between them, seemed to irritate Denham, who did his best not to show this. Daniel, smirking inwardly, composed himself and resolved to be more mature.

'Now. Something regarding Liliana, you say?'

'Yes. May I speak frankly?'

'Please do.'

Denham cleared his throat. 'As you may know, sir, I have long been fond of Miss Pevensey as a friend...but recently I have found my affections growing in another direction, and I have started to see her through different eyes.'

'Yes?' prompted Daniel politely. He wondered how this man had the gall to spin such a tale and expect him to believe it to be true. From what he had heard, Denham had shown no interest in Lily previously barring harmless flirtation—yet now that she was the ward of a wealthy man, here he was, oozing out of the woodwork, staking his claim ahead of the pack.

Denham smiled, a study in self-deprecating charm. 'I would like your permission to court her, sir. To call on her at Brook Street, perhaps take her to the theatre—with a chaperon naturally—'

'Thank you,' Daniel interrupted wryly. 'I have not been away from polite society for so long that I do not remember what courting a woman involves.'

He regarded the boy—for it was hard to see Charlie as anything else—for a long moment, and tried hard to quell the temptation to refuse. There was definitely something he did not like about Lily's would-be suitor, quite apart from his unhealthy addiction to the card table and his apparent fickleness—something he could not quite put his finger on. But then he remembered the way she had taken Denham off to dance on the night he had first met her, and how she had gone eagerly to walk with him at the picnic.

And Robbie had asked him to ensure her happiness, so, if Denham made her happy, then he supposed it was ridiculous to stand in the way of that.

He said, 'Have you spoken to my ward of your intentions?'

Denham nodded eagerly. 'She was most receptive to the idea—told me she would like nothing better.'

Fears confirmed, Daniel inclined his head. 'So you come to me for my blessing?'

'Miss Pevensey requested that I ask your permission to call on her, in the interest of propriety.'

'Did she?' Daniel tried to mask his surprise. She wished to seek his permission? Did this mean that she was at last getting used to the idea of having a guardian? He hoped so, and he could not help but be absurdly pleased that his opinion was beginning to matter to her, even if it was only in appearance.

Denham was starting to look impatient. 'So may I call on her?'

'By all means,' said Daniel, with a warmth he did not feel.

The younger man broke into a broad grin—as well he might, Daniel thought cynically, given the handsome dowry he would find in his possession if his suit was successful.

Denham, business completed, stayed only a few moments longer, for the sake of politeness, then rose to his feet. 'If you will excuse me, Major, I believe I am expected back at the card tables.'

'You said you were making a loss?' Daniel asked.

The younger man shrugged extravagantly. 'An unlucky hand, nothing more. I will recoup my losses in the next game.' He paused, as if considering. 'I don't suppose you could stand me some blunt in the meantime?'

Daniel looked at him for a long moment, then smiled tightly. 'Nothing on me,' he lied smoothly.

Denham shrugged again. 'No matter. As I said, 'twas merely an unlucky hand.'

Daniel nodded, concealing his distaste with an effort as the young man shook his hand and thanked him in the most effusive phrases. Was it uncharitable to have reservations about Denham's intentions? For all he knew, the boy could be genuinely in love with Lily; she certainly seemed fond of him. And yet... He had not been a soldier for over a decade without developing a keen instinct for the motives of others.

He frowned down at his empty glass, the relaxed mood he had been in upon Connor's departure having deserted him for something altogether more prickly. Unable to concentrate for the sudden, nameless frustration that gripped him, he put his drink aside and stood up. He would return home and see what his ward had to say on the subject of Denham.

His mood was little better after the brisk walk from St James's Street to his house but he was still determined to discuss Denham's request with Lily. Handing his coat and hat to the butler, he asked, 'Is Miss Pevensey home?'

Thomlins looked up. 'She went to Oakridge, I believe.'

Daniel hesitated. 'Did you say Oakridge?'

'I believe so, sir.'

His master stood for a moment, brow furrowed, trying to make sense of this information. 'When did she leave?'

'Shortly after you did, my lord.'

Daniel checked his watch. He had been at his club for almost three hours—had she purposefully waited for him to be out of the house before making her escape?

When he had told her she could take up residence in Richmond, he had not thought she would actually do so. These last few days they had been comfortable enough under the same roof—why did she suddenly feel the need to move?

He took his hat back from Thomlins. 'Have my horse prepared and brought round, please.'

He stood on the front steps, to wait, brow furrowed.

Why had she shown him the courtesy of making the final decision regarding Denham if she was planning to flee to the country the moment his back was turned? Could it be that she did not wish to receive the young man's attentions and hoped to put him off by referring him to her guardian? The thought cheered him disproportionately for the moment or two before he discounted it. Surely she would have spoken to him had that been the case—asked him to refuse on her behalf?

It was all most odd.

His groom appeared, leading Daniel's precious chestnut gelding, saddled and ready to go. Thanking him, he mounted and turned the horse towards the Richmond road, thoughts already flying ahead of him.

Whatever was going on in his ward's mind, he intended to get to the bottom of it.

Lily, having set every servant at Oakridge to cleaning—including John, who had professed himself ready and able to work—stood hands on hips in the hall and looked about her.

The house was magnificent, it was true, but it held a neglected air, as if the Major had lived in but a few rooms while he was here. Now that he had removed himself to London, the house seemed sad somehow—but a ball would change all that.

She smiled at the thought, imagining the place lit up, full of music and people, dancing, talking and making merry. It was just what her guardian needed.

She had thought all morning about the idea and finally decided that her first impulse—to be touched by the gesture—was the correct one. For, even if this ball was to find her a husband, it still showed that the Major was taking care of her as Robbie would have wished. She had determined to do what she could to make the event a success. So it was that, as soon as the Major had left for his club, she had summoned his carriage and made her way here to see for herself what needed to be done.

Now, warm from the exertion of dusting the expansive banister that swept magnificently downstairs, she crossed the intricately tiled hall to where the front door stood open, allowing in a cooling breeze. A few more impulsive paces took her outside and on to the wide stone steps, her lofty position affording her a perfect view of her guardian's property.

It was a beautiful late spring day, and the few clouds scudding across a peerless blue sky were reflected in the lake that lay at the end of a graceful sweep of lawn, graded by steps edged with topiary.

Something was glinting in the sunlight, to her right. Turning, her eye was caught by the chapel, off to the side of the house, tiny grave-yard edged in rosebushes. Its windows reflected the sun, as if winking at Lily, beckoning.

She had not yet been to explore there so, with a bounce in her step, she set off down the steps and across the lawn, slowing to catch her breath as she reached the small building, all rough-hewn stone and Gothic arches.

The heavy oak door was stiff, but unlocked. Pushing it open, she went in, savouring the chill chapel scent of dust, incense and stone.

Inside it was cool and charming, stained glass windows throwing rainbow pools on to the flagstones beneath her feet, an ornate cross atop the altar and a painted screen behind. She stopped to admire the carved stone on a small font that perhaps Daniel himself had been baptised in, smiling at the image of her stern guardian as a squalling infant.

She walked around a little, running her hands over the worn wooden pews and savouring the utter stillness. Then, beginning to feel a little cold, she slipped back out into the sun.

In the little churchyard, she examined the handful of headstones that slumbered peacefully in the shadow of the chapel. Some overgrown with moss, some almost clean, they stood in a cluster, the grass between and over the graves long and luxuriantly green. Making a mental note to ask John to arrange for it to be cut, Lily drew closer, the sound of birdsong soothing her as she examined the letters carved into the stone.

The two most recent were those of Daniel's parents—she recognised their names from the painting she had so admired on her last visit to Oakridge. *Roisin Westhaven* was an elegant Celtic cross—Lily remembered Daniel making reference to his family owning land in Ireland. Beside this, the stone new and untarnished by time, the crisp engraving *Christopher Westhaven* caught her eye. With a pang of sadness, she remembered the loss in John's eyes as he spoke of his master in such reverential terms. She felt sure only a good man could inspire such devotion.

Her eyes lit on the rosebushes that surrounded this tranquil place, gloriously in flower with red, yellow and peach-coloured blooms. They needed cutting back anyway, and it would be nice to lay some flowers on the graves before her.

She slipped her hand into the pocket of her simple day dress and found the secateurs she had been using earlier to trim the climbing plants in the conservatory. Working slowly, enjoying the feel of the sun on the back of her neck, she was soon totally absorbed in her task, thinking only of the beauty of the velvety petals as she hummed a simple tune that came to her lips unbidden from the distant past. She had sorely missed working in the garden since moving away from her aunt's house—it was pleasant to have such work to do again.

Crossing to the graves, arms full of roses, she knelt in a pool of skirts with the flowers in her lap and began to lay the long-stemmed blooms on each one, adding splashes of bright colour to the moss-mottled stone. She worked slowly, lost in a reverie brought about by the warmth at her back and the stillness all around.

The only indication that she was no longer alone came from a single footfall—a boot against stone flags—and a movement in the corner of her eye.

She raised her head to find her guardian watching her.

'Major!' Smiling, she gathered the remaining blooms, rose and started towards him. 'What a surprise to see you here!'

Only then did she notice the thunderous look on his face—and it stopped her in her tracks. His eyes searched her face, casting a cloud over her buoyant mood. His tone, when he spoke, was far from the friendly note of her own greeting. 'What are you doing here, Liliana?'

'Here?' Looking down at the flowers in her arms, the answer seemed obvious to Lily.

'At Oakridge,' he clarified brusquely.

'Oh.' Her brows drew together in wounded confusion. She was merely doing a little spring cleaning—she did not see what there was to so object to. 'I...I did not think you would mind.'

'Why would I not mind you decamping to the country without so much as consulting me?' he snapped. 'I thought we had decided you were to remain in London?'

'But I have not... Oh!' Confusion gave way to amusement as Lily understood his annoyance at last. 'My lord, I have only come for the afternoon, to see about setting things in order. I had planned to be home in time for dinner.'

He opened his mouth, frowned, then shut it again. 'I see.'

'Did you think I had made good my escape?' Watching his expression, she saw that was precisely what he had thought. She swallowed a smile, as he still looked thoroughly nonplussed. 'And you are here... why? To carry me home again?'

He shrugged, and there was a spark of self-deprecating amusement in his eyes now, giving light to his face. 'I suppose that is exactly why I am here.' His eyes moved from her face to the roses which lay against her bare arms, petals moving slightly in the gentle summer breeze. 'I had not expected to find you so occupied, at any rate. What brings you to the chapel?'

Suddenly self-conscious, Lily looked away. 'I was exploring. I just thought…well, the roses needed trimming…and I thought I could cut some for the graves. For your parents.'

He followed her eyes to the headstones, and there was such a softening of his face as he beheld his father's grave that, foolishly, Lily felt a tightening in her throat.

'You do not mind?' she asked huskily.

For a moment he gave no reply, so deeply lost in his thoughts that she was unsure whether he had heard her. Then he shook his head slightly. 'I do not mind.' He looked at the graves for a moment more, until he seemed to come back to himself, brows drawing together. 'Shall we walk a little, as we are here? It is a pleasant day.'

She nodded, a little surprised. 'Of course. But I have flowers left to—'

'Bring them. John will be glad of something to brighten the place up.'

He held the gate open for her to pass, closing it firmly behind him. She fell into step beside him as, slowly, they left the chapel and its tiny graveyard behind them, moving away from the house and towards the lake, where a line of trees stopped anything but the lightest breeze from reaching them. Lily, relishing the fresh country air after so long in London, tipped her chin up a little as she walked to better feel the sun upon her face.

The Major, beside her, appeared oblivious to his surroundings. His silence distanced him from her—his thoughts, she knew, had remained behind at the graveside of his father. His walk seemed somehow stiffer than usual, as if his leg caused him trouble. Lily, picturing him spurring his horse the whole way from London, determined to drag her back from her supposed flight, was not surprised.

'Would you care to sit a while?' she asked.

He slanted a glance at her from beneath lowered brows. 'What for?'

She shrugged. 'I would be glad of the rest. Perhaps you did not notice, Major, but your house is significantly less disordered than when you were last here. I have been on my feet all day.'

Without further ado, she selected a tree and settled herself under it, laying the roses beside her and busying herself with arranging her skirts so she would not see the suspicion she knew would be in his face. The grass here was long also, and there were daisies and dandelions dotted about. Lily leaned back against the trunk of the tree and sighed—in truth, it was good to sit after the feverish work of the morning.

After a moment a long pair of legs moved alongside her. The Major lowered himself to the ground right-side first, his left leg held stiffly out in front of him.

'I have told you, such work is not necessary,' was all he said.

'And I have told you, houses do not clean themselves. Some organisation is needed.'

'My staff are perfectly organised,' he retorted, gaze focused on the house across the lake. 'It was simply easier to keep the rooms we did not need shut up. No doubt John is glad of your input now we are to open our doors to all and sundry, however.'

'He seemed to be,' she assured him.

'Hmm,' he said. 'I think he likes you. And God knows it has been long enough since we had a female influence in running things.'

'When did your parents die?' Lily asked softly.

He glanced at her. 'My mother seven years ago. My father last year.'

'You were in America when he died?'

He nodded. 'I found out when I returned home. It was decided not to send word to me there, so the news was somewhat…unexpected.' The shadows in his eyes belied the matter-of-fact way in which he spoke.

'Why was word not sent?'

He was silent a moment. 'He died two days before my family received the news that I had been wounded. There was doubt as to whether I would live, so no letter was sent. They felt, I think, that to tell me in my condition would be dangerous.'

Wordlessly, Lily regarded him. She had been unaware that his injuries had been so serious. 'But you did live,' she murmured.

He nodded. 'As soon as I was sufficiently recovered I set sail for England. So I returned to the news, and my inheritance. And here I am.' He threw her a wry smile. 'At least I can be thankful that he did not live to see me this way.'

'He would have been proud!' she retorted.

For a moment he was completely still. 'That was the last thing your brother said to me.'

'Really?'

He nodded.

Lily smiled sadly. 'Well, Robbie was always right.'

Another ironic smile. 'He always knew the right thing to say, you mean. He knew I have been trying to live up to my father for my whole life.'

'He made you feel you had to? Your father, I mean?'

'Never.'

And she saw, in that one word, what he did not say—the depth of the bond that had existed between father and son—the sadness that he carried with him, and the pain such memories created for him.

'Sometimes…' she said carefully, 'you speak of Oakridge as though it is not your own.'

He threw her a look of pure, unguarded surprise. 'What makes you say such a thing?'

She shrugged. 'You said John would be glad of the flowers. As if he were master here, instead of you.'

'I'm sure he fancies so himself,' he said lightly. There was a moment of silence. Then, just as she was about to change the subject for something that would smooth out the furrow between his dark brows, he said, 'It has always been my father's house. It is hard to adjust, I suppose. Hard to feel as if I—' He stopped, as if thinking better of whatever he had been going to say. 'It is foolishness.'

'Will you tell me about your parents?' she asked.

He paused for a moment, as if considering her request. 'What do you want to know?'

She shrugged. 'What do you think of when you think of them?'

'Hmm.' Thoughtful, he shifted position, then, clearly unable to get comfortable, lay back altogether, head pillowed by the long grass. He sighed, the hard lines of his face relaxing a little, and closed his eyes. 'That's better.'

Lily drew her feet up under her and leaned one shoulder against the tree at her back. He looked so different, all of a sudden, long body stretched out in the grass, giving her an ideal view of powerful thighs outlined by fawn-coloured breeches. He was totally tranquil, almost carefree—he looked at least five years younger. She watched him for a long moment, broad chest rising and falling slowly, dark hair ruffled by the same breeze that bent the lush green stalks of grass about his face. Then, just as she was wondering whether he had fallen asleep, he said,

'We used to play at being soldiers, my father and I—and later my brothers, when they were older. I had this age-old wooden sword that I slept with, under my pillow.' Eyes still closed, he smiled. 'We would wear ourselves out upon the lawn, and he would carry us on his back, until my mother would come out and say, "What are you men up to?" She said the same thing each time, and each time I used to swell with pride at being included with my father in that one word.' He opened his eyes, cloudy with memories, and looked up at her. 'That is what I think of when I think of them.'

Lily nodded, eyes moist.

With a frown, he said, 'I did not mean to upset you.'

She smiled sadly. 'I am not upset. You paint such a beautiful picture, that is all. It made me think of my own parents.'

He raised himself up on his elbows. 'They died young, I believe?'

She nodded. 'A fire. I was fifteen, staying with a friend for the summer, Robbie was away at Cambridge. Our family home in Surrey had been in my father's family for generations, but it burned to the ground in one night with them inside it. They said a log must have rolled out of the fire-place in my parents' chamber. Several servants also died, and nothing was saved. By the time we returned there was nothing left but ashes.'

'You were young to lose your family.'

'Robbie was my saving grace,' she told him. 'He made the money that was left last as long as he could. He made sure I wanted for nothing, carried on the education my parents were eager I should have.'

'Which was?'

She tipped up her chin. 'To know all I could of the world, through books and experience, within reason. To think for myself, to solve my own problems. My mother used to say women should rely on men to govern all but their thoughts. She was a governess in her youth and in my father found a match above her station, it was said—though she was worth more than any noble's daughter. She taught me to know my own mind.'

'And what do you think of when you think of them?'

She smiled at her own words, reflected back at her, and leaned her cheek against the rough bark of the tree as she thought.

'My mother used to come into my room in all her finery before they went to the theatre. She would brush my hair and talk to me about who they would meet, and what their significance in the world was. My father would stand in the doorway and wait for her with such pleasure in his face, as if he could not believe she was his. She was beautiful, you see, though she never seemed to notice it.'

'I can imagine,' he said softly, watching her. Then, as her gaze shifted to his, 'They sound like remarkable people.'

Pride tinged her voice as she said, 'They were.' Then, because there was a lump growing in her throat at the thought, she added, 'Your parents sound similarly minded, my lord. Was theirs a love match?'

He raised his eyebrows, and settled back into the grass. 'He married her for her money. The rest, he used to tell me, was luck he did not deserve. They were deeply in love and obscenely happy all their days.'

'You never hoped for such a marriage for yourself?'

She regretted her words immediately—it was too personal a question, he would shut himself off now, and she would never again glimpse the man behind the iron façade. And indeed, for an instant, he did seem to react as she had feared—but then his face cleared, and he shrugged.

'The army was my life,' he said simply. 'It is not right to ask a wife to follow her husband to the ends of the earth on campaign after campaign. I was content as I was.'

'And now?' she asked, emboldened.

He regarded her with eyes the colour of the sky before a storm. 'Now I am content as I am. I am too old to change my ways.'

She was almost certain this was not true, yet she did not wish to contradict him and spoil the relaxed, open atmosphere between them. 'You are not old,' she chided gently.

Eyes closing again, he snorted. 'You have not the height advantage to see my grey hairs, Miss Pevensey.'

'What makes you think I have not seen them already, and am merely too polite to own to it?'

This elicited a deep chuckle, revealing crescent-shaped dimples either side of his mouth that Lily had never noticed before. The sight of them stirred something in her, something molten, buried deep. She leaned forward to regard him more closely.

The hair in question, shoulder length and tied at the nape of his neck, was nestled in the long grass, but at the front, where it was shorter, it had worked itself loose. Glossy and so dark as to be almost black, there was no sign whatsoever of the ageing to which he laid claim.

Before she had realised the consequences of what she was doing, Lily put out a hand to brush his hair gently from his forehead. It was coarser than her own, and thicker, but it felt so good between her fingers that she found herself repeating the gesture, smoothing the hair away from his temples, touching his warm skin inadvertently as she did so.

His eyes opened, very slowly, and met hers, as time slowed down and her heartbeat sped up. Slowly, she withdrew her hand from his hair. 'No grey,' she murmured and, because she could not help it, she ran the backs of her fingers gently down the side of his face, until she was touching the place where the dimples had been just a moment before. 'Perhaps a line or two,' she told him, an unconsciously sensuous smile curving across her lips.

For a moment there was utter stillness.

He said her name, very softly, and she thought for a second, as he took her hand in his, removing it from his skin, that he sounded re-gretful. He sat up, bringing his face closer to hers as she waited, lips parted hungrily. All she could think about was the last time she had been at Oakridge, alone with him in the grounds. She had not been able to forget the feel of his mouth possessing hers—the memory still crept up on her in idle moments. And now all she could think about, all she wanted, was his kiss, even if it was only one more time.

But, even as she found herself leaning in towards him, she realised he was drawing away, averting his face from hers.

'Lily…' he said again—and this time she realised he was not encouraging her, but trying to bring her back to herself.

She jerked backwards, mortified, one hand covering her treacherous lips, then scrambled abruptly to her feet, tripping over her skirts as she did so, righting herself unsteadily and backing away as if from physical harm.

'Oh, God, I'm sorry. I don't know what…' She shook her head, confusion dulling her wits. 'I'm so sorry.'

'It's all right.' He was on his feet now, braced against the tree.

'No.' Trembling now, unable to look him in the face, she wanted nothing but to be away. 'It isn't.' Her back was against a neighbouring tree now—she could go no further. 'I didn't mean to… It's just, you were so kind, and…'

'Lily.' Towering over her, hair falling in his eyes, he took her by the upper arms and bent his head to look into her face. 'Look at me.'

She closed her eyes, steeled herself, and did as he asked.

'This is my fault,' he said firmly. 'The day you visited me, and I…'

'You kissed me,' she all but whispered.

He nodded. 'I should never have done that. It was a foolish impulse and I have regretted it ever since.'

Lily felt her eyes widen. He had regretted it? She did not know why this knowledge caused her so much pain, only that it did.

'The responsibilities of guardianship are new ones for me,' he was saying. 'I mistook my feelings of affection for my best friend's sister to be something baser, and I have confused you as a result. Do you understand what I am saying?'

Lily nodded slowly.

He was saying that he felt only as a brother would towards her.

He was ignoring her incredible lapse of judgement and morality by being a gentleman and providing her with an excuse for the fact that she had tried to kiss him.

He was pretending—he *must* be pretending—to believe that she had simply wished to express her friendship following their conversation, crediting her with an innocence he must now know she could not claim to possess. She had lunged at him like a common strumpet, after all, her inexperience serving to give her completely the wrong impression of the situation.

Cheeks burning, she lowered her head. How could she have thought otherwise? What would he want with her? He was a man of the world, he must have known many women, no doubt all comely and experienced in the ways of men. She was little more than a foolish girl—how could he see her as anything other than a child, naïve and inexperienced, playing at passions she did not understand?

'I understand,' she said softly. 'You are too kind, sir.'

He released her and stepped away. 'I have to get back to London. Are you coming?'

'I...' Lily still could not look at him without shame. 'Perhaps it would be better if I stay here for a few days...until the ball. Just to make sure everything is ready.'

He stiffened. 'Is that what you want?'

It was not, really. She had been starting to feel at home in his Brook Street house, and had planned a menu carefully for his first dinner at home this evening. But how could she say this to him now?

He said, 'Charles Denham came to see me, asking if he could call on you. I have given my permission, but if he is to come here you will need a chaperon.'

She looked up, startled and dismayed. She had forgotten Denham's request with the arrival of Captain Flaherty and everything that had happened since; there had been no chance to speak to the Major about refusing on her behalf. Now, it appeared, it was too late.

'You said he could visit?' she asked.

He nodded, eyes narrowing. 'I thought it was what you wanted.'

He looked taken aback at her hesitation, she realised. Had he been relieved to hear that Denham was interested in her? It was evident, after all, that he did not expect to have to provide for her himself for years into the future. His talk was often about finding her a husband, and the last thing she wanted was to be a drain on his time and resources.

This time with him, she must remind herself, was a respite from her financial worries, but she could not see it as a solution. She could not see this as the home she so desperately craved. She still needed a husband and Denham, repellent though he was, was her only option for the present—perhaps she should accept that and at least try to become fond of him.

'Yes…it…it is what I wanted,' she said hastily. It would not do for him to believe her ungrateful, on top of whatever else he must think. And Denham was his friend—he would naturally assume such attentions were welcome. 'Of course I do. Thank you, that would be lovely.'

He regarded her for a moment. 'So you will come back to Brook Street?'

She nodded. 'If I am welcome, I would like that.'

'You are welcome in both my homes as long as you need them,' he said softly. 'I thought you knew that.'

'I do.' She smiled up at him, still finding it hard to meet his eyes fully. 'You are very kind, my lord.'

'Right then.' He drew himself up. 'I will see that the carriage is ready.'

He left her then, and she watched him walk the short distance to the house, steps uneven in the way that made his walk distinctive, so she would always recognise him, even from the back.

Lily closed her eyes. She was a fool. She must remember that he was her guardian because he had to be. The sooner she was able to find another way to survive, the better—for her sanity and, she was beginning to feel, for her heart. She must not think of him as he had been today: pleasant to converse with, kind…distractingly good-looking…

With every day that passed, there was more at stake now than her pride.

* * *

Disgusted with himself, Daniel strode in the direction of the house, muttering every profanity he could think of under his breath.

He had stood and told a pack of brazen lies to a woman who obviously trusted him far more than he would ever deserve.

He had told her he saw her only as his ward—when the truth was that it had taken every ounce of decency and moral fibre he had ever possessed to stop her innocent gesture of affection before he thoroughly took advantage of his position.

Again.

She had touched him with such guileless sensuality, the merest brush of her fingers enough to arouse him more than the feminine wiles of his most practised lovers ever had.

If Robbie could see him now, he would run him through.

He must never touch her again—he had almost chased her out of his town house for good today. If she was not in London, she could not find a husband—and then he could not fulfil his promise and, worse, she would be longer under his roof, tempting him to disgrace himself and ruin her.

His lips narrowed as he remembered what had changed her mind about remaining at Oakridge. At the mention of Charlie Denham she had been only too willing to return.

He tried to tell himself he was pleased; she would be married soon enough, safe away from him. But all he felt—as he seemed to feel lately, whenever his thoughts turned to Liliana Pevensey—was frustration.

Chapter Nine

A week before the ball, Daniel escorted Lily to the dressmakers', and found himself smiling at her ill-concealed excitement.

His own tailor had welcomed him last week as if receiving a customer back from the dead, and Daniel knew he could count on discretion from the man who had dressed his father and grandfather before him. Though he planned to wear his dress uniform for the occasion, it would not hurt, he had decided, to order some new evening wear for forthcoming events. But the occasion had not filled him with delight in the same way it seemed to with her.

'I cannot understand why women take such pleasure in clothes,' he told her as they crossed into Bond Street.

'Wait until you see my dress,' was all she said, eyes shining. 'You do not know what a pleasure it will be, after six years of making my own clothes or altering second-hand ones, to wear a dress made only for me.'

'I am convinced.' At the doorway to the dressmakers' he stopped. 'I shall let you go alone from here. Is half an hour long enough, do you think?'

She nodded, meeting his eyes only for a moment now that they were face to face. 'It should be fine.' She was more wary of him since Oakridge, he had noticed. He wished he knew what would put her at her ease, and hoped that the ball would help.

'Until later, then.'

She smiled, excitement returning, and disappeared inside.

Left alone, Daniel found himself with time on his hands. There was no point stopping in at the club for such a short space of time, and he could think of no shopping he needed to do for himself. He could pass the time quickly enough with a cup of tea somewhere, he supposed.

But his mind, of late, had been returning to a certain item glimpsed through a shop window last week. Perhaps he could go for one more look, if only to convince himself he was being foolish.

He walked on until he reached the stretch of shops he was looking for, and stood, hesitating for a moment, before he crossed the road to reach the largest of the many jewellers.

It was still there, in the window, winking at him from behind plate glass and smartly painted black window frames. Against a padded velvet bust lay a necklace of diamonds interspersed with small oval-cut emeralds, sweeping down to a central pendant of two more, much larger emeralds. These were darker and deeper than the smaller stones, one round and the other, suspended beneath it, the shape of a tear drop—both edged all around with diamonds that sparkled in the sunlight streaming through the window.

Daniel stood for a moment, wondering if he had taken leave of his senses.

He had seen the necklace a week ago, by chance—and since that day all he had thought of was how perfect it would look against the creamy skin of a woman he had sworn to put out of his mind.

He badly wanted to see these stones around her neck, reflecting and enhancing the colour of her eyes. But this was no mere gift from a man to the ward he barely knew. Daniel had been away from society for some time but he was no fool—jewels like these were the sort a man bought for his wife or—probably more frequently—his mistress. Neither thought was helpful when juxtaposed with the image of Liliana Pevensey.

Yet still he stood, as the world passed him by, and wondered what would happen if he bought this necklace for her to wear at his ball.

And in the end he was no match for the impulse that gripped him as its like seldom—if ever—did. His purchase took all of ten minutes and, before he had time to regret such foolishness, he was back on the street with a carefully wrapped package, looking at the ominously empty space in the window.

He would give it to her in a week's time, on the night of the ball. Robbie had asked him to find her a husband, after all, so it was his duty to ensure that she looked her best to attract suitors.

Ignoring the odd and most unwelcome disquiet such thoughts were beginning to provoke, Daniel secreted the package in his coat and headed off to find that cup of tea.

'Major. You wanted to see me?'

The night of the ball was finally here—a night she had been looking forward to increasingly for the last week—and Lily, singing to herself in her room as Jo arranged her hair, had been summoned by John to attend her guardian.

With only an hour before their guests were due, she had eventually discovered him in the drawing room, before the fire.

He was standing with his back to her, and as he turned Lily found her breath catching in her throat. He stood instinctively more upright in his full dress uniform, the firelight glinting off the shiny brass buttons of his scarlet coat. From the highly polished boots, to the crimson sash knotted around his slim hips, to the broad sweep of his shoulders, adorned with gold braid, he was simply magnificent.

He frowned. 'What is it?'

'Nothing.' She went forward, smiling despite herself. 'You look like your painting, that is all.'

It was the wrong thing to say, she saw that at once. His mouth twisted in self-mockery. 'That was a different life,' he said shortly. 'I have no business wearing this at all, really. I suppose this should be the last time.'

'But you look so distinguished,' she countered.

His expression relaxed a little. 'Thank you.'

As she approached, she was aware of his eyes on her body, examining her gown, the first new dress she had owned for some years.

It was also one of the most beautiful she had ever seen: jade-green silk, with darker green embroidery on the stomacher and skirt, and falls of fine, frothy lace at the elbow-length sleeves and edging the low, square-cut bodice. Since it had been delivered yesterday she had stopped often to run her hands over its intricately detailed needle-work and full skirts, now displayed to advantage over side panniers.

'What do you think?' she asked uncertainly. 'It is a little too fine for me, I fear.'

There was a new depth to his eyes as they met hers, a crackling awareness that made her unable to hold his gaze.

'Not at all,' he said softly. 'It suits you perfectly.' After the briefest of hesitations he added, 'You are wearing pearls?'

'Yes.' Her hand went to the double strand of creamy pearls about her neck, her lips curving into a wistful smile. 'Robbie gave them to me before he went to war. I have no other jewellery, it is true—but I need none, so long as I have these. I was never interested in expensive baubles, at any rate.'

He nodded, expression suddenly distant. 'I see.'

Worried, she bit her lip. 'They are not right for my gown?'

He smiled then, though it was a little tight. 'They are perfect. Forgive me, I did not mean to suggest otherwise.'

Reassured, she let her hand drop. 'Then I am ready.' She smiled. 'What was it you wanted with me, Major?'

His brows drew together. 'What do you mean?'

'John said you wanted to see me.'

'Oh. Of course. I...wanted to...' He half-turned away, then back. 'I just...wanted to make sure you were ready.'

'I am.' Lily's excitement at the evening to come bubbled to the surface. 'And the house looks lovely. Everything is prepared for our guests—all I have to do now is oversee the final touches.'

He nodded. 'Excellent. Then I shall see you in the ballroom.'

'Indeed.'

She left him where he had been when she entered, and hastened along the passage to find John and complete her last-minute tasks.

It only occurred to her momentarily, some minutes later, that it seemed odd for him to summon her merely to check she was prepared; but the thought barely had time to surface before it was buried amid the hundred other things in her mind.

Oakridge was ready for its first ball in six years—and Lily, waiting to greet the first arrivals, was ready to be its hostess.

Somewhat wistfully watching the graceful turns and steps of the dancers from her place beside the Major, Lily felt a thrill of happiness at how well the evening was going. She had enjoyed her duties as hostess thus far, greeting the guests, circulating and receiving congratulations on her good fortune to have acquired such a guardian. There was still a great deal of curiosity about Major Westhaven, that much was obvious, and people were eager, as always, to ask questions about him. Lily, trying her best to answer, was only now fully realising how little she knew about his past.

It was with this in mind that she had joined him at his post, watching over proceedings from one end of the ballroom.

'Major!' It was Mrs Thembleton, approaching with her daughter, a dimpled blonde beauty, in her wake. Beside her, Lily sensed her guardian stiffen, though no change showed in his countenance as his guest drew near. 'A truly delightful evening.'

'I am gratified to find you enjoying yourself, madam.' The Major bowed, all solicitous politeness, with just the slightest hint of irony about the tilt of his eyebrow. Lily suppressed a smile as he gestured towards her. 'You know my ward, Miss Liliana Pevensey?'

'Of course.' Mrs Thembleton smiled at her, somewhat stiffly, Lily thought. 'And I must introduce my eldest daughter, Araminta.'

Araminta, simpering demurely from beneath long lashes, received the Major's words of greeting with a charming blush, although the nod she reserved for Lily could almost be called chilly. Turning immediately back to the Major, she gifted him with a winning smile, dimples deepening. 'It is a lovely party, my lord,' she said in tones of honeyed warmth. 'And your home is just lovely! I'm having such a lovely time.'

'Lovely,' replied the Major smoothly and with an air of perfect sincerity.

Lily, unable to completely stifle a laugh, turned it hastily into a cough.

'Are you quite well, Liliana?' The Major turned a quizzical gaze upon her and, ever so slightly, twitched that eyebrow. She dropped her eyes from the wicked glitter in his, lest she succumb to a fit of the giggles. As it was, her lips were trembling.

'Quite, sir.'

'You do look a little pale, Miss Pevensey,' Mrs Thembleton interjected. 'Hosting a party can be so exhausting—why, just the other day we had but a small company for dinner and I felt myself quite faint with fatigue at the end of the night! Perhaps you should sit down a while. It is too awful of us to monopolise *both* of you.'

The implication was quite clear—Lily was in the way. Resigned, she inclined her head. 'Perhaps I will just go and—'

'Liliana was just telling me as you approached how she has been admiring your dress, Miss Thembleton,' cut in the Major smoothly, throwing her a warning look that conveyed in no uncertain terms what he would think of her if she made good her escape.

'Really?' Araminta blushed a yet deeper shade of pink and she looked at Lily with a good deal more warmth. 'This trim is all the rage in Paris, so they say, Miss Pevensey. If you would like, I can lend you some drawings so you can ask your dressmaker to—'

'Oh, they're about to play a cotillion!' It was Mrs Templeton's turn to interrupt, steering her daughter back on course. 'Araminta dances so prettily, my lord—I wonder whether you would do us the honour of escorting her to the floor?'

There was the slightest of pauses, during which Araminta gazed up at him as though she would be inconsolable should he refuse. Then the Major, drawing himself up, gave an apologetic shake of his head.

'I regret that an old war wound prevents me from dancing,' he said, smoothly enough. But Lily, who was beginning to notice such things, saw the way his face closed off—the tension in his jawline that spoke of how he hated any attention drawn to his injury.

There was a flutter of surprise and sympathetic cooing from both women.

'You must have been very brave, my lord,' ventured Araminta in a tone that struck Lily as decidedly insipid, her large blue eyes fixed meltingly upon his face.

'Not at all, I assure you,' he said briskly. 'And I am sure that there will be many other gentlemen who will take advantage of my misfortune at being unable to stand up with you, Miss Thembleton.' Araminta's mother opened her mouth once more—no doubt to make another suggestion, Lily thought wryly—but he spoke first. 'Now, you must not allow me to prevent you from enjoying yourselves. Do have a wonderful evening.'

Recognising this as a dismissal, even if she did not look overly thrilled at the prospect, Mrs Thembleton took her leave gracefully, and led her daughter off into the throng.

Lily, slanting a look at the Major from the corner of her eye, sensed from his stony features that he was no longer in the playful mood that had so surprised her mere moments ago. She stood silently by his side, watching as the cotillion got underway and trying to think of something to say that would dissipate the tension in his broad shoulders.

'Do not let me keep you from enjoying yourself, Liliana.'

She glanced up, surprised. He was not looking at her, but staring straight ahead. 'You are not, my lord.'

'You do not, then, wish to dance?'

'Oh, not for the moment. I am quite exhausted with all the excitement.'

He frowned, and she knew he had seen her lie immediately for what it was. He was facing her now, and in the depths of his eyes she saw the shadows stirred up by Miss Thembleton's invitation to dance.

'You look as if you would like to be on the floor.'

'Do I?' Looking down at her swaying skirts, she realised belatedly that she had been moving to the music without realising. 'Oh! No, truly, my lord, I am happy here. Would you like another drink?'

The tightening in his jaw would have gone unnoticed had she not been watching so closely. 'I am quite capable of fetching my own drink,' he said quietly.

Dismayed, she turned towards him, feeling herself flush. 'I know you are. I was merely—'

She was saved by the appearance of Captain O'Flaherty, cheerful and dashing in dress uniform. He bowed smartly to her.

'Connor. For God's sake relieve Liliana of her nursemaid duties and dance with her.' Major Westhaven's tone was lightly self-deprecating, but Lily thought she knew him well enough by now to see through the front he put up.

'Really, I do not—'

Her protest was cut off by Connor, extending an arm. 'That sounded like an order, Miss Pevensey. Come, I'd be honoured to stand up with my beautiful hostess, if you'll have me.'

With a glance at Daniel—impassive as always—Lily acquiesced. 'Very well. Perhaps just for one dance.'

As they walked down the long room towards the dancing, Connor leaned in a little and, without turning towards her, said, 'You're not doing him any favours feeling sorry for him, Miss Pevensey. He does that well enough for himself.'

Surprised, she turned wounded eyes on him. 'I was not trying to… I merely… I was very rude to him when first we met and I asked him to dance. I thought he refused because he was miserable when really…' She sighed. 'And now I fear I have offended him again.'

'Ah.' Connor grinned at her as they took up their places for a minuet. 'I wouldn't worry. It won't do him any good to be taken too seriously either.'

As the dance began and they promenaded together down the long ballroom, there was ample opportunity to talk, provided Lily kept a careful watch on the other dancers.

Connor was grinning by the time they were a few steps into the dance. 'What is it?' she asked.

He inclined his head. 'He's already fighting off another one.'

Lily followed his gaze to where the Major stood, in conversation with a shapely raven-haired creature who made Araminta Thembleton look positively plain. The bad humour of moments ago seemed to have deserted him, for his smile was charming—although he was probably putting up a front, she decided. An odd feeling uncurled itself, just beneath her ribs, as the girl tipped up her dainty chin and laughed at something he was saying. She transferred her attention back to the dance, just in time to stop herself going off course.

'He's chosen that one well,' Connor commented, also still watching.

'I think they're choosing him,' Lily said lightly, although the Irishman's obvious appreciation for the dark-haired beauty pricked at her further.

'Who is she?' His eyes were still across the room.

'Caitriona O'Neil. Her family owns half of Ireland.' She tried not to purse her lips. 'At least, that's what she tells anyone who'll listen.'

'A countrywoman!' He looked pleased at the thought. 'Perhaps I'll introduce myself later on.'

'If she can tear herself away,' Lily said without thinking, then bit her lip as Connor flashed her an amused look.

'Well, he always was popular with the ladies,' he told her, grin tempered with nostalgia. 'I've long envied the way he fills a uniform. Not that he relies on that—he can turn on the charm almost as well as I can when he's a mind to—and I've the luck of the Irish with me.' He winked conspiratorially at her. Lily attempted to smile back, unsettled by the feeling of discomfort that such words awoke in her. Of course Daniel was popular—he was very handsome…wealthy…and intelligent… It was only natural that women should be drawn to him. Lily almost missed a step, righting herself just in time.

'Are you all right?' Connor's eyes met hers.

She nodded brightly. 'Perfectly.' She pretended to be concentrating on the steps then—though she could have performed them with her eyes closed—while she collected her thoughts. They danced the rest of the minuet in silence—Lily making an effort not to look over at her guardian again—and applauded the musicians with the other couples as it ended.

'Shall we walk a little?' asked the Captain as he escorted her from the floor.

She nodded, still turned away from where the Major had been. Connor took her arm and led her on a circuit of the large room.

'Have I said something to offend you, Miss Pevensey?' he asked softly. 'You must make allowances for me if my talk is improper— I've not been much in the company of ladies recently.'

Lily, feeling guilty now for her silence, smiled up at him. 'Of course not, Captain. Forgive me if I am distracted—my duties as hostess are new to me.'

'You're doing grand,' he told her warmly, with a squeeze of her hand that, foolishly, brought tears to her eyes.

Lily blinked hastily. This was irrational—what was the matter with her? Her guardian had a perfect right to speak to anyone it took his fancy to—she should be pleased that he was integrating himself back into society, finally. She must get a hold of herself and start behaving like a rational adult.

'Have you known the Major long?' she asked eventually.

Captain O'Flaherty nodded. 'The 63rd was stationed in Ireland before the war—it's where they recruited me. I've known him ever since. We were both in America from the outset. Hasn't he told you that he saved my life?'

'No!' Surprised out of her gloom, she glanced at Connor. 'When?'

'Our last battle together. Hobkirk's Hill.'

She knew that name, and all at once all other thoughts were cast aside as she came to a halt. 'The same battle where Robbie died?'

He nodded.

Lily's heart began to pound. She had thought she would never want to know—but suddenly she realised that she needed to hear the full story in order to understand not only Robbie's last moments, but also what Daniel had been through, how he had received the injuries he guarded so fiercely. 'Please,' she said, because she could not help herself. 'Tell me.'

He looked uncertain. 'It's not really ballroom talk, Miss Pevensey.'

'Please?'

He shrugged. 'If it will help.'

'I'd like to hear how he saved your life.'

'What's Daniel told you?'

'Little. Only that you were under fire from grapeshot.'

He nodded, eyes glazing over as he saw again the field of battle, so many thousands of miles away. 'We came out of the woods to take Washington's rebels on the offensive. We went at them as usual, shoulder to shoulder, in formation. They allowed us to advance, but as we got close their front line fell back to reveal their cannons—and they starting firing upon us.' He looked at her to check she was following.

She nodded. 'Go on.'

'Daniel was ordering the men in our company back and to the side—to surround them, y'see—even as their infantry was coming at us. I took a musket ball in the shoulder and I fell, right in the area we were trying to keep clear, where the rebels would be at any moment. Daniel ran straight in, and dragged me out by the straps of my pack. He was hit by grapeshot from one of the cannons as he got back to the lines. I could see him lying unconscious and covered in blood not far from where I was. Captain Pevensey…' He looked at her and his face softened, as if he had forgotten for a moment how close she was to the unfolding tale. 'Robbie took command, kept trying to draw forward and surround the enemy as we had been ordered, but…' he glanced at her sympathetically '…he didn't get much further before he was hit also. We lost a great deal of men that day.' He smiled sadly at Lily, still silently watching him. 'Daniel saved my life at his own expense. I'll never forget it.'

At his own expense… Lily frowned. It was so similar to something John had said about his master and his participation in the war. She was about to ask him what price the Major had paid when someone approached them from the side, and she found herself looking up into the face of Charlie Denham, boyishly handsome in a new jacket, heavily embroidered. 'Miss Pevensey. You are radiant this evening.'

She forced herself to smile charmingly at him, trying not to resent his interruption. 'Thank you, Lord Denham.' She gestured to the man at her side. 'Do you know Captain Connor O'Flaherty?'

'We've met at White's.' Denham smiled dismissively at Connor. 'I wonder, O'Flaherty, could I steal Miss Pevensey from you for a dance?'

'Certainly.' Connor turned to Lily and bowed. 'It was a pleasure.'

She smiled into his warm hazel eyes. 'Thank you for our talk, Captain.'

'I was glad to be of service.'

She turned to Charlie as Connor departed, her most sparkling smile ready. 'What a pleasure to see you again, Lord Denham. I did so enjoy our trip to the theatre last week.'

This statement was so untrue it almost choked her to utter it. They had gone with Kitty as a chaperon, and Lily had tried hard to enjoy the evening's entertainment—but although the play had been excellent and many of her friends had been there, nothing had been able to redeem the evening. Denham had been solicitous to the point of smothering her—and although she had wondered what they would find to talk about, he evidently had no such worries. He spoke at length about himself and his interests, his skill at boxing, his new hunter, his top-class education and connections, the princely inheritance that awaited him when he succeeded his father as Earl of Ashburton—and countless other such thrilling subjects.

He had not thought to ask Lily a single question about herself for the entire evening. She had gritted her teeth and told herself firmly that once they got to know each other a little better such things would progress naturally—he could not really be so preoccupied with clothes and horses, surely?—but the whole evening had been a strain and she had been very grateful to leave him at the end of it.

'It was, indeed, a marvellous evening.' He looked around him. 'And as for tonight—you make a ravishing hostess, and the house looks wonderful.'

Lily dipped her eyelashes in response, suddenly conscious how alien such posturing seemed to her now. Living with Daniel these last few weeks, she had been increasingly able to behave as herself. He did not seem to expect her to perform as other men did.

'I will pass your compliments to Major Westhaven,' she said demurely.

Denham nodded approvingly. 'How lucky he is to have you to

support him and bring him out of himself—who could have said at the beginning of the Season that he would be holding his own ball tonight? You have worked wonders.'

Lily, surprised at such a comment, followed his gaze to where Daniel was standing in a small group—mostly of ladies—engrossed in conversation.

'The ball was his idea,' she protested. 'I did little but supervise the flowers and see to the music, I assure you.'

He threw her a devastating grin. 'Beautiful and modest. I envy him such a companion.'

Lily, uncomfortable at the way he was looking at her, only smiled.

'Would you care to dance?' he was asking now.

'That would be lovely.' With relief at no longer having to speak to him, she took his arm—trying to grit her teeth and disregard the way he laid his hand over hers in a proprietary manner—and allowed him to lead her to the floor.

Daniel, left alone for a moment, swept the room with his eyes, looking for Liliana—and came to rest on her in the middle of the dance floor, dancing a cotillion opposite Charles Denham. The tiredness she had feigned earlier was now a distant memory, he noted sourly; currently she was all charm and gaiety, cheeks flushed and eyes sparkling with pleasure from the energetic dance. Or perhaps the change was simply due to the delights of her handsome partner who, as always, Daniel found immensely irritating, prancing opposite her, arrogantly secure in his own talent for this dance with its quick intricate steps.

And they did make an exceptionally handsome couple, though it galled him to admit it, even to himself. Eyes all over the ballroom were drawn to them, and comments about their suitability, no doubt, now that they had been seen about town together.

Connor appeared at his elbow, drink in hand, saw where his attention lay, and smiled. 'Dances well, doesn't she? I was most impressed.'

'She's certainly in demand,' muttered Daniel, jaw tight.

Connor shrugged. 'She's a beautiful girl. I'm only surprised you chose to make her your ward and not your wife.'

Daniel glared at him. 'Don't mock me, Captain.'

'Do I sound like I'm mocking you?'

He averted his eyes from the dance floor. 'As you can very well see, her affections are engaged elsewhere.'

Connor arched an eyebrow and made a sound deep in his throat. 'You sure about that?'

'Oh, I'm sure.' Daniel heard the bitter note in his own voice and despised it. Where had it come from, this sudden longing for a future he had long accepted would not be his?

Connor, arms folded, watched the dancing in silence for a moment. 'She's fond of you, any road.'

Daniel turned to him with a frown. '*Fond* of me?'

Connor looked amused. 'You hadn't noticed? She worries about you.'

Alarmed, Daniel glared at his friend. 'What have you said to her?'

'Don't worry, Major, I made you sound brave and dashing in all my stories.'

'*Captain.*' Taking him by the elbow, Daniel moved back from the room. 'For God's sake, tell me what you said to her!'

'She wanted to know about Hobkirk's Hill.' Connor frowned, perplexed. 'I don't remember what I said, exactly. Is it important?'

Daniel did not answer for a moment, and light dawned in the younger man's face.

'You haven't told her you lost your leg, have you?'

'Keep your voice down,' Daniel growled. 'Come outside.'

Connor followed him out on to the terrace and down the steps that led to the lawn, watching as his friend lit a cigar and blew smoke into the semi-darkness.

'Why haven't you told her?'

Daniel leaned against a stone urn and regarded the man who had pulled him off a blood-soaked battlefield and dressed his wounds with his own hands. Even now he clearly remembered the aftermath of Hobkirk's Hill: the blinding, bright white agony, matched only by the delirious heat that seared him in every bone, every joint of a body that had felt irreparably broken for long after.

The memories themselves blurred into one, but he would never forget the details imprinted on his senses: the smell of the sickroom, the moaning all around; the constant stabbing ache after the surgeons had taken his leg. He could hear himself now, grief and pain making him blunt as Death waited at the foot of his bed, inviting him on his final journey with an outstretched hand:

'What's the damage? Don't lie to me.'

And Connor's cheery reply, *'You'll live, sir. God willing'*, as if words spoken gently could heal his shattered body. But they had.

This man had been with him through it all—more than anyone else he should understand.

'Major?' There was a hand on his shoulder.

He shrugged it off. 'You were there, Connor. It's not exactly a subject for dinnertime chitchat.'

'I doubt she'd faint. She seems made of sterner stuff.'

'Nobody knows. I've been at Oakridge this past year, learning to walk again.'

'People you meet in ballrooms don't need to know.' Connor sighed. 'I'm not expecting you to put it on your calling card, I'm only suggesting that your ward might appreciate some honesty.'

'It's not relevant to our relationship.'

A snort of derision told him what the other man thought of this.

Daniel gritted his teeth. 'I don't need anyone to worry about me, as you so euphemistically put it.'

'But she'll find out, surely.'

'Why? She does not need to. You saw her with Denham. Now she has my money behind her she'll be married before long and out of my house.'

'And that's what you want, is it?'

'It's what Robbie wanted,' came the curt reply. 'I'm her guardian, Connor, that is all there is to it.'

'You're content as just her guardian?'

Daniel pushed aside the image of Lily, deliciously curvaceous in the gown he had paid for, capably organising staff and guests alike. 'I'm not sure what you're alluding to. If you are trying to say something, just say it.'

Connor held up his hands, palms up. 'I'm saying nothing.'

Daniel looked at him for a long moment. 'She is my ward. She does not need to know the details of my personal life.'

''Tis a little more than a detail.'

'Enough.' Daniel held up a hand. 'It is my decision.'

'No argument there.'

'For a change.' He smiled wryly. 'You don't follow orders as well as you used to, Lieutenant.'

'Captain.'

'My apologies. Old habits die hard.'

'You should know.'

Daniel shook his head in fond exasperation and finished his cigar. 'Can we leave it at that?'

Connor shrugged. 'Of course.' He clapped his friend on the back. 'Come—shall we rejoin your guests?'

Daniel gestured to the stairs. With any luck Denham would still be engaged on the dance floor and he would be spared the dubious pleasure of his company. 'By all means,' he said, with only a hint of irony. 'Although I would like them a good deal better if they would stop pushing their daughters in my path. I've been fending off requests to dance all evening—I'm beginning to feel like an infirm old man.'

The Irishman grinned. 'Serves you right for being such a handsome devil, doesn't it? Lead the way.'

'Major Westhaven?'

Daniel, having freed himself from one Miss Ottalie Flinders, a girl imbued with an excess of diamonds as sparkling as her wits were dull, had just slipped out of the ballroom and into the hall. He was on his way below stairs for a moment of peace and a glass of hard liquor—so the sight of Charles Denham coming toward him, earnest and sober-looking, was a doubly unwelcome one.

He stopped. 'Lord Denham.'

'Is this a good time to seek an audience with you?'

'Now?' Even the boy's lack of tact should allow him to see it was a spectacularly bad time. Daniel could feel his mood was rapidly deteriorating as he stood, regarding this man who could so easily bring a smile to Lily's face. What on earth did she see in him, trussed up in such a manner?

'If you have a few moments…' It seemed finally to dawn on Denham that his suggestion was not being received favourably. 'Or would you would prefer that I—'

'Come, then,' Daniel cut in. It was as good a time as any, he supposed.

He drew himself up and led the way down the hall to the library—his father's favourite room and always, for Daniel, a place of business. And, surely there was only one reason why this man would seek him out at such a time.

Denham took up a position before the desk in what he obviously considered to be an upright stance. Daniel, after years commanding a company of men, itched to point out the flaws in his carriage. He walked slowly to his chair, knowing his limp was less obvious at an unhurried pace, and sat down leisurely.

In the silence that followed, he fixed a stern stare upon the younger man.

'Thank you for allowing this interruption to your evening.' Denham looked slightly intimidated, as was Daniel's intention.

'Won't you sit down?'

'No, thank you. I am content as I am.'

'Fine.' Daniel sat back in his own seat. 'Then perhaps we can discuss why you wished to speak to me? I have guests to attend to.'

'Of course.' Denham stood taller. 'I have come to ask for Miss Pevensey's hand in marriage. If you agree, I would like to propose to her tomorrow—when she has had ample time to recover from tonight's exertions, naturally.'

There was a long silence as his words rang in the quiet room. Daniel, sitting quite still, could hear nothing but the ticking of the grandfather clock in the corner—and the shrill voice shouting objections in his mind.

'Why?' he said at last, when Denham was beginning to squirm.

The younger man's eyebrows drew together. 'I beg your pardon?'

'Why do you want to marry Liliana?'

'Well…because I love her.'

'I see.' Daniel looked at his desk for a moment, to hide the disbelief in his eyes. 'And she loves you?'

'I think she cares deeply for me, yes. And I would make her an excellent husband. She would be well provided for, I assure you.'

All good answers, Daniel told himself. And it was possible that everything the boy said was true. Lily did seem to care for him, for some reason. But did she not deserve something more than this somewhat insipid young man, who was so clearly only infatuated with her money—who would no doubt lose interest in her within the first year of marriage?

He knew it was none of his business—if she wanted him, she must have him.

Yet every bone in his body told him this was not what she wanted. Even though she was enthusiastic whenever the subject of Denham was raised…even though she smiled prettily at him, danced with him and listened patiently to his over-polished ramblings about how beautiful she was… It was wrong. She deserved better.

'I'm sorry,' he said firmly. 'I am going to have to refuse your offer.'

Denham blinked. 'You're…what?'

'I have decided it would be better to wait another year before finding my ward a husband.'

'I…I don't understand…' The younger man looked completely nonplussed.

'Liliana is not ready for marriage,' Daniel told him.

'But…' A pink flush was creeping up the boy's neck. 'The whole of society knows you're trying to marry her off!'

'I have changed my mind.'

'Should you not ask her what she wants?'

'What makes you think I have not asked her already?'

Denham froze. 'She would not refuse me! I do not believe you!'

Daniel sighed deeply, as if this was taking up far too much of his valuable time. 'Unfortunately, Lord Denham, it is not her decision to make, even if she did wish to marry you. I am her guardian, and I say the match is not a desirable one.'

'Not desirable?' spluttered Denham. 'I am the future Earl of Ashburton! She will be a Countess! She will want for nothing—I will see she wants for nothing!'

'With goods paid for by her dowry?'

Denham looked like a spoilt child on the verge of a temper tantrum. 'I have money in my own right, I assure you. I receive a generous allowance and I will be very wealthy when I come into my inheritance.'

'Indeed.' Daniel was still icily calm. 'But I have seen your name too many times in the Betting Book at White's for comfort. And when I passed your father on the Strand the other day he was the picture of health and did not look ready to give up the ghost—or his riches—at any point in the near future. So no, Lord Denham, you are not what I would look for in a husband for my ward.'

'How *dare* you?' Thoroughly red in the face now, Charlie was fit to burst.

'I dare,' said Daniel calmly, 'because this is my house, and Liliana is my responsibility. Perhaps if she is still unmarried when you eventually do come into your inheritance we may speak again.'

For a moment the younger man stood, quivering with impotent rage, before his desk. Then, clenching his fists, he turned on his heel. 'I will see myself out!'

'Do, there's a good chap,' Daniel muttered. As the door slammed behind Denham, he leaned back in his chair and allowed himself a satisfied smile. His dark mood had vanished—and the rest of the ball would be infinitely more enjoyable if he did not have to see that jumped-up fool fawning upon Lily every time he turned around.

It was only as he thought of her, resplendent in her jade dress, effortlessly pleasing his guests with her grace and probably wondering where the suitor that had dogged her footsteps all night had vanished to, that Daniel began to wonder if acting without consulting her had been the right path to take. There was, after all, every chance that he had interpreted her wishes wrongly.

Guilt started to seep into his feeling of well-being. He had always prided himself on his ability to read people—it had made him a formidable opponent at the card table, in the days when he had indulged in such things. And, despite her show to the contrary, something still told him he was not wrong.

But what if it was nothing but his own foolish mind creating obstacles?

His judgement was clouded when it came to Lily—even he could admit that, if only to himself. What if she did want Denham after all?

Muttering a profanity under his breath, Daniel pushed himself to his feet. It was done. He would speak to her tomorrow and, if necessary, he could reverse his impulsive decision. Nothing was set in stone, after all.

For now he was returning to the ball, his guests and his ward—and he was going to enjoy himself if it killed him.

Dismissed like a servant, Denham strode from Oakridge Park with a snarl of impotent fury on his lips.

How dare Westhaven speak to him so? The man was outranked and outclassed—the very least he could do was have the decency to acknowledge how satisfactory a match this would be for his succulent ward.

At the thought of Liliana, and all he would be denied, Denham ground his teeth in frustration. Quite apart from her newfound wealth, he had been shown tonight exactly what he would be getting in his Countess. And he had liked what he had seen.

He halted, seething, on the steps of the house. Why should he accept such an injustice? Why should he have to bow to the idiocy of her arrogant guardian? Why could he not have what he wanted, when nothing but the whim of a lame old soldier stood in his way? Westhaven was clearly not in his proper wits, suggesting she would not favour the match—no doubt jealousy of Charlie's looks and popularity clouded his judgement. Liliana would want what she was told to want—and besides, what woman would not jump at the chance of marriage to Charles Denham? He was the most eligible bachelor in town—to suggest otherwise was ridiculousness.

So why *should* he allow such a ruling?

'My lord?' His carriage had pulled up at the foot of the steps, Charlie realised; his coachman looked up at him quizzically. 'Are you ready to go, sir?'

A frown settled on Denham's brow. He would not allow himself to be dictated to. He was the future Earl of Ashburton—if he wanted Liliana Pevensey, who was Westhaven to stop him?

He would have her, and the consequences be damned.

'No,' he said, waving a dismissive hand at his driver. 'Wait a while longer, Hopkins. I think I shall have another drink.'

Chapter Ten

By five in the morning the last of the guests were departing and Connor and Daniel sat together on a *chaise longue*, exhausted but content.

Connor, slumped against a cushion, drained the last of his brandy. 'Good party.'

'Praise indeed,' said his friend, with a wry grin. 'Especially as I know you are used to merrymaking of a somewhat wilder sort.'

The Irishman raised his glass. 'Don't try to tell me you don't miss army life, my friend, because I'll not believe you.'

'I wouldn't dream of it.'

'Not, of course, that you're not getting your fair share of attention here. That little blackheaded one'd have swooned in your arms if you'd just have batted your eyelashes a little harder at her.'

Daniel gave a snort of cynical mirth. 'I've no interest in batting my eyelashes, as you so charmingly put it, at anyone. Those days are past. Besides,' he added, stretching his long legs out in front of him, 'they soon lose interest when they learn I don't dance.'

'I'm sure they just think you're doing it to add to your air of mystery.'

Another deep chuckle. 'I'm sure they do.'

There was a comfortable pause, during which Connor studied the older man in a contemplative fashion. 'There is, of course, one dance you could do with your injury.'

His friend eyed him. 'And that would be?'

'The waltz.'

Daniel threw up his hands in exaggerated glee. 'Perfect! Why don't we turn Oakridge into a Viennese brothel while we're about it?'

Connor struggled to his feet. 'I don't mean when anyone's here to see it—I'm not suggesting you start a new fashion. For yourself, at home. It's perfect—you'll have someone to lean on. Come.' He held out his hand and fluttered his eyelashes prettily.

A smile tugged at Daniel's lips. 'You're drunk, Captain.'

'Maybe I am. Just a little. Yet would you deny me this dance?'

With a sigh, Daniel hauled himself to his feet and approached his friend. 'I don't believe I've ever waltzed,' he said.

Connor grinned. 'Then I don't believe you've ever lived.' He placed Daniel's right hand on his waist, and took his left. 'I'll be the lady.' His left hand came to rest on Daniel's shoulder. 'Watch my feet and mirror me—you can do it with your leg straight if needs be.'

It did not take long—within ten minutes they were twirling slowly about the dance floor, Connor humming a simple tune—and Daniel found himself dancing for the first time since his army days, over a year ago.

Granted, his body had little of the grace he was sure the dance deserved; his steps were small, his left leg stiff—but it was possible, especially with a partner to steady him through the turns and when his weight fell on his left side.

Despite himself, there was a smile on his face. Connor, seeing it, grinned. 'Didn't I tell you?'

'It is of little consequence,' retorted Daniel, though he had to admit the Captain was right. 'What hope has London of embracing such a dance when it is still shunned as scandalous indecency even in Paris?'

'Behind closed doors who is to know what you get up to?' Connor winked.

'You are a terrible influence.'

'But an excellent teacher and exemplary dance partner, you have to admit.'

Before Daniel could reply there was a flurry of skirts behind them as Lily entered the ballroom, gliding across the polished wooden floor in her dream of a dress.

'That's the last of the guests sent on their way,' she said, then stopped short, mouth open in surprise. 'Goodness, gentlemen! What *are* you doing?'

'Teaching the Major to waltz.' Connor grinned at her over his friend's shoulder.

'Waltz?' She came forward, and Daniel found himself wondering how she still looked so fresh after hours of merrymaking. Her eyes were fixed on their feet, and he could see her watching the steps, taking them in as they twirled slowly. 'I've never seen such a dance before—may I try?'

Daniel stopped, abruptly pulling himself free of Connor's clutches. 'Absolutely not.'

'Why not?'

He straightened his uniform. 'It is not at all a suitable dance for a young lady. Any kind of lady, in fact.'

Amused, she asked, 'Is it designed for two gentlemen, then?'

'Not at all.' Connor grinned at her.

She turned to him. 'Will you not show me, Captain?'

The glint in the younger man's eye said that he would like nothing better.

Daniel stepped forward. 'Fine. I'll show you.'

Connor threw him a wicked smile. 'Excellent.' He went behind Lily and took her by the shoulders, positioning her. 'So, you stand like this...a little closer...' He eased her forward. 'And he holds you like so...'

Lily raised startled eyes to Daniel's face as he lightly rested a hand on her waist and she found herself encircled in his arms, her small right hand clasped in his larger left one. There was less than a body's width of space between them; she looked as if she was beginning to see why he had been so reluctant to allow it. Doubtless she had had no idea that a dance even existed where such close contact was allowed between partners—the whole of her bare arm lay atop his, with only his sleeve between them, and he could see that she was as aware of this as he was, despite the curiosity still alight in her eyes.

'Where did you say you learned this?' she asked Connor.

'Vienna,' he answered smoothly. 'It's a simple box step, much easier than the dances we do here, as you will see—Major, let her follow your lead.'

Daniel frowned, his eyes searched Lily's face for a moment. 'I'm not sure this is appropriate, Miss Pevensey.'

She smiled at his concern. 'Show me. I trust you, my lord. Besides—' and here her eyes glinted wickedly '—there is no one here to see, even if it is a little *risqué*.'

He shrugged. 'Let it not be said that I corrupted you.'

So they danced, slowly at first, then a little faster as Lily picked up the steps; Connor sang in a melodious baritone to keep them in time, slurring his words only slightly. Daniel was actually starting to enjoy himself, his movements becoming looser as he grew accustomed to the rhythm of the dance. She moved with him perfectly, matching the size of her steps to his, body held gracefully, allowing him to lead as if she waltzed every day.

Everything was going well until Connor abruptly stopped singing. Daniel glanced up, frowning, as a sonorous snore reached them. The Irishman lay splayed on the *chaise*, mouth hanging open, empty bottle beside him.

Lily, following his gaze, smiled affectionately and Daniel, although he despised himself for it, felt a shard of pure jealousy twist within him that she could look at his friend with such tenderness on her face.

'We should stop,' he said gruffly.

She looked up at him, eyes very green in the light of a hundred lamps, cheeks flushed with pleasure. 'But I was just starting to feel at home with the steps!'

'We've no music,' he managed.

'Shall I sing?'

She had been joking—he realised that as soon as he nodded. But, seeing the slight inclination of his head, she shrugged, and began to sing, very softly at first, a little shyly, then increasing in volume as her confidence grew.

It was a simple folk song, not one he had heard before; her voice was sweet, lower than was fashionable, but clear. They waltzed more slowly now, and after a while he ceased to be aware of Connor, snoring softly to one side.

He concentrated only on the steps. And on the woman in his arms.

This dance was more than slightly *risqué* in the eyes of society, he knew—and to perform it with an unmarried virgin of Lily's class was nothing short of scandalous. But here, holding her in his arms, nothing about the way they moved together felt remotely shameful.

Then he realised what she was singing.

It was a love song. A song of passions divided by a fathomless ocean—not a particularly unusual or original theme, but one that spoke of longing and loss in a manner Daniel knew all too well. Drawn in by the notes she shaped so sweetly, he made the mistake of looking down at her just as she glanced up, and her green gaze merged with his. She smiled at him as she sang, ever so slightly, her full lips curving in a way that was made all the more sensuous by the fact that she was clearly unaware of the effect of such a movement.

He returned the smile and suddenly found he was having to make a conscious effort to stop the hand at her waist from drawing her closer.

And, more dangerously still, out of nowhere, he wanted to kiss her. In fact, he could not remember ever wanting anything so clearly, so intensely, as he wanted this now.

He wanted to forget the vow he had made to protect her. He wanted to take her up to his room, pull the emeralds from their leather case, put them around her smooth, white neck, and undress her so she was wearing nothing else.

He wanted to lose himself in her. To forget what he was, and be with her what he could have been had he never gone to war.

But all the while, in his mind, he saw her laughing with Charles Denham.

Handsome, whole Denham.

Distracted, he stumbled, pulling him towards her as his arms tensed. She veered hard up against his chest, hands coming out to steady him, her song stopping abruptly as her lips parted in a gasp of surprise.

'Forgive me.' He made sure she was steady and stepped away, putting much-needed distance between them. 'I have had too much to drink, I fear.'

She smiled, inclining her head in Connor's direction. 'Not as much as some, it seems.'

He said, 'I have not heard that song before.'

'It was just something my pianoforte teacher taught me, a long time ago. It was the first thing that came to mind.' She was rubbing the top of one arm absently with the opposite hand; he frowned slightly.

'Are you cold?' Unthinking, he covered the tops of her arms with his hands—her skin was cool and silky beneath his rougher palms.

She shook her head, eyes liquid, lips parted ever so slightly. For a moment he stood, mouth inches from hers, and they swayed together as if dancing still, pulled in towards one another, her gaze locked with his. All he could hear was her breathing, somehow soft and harsh all at the same time, threaded raggedly within and around his, in time with the pulse that throbbed faintly, sensuously, in the hollow at the base of her throat.

He wanted to touch her there, just there, where the rhythm of her heart betrayed her. With his fingertips, with his mouth. Until she wept with pleasure. Until he forgot his duty and every promise he had ever made, lost in her sweet scent and the taste of her skin, musky with perfume and dancing, leaving the tang of salt on his tongue. Until he forgot how she looked at Denham; until she forgot she had ever looked at another man at all; until she was his not for safekeeping, not because she had to be, but because every inch of him had claimed every inch of her.

He wanted to kiss her. It was all he needed—and the last thing he could allow.

Daniel took his hands off her before he did something he knew they would both regret.

He stepped back, clearing his throat, willing his body back under his control.

'Well, I'm for my bed,' he said with a nonchalance he was acres from feeling.

Lily nodded. 'I will join you, I think.' Then, realising the connotation of her words as Daniel looked sharply at her, she flushed a deep red. 'I mean...I will retire also.' She dropped her eyes and for a moment they stood frozen, he still too aware of her for his own good, she mortified.

He sighed. 'I bid you good night, then.'

It was not particularly appropriate, as the first fingers of dawn were already stealing into the ballroom—but he could think of nothing else to say.

She nodded. 'Thank you for my ball.' She cleared her throat; he could see that she had something more she wished to say.

'What is it?' he asked.

She shrugged. 'Only that...you...you've made me feel at home here—and at Brook Street. I just wanted to...' As he watched, her eyes filled with tears and she stopped, a catch in her voice.

'It's not necessary to thank me,' he said gruffly, wanting desperately to be away before his lips sought hers of their own volition.

She nodded, and now a single tear slid down one cheek. 'I know. My brother.'

His duty.

Daniel wanted to laugh out loud that she could still believe such a thing. His promise to Robbie could not be further from his mind. 'You are welcome,' he said.

Another tear followed the first. Without meaning to, he heard himself say her name.

She lowered her lashes. 'Forgive me. I'm tired, I think.'

And the next thing he knew his arms were around her, claiming her not for the kiss he so craved, but in an embrace that drew her body up against his. She protested just for a moment, her limbs stiff, but as her cheek made contact with his chest she stilled, melting into him, accepting his arms around her, even returning the pressure with which he folded her closer.

Her scent rose up around him, swiftly making this embrace—a gut reaction to her tears—into a sensual torture. The softness of her body against his began to distract him, and, before he knew what he was doing, he found one of his hands on the back of her head, long fingers buried in the silky hair that was pulled up from the nape of her neck.

Then she made a sound—very soft, against his chest—and he recognised the danger he had put himself in, almost without realising, so soon after vowing to make good his escape.

He pulled away before his body could react as his senses were, and watched as she came back to herself, as if waking up from a long sleep, looking dazedly up at him.

'It has been a long night,' he said gently.

She nodded.

'Go,' he told her. 'Get some sleep.'

She smiled faintly, stepped away, then turned back, eyes enquiring. 'Did you enjoy yourself tonight?'

Looking down into her hopeful face, he heard Connor's words from earlier: *She worries about you.* As one worried about an elderly relative, perhaps, or someone who was out of their depth in social situations. That was all. She did not see him as a man—she would not have danced such a compromising dance with him otherwise.

Realising she was still awaiting his verdict on the ball, he forced himself to smile. 'I don't remember the last time I enjoyed myself so much.'

It was the truth, in some ways. In others it had been sheer torment.

His answer had pleased her. 'I am glad.'

Daniel closed his eyes as she left the ballroom, berating himself for his idiocy. He was her guardian, that was all. The man who made her feel at home until a real home could be found.

That was all.

He would tell himself until he understood. This was how it should be.

So why did he feel this churning, regret-filled desire whenever he thought too long about her? Why was he having such trouble fulfilling his role?

He must stop allowing his body to rule him and focus on what he had sought her out to do a year ago—the reason he was here, dressed in his outdated finery, enduring the curious stares of society. He was to ensure her happiness, protect her from rakes and fortune hunters, and secure her a good marriage.

Anything more was a fantasy that he of all people should know better than to indulge.

Walking away from him was the right thing to do, Lily knew that. His gesture of comfort had both soothed and tempted her—all she had wanted was to close her eyes and raise her lips to his. But she knew where that would end; and she did not wish to spoil what had been close to a perfect night by making a fool of herself as she had that day at Oakridge—the last time she had tried to kiss him.

So she concentrated on making her steps even, guiding them towards the safety of her bedchamber, though every sense within her screamed at her to turn around.

'Lily?'

The abbreviated form of her name, spoken so rarely that it sounded altogether new framed by his deep voice, wound its way inside her, pulling her back. She slowed.

'There is something you should know.'

She froze as if her feet had been bolted to the floor. Could it be that she had not been mistaken? Were these tangled, uncertain feelings that she had for him reciprocated?

'Yes?' she prompted softly. But when she turned back to face him there was no sign of the tender way he had looked at her moments ago. Instead, his expression was carefully controlled, formal almost.

He hesitated as he sensed her confusion at the change. 'Perhaps we should talk about this tomorrow.'

She frowned. 'What is it, my lord?'

He said, 'Denham has asked my permission to propose to you.'

'Oh…' Lily's heart sank. She had forgotten about Denham. But now, in a flash of insight, she knew without a doubt that feeling would never blossom between herself and the future Earl. The last thing in the world she wished to do was to have to refuse so ardent a suitor, but she must steel herself to it—at least she knew the Major would respect her decision when she explained why she could not become the Countess of Ashburton.

And yet…as she looked up at him she had to wonder why he was telling her this now, when he had held her in his arms not a moment ago? Was this evening his farewell—had he let his guard down because he believed she would soon to be married and away? Was that all that lay behind his embrace: relief that he had discharged his duty?

'When?' she asked numbly.

'Earlier tonight. He approached me at the ball.'

'No.' Momentarily, she closed her eyes. 'I mean when will he come to propose?' She wished to know how much time she had left to compose herself—to think of the right words to say to Denham. To explain to Daniel why she had agreed to be courted by a man she did not even like, let alone hold in any regard. It seemed so foolish now.

'I have refused,' he said flatly.

Lily blinked. 'You have…refused?' Her brain was fuzzy after hours without sleep; for a moment she did not understand. Then, as realisation of what he was saying slowly sank in, she waited for a moment to feel the relief that such a statement should have provoked in her.

Instead, all she could hear were his words in Hyde Park, so long ago it seemed now, soothing her worries about potential suitors: *I will decide nothing without consulting you. You may depend upon that.* 'Refused his offer for my hand?'

He nodded, wordless.

'Without speaking to me?' she clarified, because she could not quite believe it.

Again, he nodded, and now there was something guarded in his eyes. 'I have informed him that I do not wish to find you a husband just yet.'

Eyes wide with disbelief, Lily stared at him. '*You* do not wish it?'

'Liliana…' He looked weary, suddenly. 'It is late—we can discuss this in the morning, when—'

'No!' She held up a hand. 'My lord, you promised me control over my own fate! It was not your place to tell him not to propose—it was mine to refuse him if I did not desire him!' Tears pricked her eyes— she had thought he respected her independence.

He nodded. 'I understand you are disappointed.'

'Disappointed?' Something further struck Lily. She had never told the Major that she had no interest in Denham—he had refused on her behalf *even though he must believe she would welcome Charlie for her husband.*

She shook her head, trying to contain the welling feeling of betrayal. She knew she was being irrational—she did not want Denham, after all. But she wanted even less to have her guardian look at her so—as though she was a child who did not know what was best for her. 'The whole purpose of this ball was to be to find me a suitor, was it not? Now you suddenly decide you do not *wish* me to marry?'

'Do you wish to marry him?' It was the question she had been waiting for, but she was too angry now to answer it.

'*This* is why I did not want a guardian!' she flung at him. 'You cannot make this choice for me—without so much as mentioning it to me before it has been made.'

His hand closed about her elbow, sending a jolt of awareness up her arm, stopping her with her mouth open. 'You deserve better than the likes of Charles Denham,' he ground out, jaw tight now.

'I *deserve* to have my opinion considered!' she shot back, face inches from his. 'I know the law gives you power to dispose of me as you see fit—but I did not believe you would go back on your word!'

His grip tightened. 'He would gamble away your dowry and bring shame upon you both. It would be irresponsible of me to give you into the keeping of a man who would make you miserable.'

'And *this* will make me happy?' she flung at him. 'Being kept closeted from my own life? Having you justify your choices *after* you have made them? If I have no free will, I am as good as the prisoner you swore to me I would never be!'

He let her go, so abruptly that she had to stumble to right herself. 'Nothing keeps you here,' he said quietly, his voice bitter. 'If you want to go, then go.'

Then he turned and strode from the room as fast as his damaged leg would let him, leaving her staring in his wake.

Lily, still wide awake, wrapped a shawl about herself and stepped out on to the terrace to watch the sun rise.

Her ball—the closest thing to a perfect evening she had ever experienced—had disintegrated into dust at her feet. The laughter, the dancing, the praise of the leaving guests, complimenting the event in the most effusive phrases…that other, dangerously *risqué* dance when all the guests had gone—it had all fallen apart so completely, just like her hopes that, finally, she had found herself a home.

Lily closed her eyes on tears that threatened to fall and felt herself again in Daniel's arms, their bodies so close together. Of course, she knew such a dance was very wrong and she would not have done it with any other man, or at all if Connor had not been there also. But her words to the Major had been true—she did trust him. She had been so sure he would never do anything to compromise her. And Lord, he had been so close… If she turned her head just so she could still catch his scent where it clung to her bare skin.

But she would never forget the look in his eyes when she had accused him of holding her prisoner, the hurt that, for a single clear moment, had revealed his thoughts to her before he shut himself off. He had told her to go.

Surely he had not meant it. Later, when they were able to speak without the raw emotion that had tipped them over the edge this past night—surely he would tell her himself that the words had been formed in anger…

She should never have spoken to him so, despite the feeling of betrayal his refusal to consult her had awakened. She would apologise as soon as possible.

There was a movement from behind her, and Lily's heart began to pound. He had returned… If he touched her again, she would not be able to resist.

'Miss Pevensey.'

Startled, she whirled around. Where she had expected her guardian, there stood Charles Denham, his face dark.

Confused, Lily frowned. What on earth was he still doing here? She had not seen him since he disappeared hours ago—the other guests had long ago departed. Had he fallen asleep somewhere and only now awoken? 'Why, Lord Denham!' She managed a smile. 'You frightened me. I thought you had left!'

'I could not.' He came closer and she saw with alarm that he was drunk. 'I have asked for your hand in marriage,' he said, coming forward faster than she could back away and seizing her hands in both of his own. 'I told Major Westhaven that I deeply admire you, and that I want to make you my wife. He has refused.'

'I know,' she said gently. 'I believe you spoke to him last night?'

Charlie nodded, youthful face clouded with resentment. 'He called me a reckless gambler and accused me of plotting my father's death for the inheritance money. He suggested that I wanted you only for the dowry you will bring! Have you ever heard anything so unbelievable?'

'Lord Denham…' Lily's hands were being crushed in his ardent grasp, and the liquor on his breath was making her feel slightly nauseous. 'You have not slept—perhaps you should go home and we can continue this conversation tomorrow.'

'You must speak to him, Lily,' he was saying now, ignoring her words, eyes hungry, imploring. 'You must tell him you want to be with me—that you will not be happy if we are not together. It is the only way he will allow it.'

Lily hesitated. She did not recognise the desperate man before her. 'But…'

'You do want to marry me, do you not?' Desperation flared in his eyes, and Lily immediately felt guilty. It was, after all, what she had led him to believe, also.

'Charlie,' she began softly.

'Well, do you or not?' For a moment the look of hopelessness fell away, to be replaced with a hostile flash of irritation, and she drew back, surprised. Immediately, he caught her hands with his again, chagrined. 'Forgive me. I have been tormented these past hours.' From his pocket he drew a flask and offered it to her.

She shook her head. 'No, thank you.'

He frowned. 'What is it? You will not share a drink with an old friend? Do you think I seek to poison you?'

Perplexed, she shook her head. 'Of course not! I only—'

'Then drink! Let us live a little before we die!'

Lily, for whom events were becoming too much, accepted the flask under sufferance as it was thrust into her hands, and, because he was watching her, sipped the strong-smelling liquid within. It was whisky, and though the taste made her cough and wrinkle her nose in distaste, it did work to warm and steady her.

'Now then,' Denham said, leaning against the balustrade and all but leering at her, 'we will have a little chat and plan our future.'

'Our…future?'

He nodded. 'When we are married.'

Lily took a deep breath. 'My lord…I have not been honest with you,' she began. 'I thought that we could perhaps find something in common, but…'

'But?' He was very still, all of a sudden, and she did not like the look on his face at all.

She inched back a little. 'Really, I think we should speak tomorrow.'

'I saw you kissing Westhaven just now,' he said softly.

'What?' Shocked, she stared at him.

'You as good as promised yourself to me, Lily.' His eyes were glittering with malice. 'What kind of woman are you, to dangle two men along together?'

'No…' Horrified, she shook her head. 'I was…I was not kissing him. We were merely… You were out here all that time?' Stepping back, she stumbled—the ground did not seem quite level, for some reason. She could not be drunk, surely, after one sip of whisky?

Yet her vision was not quite clear.

'I was here,' he confirmed. 'I saw everything. I saw how you danced so immodestly with him—shamelessly, some might call it. People would be surprised at you, Lily, if they knew.'

'How dare you?' She tried to draw herself up, though she was becoming dizzy. She must pull herself together—if Charles told the whole town in a fit of pique, her reputation would be in tatters. 'I would never…'

He smile was condescending. 'I know it was his influence. But do not worry, you are safe now. He told you to leave—he as good as gave you permission to marry me.'

'I don't think that is what he meant.' Lily swallowed, breathing heavily. The last thing she felt, standing here with him looking at her so, was safe. And she was feeling stranger by the minute… Was she ill? Was it the shock of his revelation? She closed her eyes momentarily. 'My lord, I really think I should go to bed. Perhaps if you called on me tomorrow…we could…'

'Tomorrow will be too late,' he said gently.

'What?' Lily blinked, trying to make her eyes focus on his face. Was he swaying, or was she?

'You seem unwell,' he said, expressionless now, unsurprised.

Something was very, very wrong.

Panic bloomed inside Lily when she tried to cry out and realised she was past speech, past calling for help as Denham's arms reached out to steady her, past screaming the name of the man who could protect her—who had tried, she saw that now, only to shield her from the very creature now cradling her to his chest as though she was there by choice.

'Relax,' he whispered. 'It is almost over now.'

Her sight was receding into a tunnel of confusion as everything started to spin uncontrollably. Tears ran down her cheeks as she thought of Daniel, held his face in her mind, wanting it to be the last thing she saw if she was to see no more.

She slumped against Denham and felt her head fall forward into nothingness.

Chapter Eleven

Daniel rose at midday and went downstairs to find Connor seated at the grand dining table, eating a meat pie just out of the oven with his fingers and looking decidedly worse for wear.

He grinned wryly, stifling a yawn. 'Good morning.'

'Good afternoon,' his host replied.

The Captain made a face. 'As you like it.'

Daniel poured himself a cup of tea and sat. 'How long have you been up?'

Connor looked blearily at the clock on the sideboard. 'Fifteen minutes, I'd say.'

'No doubt Liliana has been up for hours?' He was not surprised to find her nowhere in sight after their heated words the night before. He would seek her out, speak to her alone somewhere private.

Connor shrugged. 'Haven't seen her.'

John entered as he spoke, bearing Daniel's breakfast on a silver tray, nodding as his master bid him good morning. 'John, have you seen Lily?'

'She's still abed as far as I know,' replied the old man, setting a plate of eggs on the table. 'Shall I send up and see if she'd like her breakfast sent in?'

Daniel frowned. It was unlike her not to have made an appearance, even after such a late night. He had pictured her already at work, unwilling to leave everything to John and the servants. Was she still abed because of him? It was not like her to hide away from conflict—but, seeing again the hurt in her eyes as he had told her about Denham, he would not blame her on this occasion.

'Do,' he said. 'And tell her I would like to speak with her when she has a moment.'

'Very well.' John left the room as silently as he had appeared.

When Daniel next looked up, Connor was watching him, looked troubled.

Daniel scowled at him. 'What?'

'Something happened last night,' said the younger man.

'We had a ball,' Daniel said slowly. 'How much did you have to drink?'

Connor snorted. 'I wasn't that drunk.' He was still frowning. 'I woke up and Lily was shouting at you.'

Daniel dropped his gaze. 'It was nothing. A misunderstanding.'

'It didn't sound like nothing.'

His friend sighed. 'Denham proposed. I refused on her behalf. She was…less than pleased.'

'So this morning…'

'She's avoiding me.' Daniel picked up his fork, discovered his complete lack of appetite, and put it down again.

'She actually wants to marry that eejit?'

'Apparently.'

'And you…?'

'I am beholden to her brother,' Daniel told him firmly. 'Anything else is irrelevant.' He looked across at his friend. 'You didn't speak to her after I left, did you?'

Connor shook his head, looking sheepish. 'I passed out again.'

'Hmmph,' said Daniel, and tried again to eat his eggs.

'My lord.' Both men looked up as John entered, with Jo close on his heels. 'Miss Liliana is not in her room,' John told them.

'Her bed's not been slept in, sir,' added Jo, worry creasing her face.

Daniel sat up straighter, frowning. 'She did not go to bed last night?'

'There's no sign of her,' said the maid. 'She didn't call for water this morning, but then I thought, as she was up so late...'

'She's probably just walking in the grounds.' Daniel tried not to let the blossoming sense of dread within creep into his voice.

There was a short pause while the servants exchanged glances and Daniel's heart lurched in his chest. He pushed his chair back and got to his feet. 'What is it?'

'The dress she was wearing last night...'

Unbidden, a picture of Lily, floating across the room in her layers of emerald finery, tugged at Daniel. He had spoken so harshly to her... 'What about it, for God's sake?' he prompted, impatience making him curt.

'It's not there, my lord,' John told him.

Daniel stared at him for a long moment. 'She's gone, then,' he muttered.

'Gone where, my lord?' Jo's eyes were round.

'If I knew that, I would not still be standing here!' he snarled, then rounded on John. 'Make sure she's not in the house. And send someone to check the chapel.'

The butler inclined his head and exited.

'I'll check the stables,' said Connor, getting up from his chair and leaving the room at pace.

Assailed by an overwhelming feeling of restlessness, Daniel swore under his breath and headed for the staircase, Jo at his heels. He knew it was ridiculous, but he needed to see for himself that she was not there.

He barely noticed the stairs, covering the distance from them to her room in a few long strides, his leg for once the furthest thing from his mind. He paused in the doorway of her chamber, because it seemed odd just to walk in, whether she was there or not.

Jo had drawn the curtains and light streamed in through the latticed windows, pooling on the carpet at his feet. Daniel stepped over the threshold and looked about him. The bed was immaculately made and did indeed appear not to have been slept in. Her hairbrush lay on the dresser, a few strands of golden hair still tangled in its bristles. A myriad of tiny pots and bottles were clustered about it, and the scent that rose up from them was unmistakably hers.

The whole room smelled like her, in fact. And all he could see in her mirror was his own memory of the hurt in her eyes when he had told her to go.

Jaw clenched, Daniel turned back to Lily's maid. 'You did not attend her last night?'

She shook her head. 'She told me not to wait up. And then this morning…I did not like to disturb her…'

He nodded, hands clenching into fists at his sides.

She was chewing her lip now. 'I'm sorry, sir.'

He shook his head. 'It's not your fault.' He sighed. 'Forgive me…I didn't mean to speak to you so harshly downstairs.'

'You're worried about her,' she said softly.

He opened his mouth to deny it, but the words would not form. Instead he turned away from her searching gaze and back to the dresser, as if something there would give him a clue.

John stepped into the room, breathing heavily from his ascent of the stairs. 'The house is being searched, my lord.'

'Thank you.' Running a hand through his hair, Daniel remembered with a wild jolt of hope the last time he had thought her gone. 'She's most likely gone to London, to my house in Brook Street.'

'If she has, then she's walked there.' It was Connor, reappearing in the doorway. 'Both your carriages are there and all the horses are accounted for.'

'All of them? You're sure?'

The Irishman nodded. 'The grooms say the carriages have not been out. Say they'd know.' He frowned. 'Could she have arranged for a friend to call for her? Sent a message somehow?'

Daniel froze. Lily's face filled his mind once again—the horror in her eyes when he spoke of his denial of her suitor. 'Denham.'

'What about him?' asked Connor, but his friend was already out of the room and heading for the stairs. He followed. 'You think she has run off with him? They would not be so foolish, surely?'

Stopping in mid-flight, Daniel rounded on him. 'Then where is my ward? Tell me that, Captain!'

Connor grimaced.

'Precisely.' Daniel resumed his descent.

'Well…where are you going now?'

'To London.' Daniel flung over his shoulder. 'To get to the bottom of this.'

Lily awoke to a throbbing headache and a churning nausea low in her stomach, not helped by the fact that she seemed to be lurching back and forth in a most disconcerting manner. With a little moan, she squeezed her eyes open.

She was in a carriage, slumped low on the seat, and the thing she noticed immediately was how different the light was. The sun was high in the sky, slanting bright early afternoon rays into the carriage, their dappled play across her face making her screw up her eyes in pain. That was not right, surely? It had been early…very early… barely light…

She turned her head and, with a jolt of fearful recall, saw Charlie Denham, gazing moodily out at the view opposite her, playing idly with a jewelled necklace held carelessly in one hand.

Shivering with shock, she pulled herself upright and as far into the corner as she could get, temples throbbing all the more as she moved. Alerted by her movement, Denham turned his head; Lily made an effort to keep the fear out of her face as, slowly, he pocketed the necklace and ran his eyes over her.

'Ah. You're awake. I trust you feel a little better?'

Memories of the early hours of the morning filtered back through the fog in Lily's mind. She had felt so ill, so suddenly. He had not reacted, almost as if he had expected it. He had insisted she drink the whisky, yet he had taken none himself. 'You *drugged* me,' she managed, voice hoarse. 'How could you?'

'You were taken ill,' he said soothingly. 'It must have been the stress of your argument with Westhaven. I saw the way he spoke to you—

such handling would be most distressing to anyone of your delicate sensibilities.'

She regarded him, mouth open. He really had seen it all. Had he taken her anger at Daniel to mean she would welcome this…this *kidnapping*? 'Where are you taking me?' she croaked.

He did not reply.

She looked out of the window, hoping for a clue, and was dismayed at the sight of rolling green hills and winding country lanes, with fields and hedgerows flying past the window. Was he taking her to London? If so, by which route? 'Where are we? Lord Denham—'

His face rearranged itself into a smile. 'There is no need for such formalities, my dear. We are to be man and wife, after all.'

She stared at him, unable to believe the evidence of her senses, still nauseous and groggy. 'What…?'

His face smoothed into a paternal smile. 'Your guardian does not want you. And yet, once he realises we are together, he may try to take you from me, and spoil our love. I have decided it is best if we marry as soon as we can. Wednesday, if possible.'

'*Wednesday?* But…today is Saturday!'

'I am quite aware of what day it is, Liliana.'

She stared at him, amazed that he seemed not to know the protocols. 'Lord Denham—you have to get a licence—the banns must be read—even if I wished…I mean…we could not be wed for three weeks at the very soonest.'

'I am aware of that, also,' he said, and she did not like the hint of disdain in his tone. 'But there are ways around such things.'

It was only then that she understood. There were no buildings outside the window because they were not going to London. They were going in the opposite direction—north. So far north that they would no longer be in England.

'Gretna Green?' she whispered, desperate to be wrong.

He smiled, pleased at her reasoning skills. 'It is a lovely day for a journey, after all.'

'But…' Lily knew she had to prevent this or she would certainly become Lady Denham, the future Countess of Ashburton—and swiftly, at that. The vast majority of her peers would have given their carefully curled ringlets for such a title, but the thought of it filled her with dread. 'My lord—we have not discussed this!'

'It merits no discussion,' he said briskly.

There was something about the glitter in his eyes that made her feel very uncomfortable. He spoke of love...yet he had drugged and carried her off.

Her eyes fell on the door of the coach. How fast were they going? If she jumped, would she be able to run any distance at all before he caught her? And how would she know which direction to run in?

Lily fought down the lump of panic in her throat.

Perhaps she could persuade him to rethink his plan... If she could make him turn around and head back to London, escape would be much easier.

'Why the hurry to be wed, my lord?' she asked lightly. 'Major Westhaven will not stand in our way, I am sure.'

'I am not prepared to run such a risk,' he said smoothly. 'Better to ensure we can be man and wife than risk a parting, do you not agree? The Major will have no choice but to accept what is already done.'

Lily tried to smile, but the sheer malice in his face when he spoke of her guardian made the hairs on the back of her neck stand on end. 'But what about your father?' she tried. 'Will he not be disappointed not to attend the wedding of his heir?'

'My father,' he said sourly, 'is an interfering old goat who does not allow me the free rein I deserve.'

Shocked, Lily regarded him. 'How can you say such a thing?'

Denham shrugged. 'It is the truth. He will be pleased enough when I provide him with a grandson.'

'But...' she tried again, desperately, 'will it not look odd to society, as if we have something to hide by marrying this way?'

He shrugged. 'People love something to talk about. At any rate, we can always have a proper wedding later.' He looked sympathetically at her. 'Is that what perturbs you? That you will not get the opportunity to parade in your finery before your envious peers?'

'No!' Lily clenched her fists in frustration. 'It is not that at all!'

'Then what is it?' He was beginning to look irritated. 'Why do you have so many objections, Liliana?'

She took a deep breath and prayed that he would listen to reason. 'Because I do not wish to marry you, my lord.'

He stared at her, stunned. 'Do not wish…? You do not mean that—you are upset. You will be a Countess—you will be accepted in the highest realms of society! What girl would not wish it?'

'There is more to life than being a Countess,' she said. 'If you would just take me back to London, let me think on this a little…'

'Liliana—what choice do you have? Now Westhaven has washed his hands of you what will you do—live as a pauper?'

'At least it will be a life I have chosen!' she cried. 'Please, I want to go back to London!'

'Do not be foolish.' There was something steely in his voice now. 'We will go back to London once we are man and wife.'

She nodded blankly. This was her own doing. She should have simply told Charlie in the first instance that she would rather they remain friends, that she could not consider him for a husband.

'You should be glad,' he was telling her now. 'You are free of him.'

'What makes you think I wish to be free of him?' she snapped. 'He has been kind to me, though he never asked for the burden that was placed upon him!'

She had never spoken so sharply to him before, and she saw the surprise and dismay in his eyes. Had he thought to get himself a biddable wife in her?

'You should be careful how you speak to me,' he told her softly, but there was ice in his voice. 'I have been very pleasant to you thus far.'

Their eyes met across the carriage—and all of a sudden Lily realised just how much danger she was in. This was not a gentleman, looking back at her. This was a bitter, thwarted man who no longer knew why he wanted her.

She lunged for the door, hand closing about the handle, steeling herself for what she must do to escape him.

It was almost as if he was expecting it.

Within the blink of an eye, Lily found herself propelled backwards, gasping, his hand locked about her throat, pinning her to the wall of the carriage. He was very close to her as she fought for breath, the scent of whisky and unwashed skin only adding to the nausea that had not yet abated.

'Where are you going, Liliana?' he murmured. 'We are not nearly there yet.'

'My lord,' she choked out. 'You're hurting me!'

'I told you to mind your tongue,' he told her, almost tenderly, his fingers like bands of iron, digging into the soft skin of her neck as she gasped for breath and found none.

'Please…' she managed, hating herself for begging.

Unperturbed by her distress, he raised his other hand to brush her hair from her temples. 'You always did have ideas above your station,' he murmured. 'Do you know what I thought the first time I saw you?'

She could only manage a strangled sound, eyes wide.

'Such airs,' he mused, almost to himself. 'Parading about as if you had a fortune to back up those perfect curves when everyone knew you to be penniless… You would have made me an enviable mistress, had you stayed where fate put you.'

Lights were dancing before Lily's eyes.

Abruptly, he let her go.

'But now you have a fortune,' he said pleasantly, sitting back, watching her as she fell, gasping, into her seat. 'So you will have a handsome husband, and I will not have to go begging to my father for every scrap he sees fit to throw me.' He smiled. 'And, of course, I will have access to those curves, at last.'

'You will have access to *nothing*!' she told him through tears of rage, drawing herself as far back as possible into her seat. 'How *dare* you?'

To her horror, he actually smiled. 'I like this fire I see in you now,' he remarked. 'It will make our married life most…interesting.'

'I am *not* going to marry you!'

'We shall see,' was all he said, smile full of cunning.

Lily slumped back against the seat.

She had to get a message to Daniel, to tell him where she was. She did not know if he would help her, or care for her plight after what had passed between them—but she could think of no other way to escape being taken all the way to Scotland.

As if by magic, an inn appeared by the side of the road.

'I'm going to be sick,' she cried, sitting upright, and putting a hand to her mouth.

'What?' His eyes narrowed.

'Please, stop the carriage!'

His eyes were suspicious.

She clutched the hand tighter to her lips and jerked forward, sickness suddenly not such an idle threat. Across from her, Denham shot sideways with a look of disgust on his face, and banged hard on the roof to stop the driver.

'Get out,' he said brusquely. 'But remember I am here, just behind you.'

She fled, out of the carriage and on to her knees in the long grass verge beside the road. Since she had eaten nothing since the previous night, and little then, nothing came up—but, conscious of him standing behind her on the carriage steps, she was careful to make all the appropriate noises.

At last she sat back on her haunches, wiping her mouth.

'Are you finished?' His tone still held a definite note of distaste for such a performance. In a flash of temper Lily wished she had truly been sick—she would have tried her best to spoil his fine waistcoat. Closing her eyes, she remembered the concern on Daniel's face when she had been taken ill at the ball. He had not minded her, flushed, damp with fever. He had put her to bed himself. The man behind her thought only of the inconvenience.

She stood, returning slowly to the carriage. 'There is an inn there, look.'

He stepped down into the road, peering across at the squat thatched building. 'What of it?'

'Can we not stop so I may sit down a while? No doubt you would welcome something to eat—and I would be grateful for some bread to settle my stomach.'

'What—so you can throw it up again as soon as we get on the road?' he sneered.

Lily fixed him with a beseeching look.

He sighed. 'Can you not wait until we stop for the night?'

'I have not eaten anything all day,' she said softly, one hand to her head as if to ward off dizziness. 'I feel quite faint.'

As she swayed against him, Denham swore. He was, she hoped, weighing up the humiliation of having her collapse in the road in plain view of an inn full of people with the inconvenience of stopping. 'Fine,' he said eventually. 'But no more than half an hour at the very most.'

'Thank you.' She offered him a weak smile and, although his touch made her flesh creep, allowed him to help her away from the carriage.

'Please order me some simple food,' she said, 'I must just go and…'

He nodded impatiently. 'Go. I will order something cold. We do not have time to wait for them to cook us a meal.'

Lily nodded and walked unsteadily around the back of the inn, pretending to look for the privy. There were stables here, and a couple of stable boys who looked to be about twelve and fifteen respectively lounged against a bale of hay.

They straightened when she appeared, the one nudging the other into life.

'Can we 'elp, miss?' asked the taller.

'I hope so.' Lily looked at the small one. 'Can you bring me paper, and ink?'

Eyes wide that such a lady would be addressing him, he nodded, and disappeared. She turned back to his friend, who was taller than she was.

'You work here?'

He nodded silently.

'Can you ride?'

He looked offended. 'Of course I can, miss. Fast as you like.'

'Good.' She took a deep breath. 'If I give you a note, will you take it south for me, to Richmond?'

'Richmond?' He looked unsure.

'You know where it is?'

'Aye, I knows where it is…' He hesitated. 'But I won't be back in time for me supper, miss.'

'They will feed you well there,' she said. 'And they will pay you handsomely, I promise. It is very important.' She broke off. 'What is your name?'

'Jack.'

'Jack, my name is Lily.' She smiled winningly at him. 'Please, will you carry a note for me?'

She knew he was charmed by the flush that travelled up his neck. 'All right. Not much else to do around 'ere, I suppose.'

She sighed. 'Thank you.'

The younger boy was back with a pen, inkwell and piece of paper. 'Here y'are, miss.'

'Thank you.' Sitting on the bale of hay, she dipped the pen in the ink, hastily scribbled a few lines, then blotted it with another piece of paper. Folding it, she addressed it to Daniel and turned back to Jack.

'Can you read?'

He shook his head.

'All right, then you can remember what I tell you?'

'Of course.'

She described the location of Oakridge to him, and told him to give the letter to the first person he saw at the house, to say it was from Lily and ask for payment.

He nodded, and she could see that he sensed the importance of the task and was pleased to have it entrusted to him. 'I'll get there fast as I can, miss.'

'I will be forever grateful, Jack.' Standing, she brushed the tell-tale bits of straw from her dress. 'Now I must go.'

The boy was already leading out a horse as she went into the inn, hurrying now, locating Denham sitting at a table by the window looking surly.

'You were a long time,' he said.

She nodded, trying to look faint as she sat beside him. 'I still feel very dizzy.'

'Hmmph,' he said, but seemed satisfied with her excuse. 'The cook is bringing us some cold chicken. Eat quickly, we need to travel as far as we can while it is light. There will be plenty of time for rest later.'

Something about the way he said the word 'rest' made Lily uneasy.

'My lord, I am to have my own chamber when we stop for the night, am I not?'

He looked at her for a long moment. 'Why are you concerned about that?'

'Oh, no reason.' She smiled. 'Of course, I know you are a man of honour.'

'Hmm,' he said, eyes still on her face, and she had the most awful feeling that she had planted an idea in his head. 'We cannot have you sleeping unprotected, however…and we are to be man and wife…'

'But we are not yet!' Lily sat up straighter. 'My lord, my guardian would not approve of—'

'Ah, but he does not approve of anything you do any more, does he?' Denham smiled lecherously as a pretty serving wench brought over their meal and tossed her a coin. He tore off a chicken leg and bit into it. 'We will discuss it later. Do not fret, Liliana. It does not befit the future Countess of Ashburton.'

Lily, her appetite banished entirely, could do nothing but nod numbly. She closed her eyes and prayed with all she was worth that Daniel would receive her message—and that he would come. For, even if he did receive it, had he not looked at her with disgust when he had told her to go?

But she had to have faith in him. What other option did she have?

Daniel, knuckles tight around his reins, drove his horse forward for the last stretch of driveway to Oakridge.

It was four o'clock—he had searched all afternoon and found nothing. He had been to Denham's town house in London, where none of the servants had seen their master since he set out for the ball at Oakridge the previous evening; and he had also called on the London residence of Lord and Lady Ashburton who, somewhat confused, told him they had not laid eyes upon their eldest son for some days. Leaving messages at both residences that he be contacted in the event of Denham's return, he had visited his own house at Brook Street, where all expressed concern but had not seen their master's young ward, White's—on the off chance that Denham had left Lily somewhere and been seen there—then to some of the more respectable boarding houses in the city. He had even stopped at Lily's old Highgate cottage, which stood silent and empty, leading no clue as to where its erstwhile mistress might be.

Eventually, when he could ignore the growing evidence of their flight no longer, he had at last made his way back to Oakridge as fast as his exhausted horse would carry him, still hoping desperately all the while that she had come home.

On arriving at the house he threw the reins to a groom and hastened inside.

John met him in the hall, and he knew from one look at the old man's face that his hopes were in vain.

'What news, my lord?' The butler followed his master through the house to the drawing room, where, peeling off his gloves, Daniel flung them at a chair.

'No sign of her. Or Denham either,' he said, raking a hand through his hair. 'She's with him. She has to be.'

'What are we to do?'

He shrugged, crossing to the window and staring unseeingly out at the still-light sky. 'What is there to do? She has chosen her future.'

The old man sighed. 'I am sorry, my lord.'

Daniel met his eyes, and the concern there touched him, just for a moment. He nodded. 'It is I who should be sorry, John. I was wrong about everything. I thought I knew what she wanted.' He shook his head. 'Did she think me such a monster that I would continue to object to the marriage if she had simply told me she wanted it?'

'You did what you thought was best,' John told him.

Daniel snorted. 'Best for whom?'

'You must be exhausted,' the old man said gently. 'I'll have some tea prepared.'

'Don't bother. Just see that Connor has all he needs.'

'Very well.'

As if from far away, he heard the door close and John's footsteps retreating, but it was a long time before he moved from his place by the window. When he did, slowly, come back to himself from the quagmire of dark thoughts that raged within him, so much time had passed that his leg was stiff.

Slowly, numbly, like a man who has been drugged and beaten, he turned back into the room—and it was then that he noticed what he had not before.

The emerald necklace was gone.

The case stood there, where he had left it—but empty, a testament to the gesture he had meant to make and its stark, ugly reality.

The additional betrayal stabbed him like a dagger through the heart. He had not thought her capable of theft.

He had not thought her capable of any of this.

Daniel sighed. How had he allowed himself to hope? Since the war he had known what his future would be—and that he would spend it alone.

Yet since she had come into his life…he had started to see that he still wanted, deep within, the thing he had always yearned for before he lost his leg—what his father had had. A home, a wife—children to carry on the family name that had been so important to Kit Westhaven. His father had brought him up to believe that the essential thing was to find a good woman, and the rest would take care of itself.

So he had allowed himself, in the secret crevices of his heart where the light no longer penetrated, to believe that it might be her.

But of course, it was not. She was young, beautiful. He had nothing to offer but his wealth and his own broken body—and she could marry for money wherever she chose. Denham was a scoundrel, that much was obvious, but he should have never tried to prevent the match. It was clear what she wanted—only his own jealousy and prejudice had led him to think otherwise—and by refusing he had only pushed them closer together.

He closed his eyes on the thought of them locked in a passionate embrace, fleeing together from the ogre that had kept them apart.

It was the one thing he never, ever wanted to see—Lily in another man's arms. Which was somewhat ironic, given that all his efforts of late had been to bring about exactly that.

He should not have spoken so to her last night. She had been visibly upset, but the jealous surge of anger in him had been inescapable. He should never have brought Denham up then—should have left the issue until the morning. But after feeling her body against his he had wanted...what? Deep down he knew he had mentioned Denham's proposal because he wanted to see her reaction, then and there, her cheeks still flushed from his embrace, to hearing the other man's name. What had he expected—that she would tell him she no longer cared for her handsome suitor? That she would say instead...

It was too humiliating to even think. He had allowed the seething emotion within to rule him, swamping any vestige of common sense.

And now she was gone.

He lowered himself into a chair and put his head in his hands.

Where did he go from here? His gut told him to cut her off without a penny, to betray her as she had betrayed him. But Robbie would never forgive him, and he still owed it to his friend to make the best of this nightmare. The dowry must be paid. For Lily's sake, this marriage must be respectable. He must appear happy for her, even if he never spoke to her again.

Another thought pricked him. He would have to see them about town, parading their happiness. He would have to watch as she danced with Denham, hosted his parties, bore him children... Perhaps she would even wear the necklace as she entertained her husband's guests, as a final insult.

Very slowly, Daniel lifted his head, a crease taking root between his brows and growing deeper as the thought it heralded developed.

Something was not right about this picture.

Lily would not steal from him.

Even if she had been upset she would not want to support herself in such a way. His mind flew back over the weeks to the girl who would rather live in poverty in a ramshackle cottage than accept his help. She was proud. His first instinct had been the right one—he had not thought her capable of theft because she was not.

And he was sure that she would not allow Denham to steal from him either.

Which meant there was something more to events than he had first assumed.

A slow dawning horror seeped into the pit of Daniel's stomach. Could it be that he had read this wrong?

'My lord?'

He looked up. It was Jo, Lily's maid, interrupting his churning thoughts.

'Leave me, please.'

She remained where she was.

'I told John I do not want any tea,' he snapped, patience fraying. 'Leave me!'

'I haven't…' She made a small frustrated sound and tried again. 'It's about Miss Lily!'

'What about her?'

'Sir, I don't think she went off with him of her own accord.'

'What? Why?' he demanded, startled to have his dawning thoughts reflected back at him in such a way.

'Her clothes, my lord, her things. They're all there. She's taken nothing.'

'He is rich,' he said, as much to convince himself as her. 'He will buy her all she needs. She knows that.'

She shook her head, standing her ground in an attitude reminiscent of her mistress. 'She wouldn't leave this.'

She held out a small oval frame. Rising, Daniel crossed the floor and took it from her, looking down into Lily's painted eyes. It was as familiar to him as if it was his own, this painting. He had carried it all those miles back from America, after all—the last gift her brother had sent her. The slow trickle of dread within him intensified.

'The letter he sent was there as well,' the maid was saying. 'It isn't right, my lord. She'd not go without either.'

She was right. Lily would not leave these things, even if she was forced to flee in a hurry. Daniel ran a hand through his hair, swearing under his breath. Could it be true, what he now suspected—that she had not summoned Denham to her aid? That he had forced his attentions upon her? That she was with him against her will?

What on earth had he been thinking, believing things as they appeared?

Jo was frowning at him. 'My lord?'

'What have I done?' he muttered, mind racing back to the previous night. What time had he gone to bed? Five? Six? If Denham had returned after the ball—or simply lain low after Daniel had dismissed him—then she had been with him almost twelve hours by now, under God knew what kind of duress.

'I'll find her,' he said to Jo. Then he turned on his heel and fled from the room.

Stopping only to don a cloak, hat and some coin for the journey, Daniel left the house, hoping to God that it would be the last time he stood in it without her. Outside he headed straight for the stables, fastening the cloak about his shoulders as he did so.

'My lord!' The shout had come from the direction of the servants' entrance, where he now saw John, in earnest conversation with a young boy.

The old man was beckoning him across. 'My lord, a letter.'

'From Denham?' Daniel was at his side in seconds. He snatched the unsealed piece of paper.

'From Miss Lily, it appears.'

John was right. The handwriting was delicate and feminine—but hurried, as if she had written these few lines under duress.

Daniel,
Denham was waiting for me after the ball. He has taken me against my will—we go to Gretna Green.
Please forgive me,
Lily

Daniel looked up at his butler, face white. 'He's taking her to Gretna. The man is insane—such a journey will take days—perhaps a week!'

He turned his attention to the boy beside his butler who stood, mouth agape, thin limbs full of the awkwardness of youth.

'Did you bring this?'

'Yessir,' said the lad, eyes wide.

'It was given to you by a fair-haired lady with green eyes?'

A firm nod. 'Watched her write it meself, sir.'

'And how did she look?'

The youth shrugged. 'She was right pretty, sir.'

Daniel gritted his teeth. 'How did she look, boy, not what did she look like!'

John laid a gentle hand on the lad's shoulder. 'Was she happy, for instance?'

'No, not 'appy. Not at all.' The boy shook his head, frowning. 'Though her manners was lovely,' he added, with a pointed look at Daniel. 'But I'da said she was nervous of something. Frighted, almost.'

Daniel muttered a profanity that made the lad's eyes widen in newfound admiration. 'And where was she when she wrote this?'

'Hertfordshire, sir—at my master's inn near Hatfield. But that was a couple o' hours ago—I rode hard, but I reckon they'll be further along by now.'

Daniel thought about this a while. On horseback he was some three times faster than they were in Denham's carriage. With luck he could catch them before dark.

'She's in trouble, ain't she, sir?'

Daniel nodded. 'She was abducted, and the man she's with is a scoundrel.'

'Thought as much.' The boy looked pleased with himself. 'That's why I told me brother to loosen a wheel on their carriage. That'll slow 'em down some.'

'Did you now?' Despite the gravity of the situation, Daniel allowed himself an incredulous smile. 'How hard can you ride, boy?'

The lad looked him up and down, taking in his fine clothes. 'About as hard as you, I reckon.'

Daniel's lips twitched. 'We shall see. Ready your horse—you can point me in the direction of your inn and set me on the road to Scotland.'

'You're riding to Scotland tonight?'

'I'll go as far as I can before I have to stop.' Daniel fixed John with a solemn look as the lad sprinted away to find his mount. 'I cannot believe I did not see this situation for what it was immediately,' he muttered.

'Done is done,' the old man told him. 'What matters now is that you find her and bring her home safely, Lord Westhaven.'

Daniel frowned. 'John—why must you insist, even now, on calling me by my father's title?'

The old man smiled. 'Because you are your father's son, my lord. Through and through.'

For a moment they stood, looking at each other across years of understanding.

'Shall I have your horse tacked up?' John asked.

Daniel smiled wryly. 'Absolutely.' He looked at his father's man-servant, face grim. 'I'm going to find her, and bring her home. And then I'm going to make that spoilt, upstart boy rue the day he ever crossed me.'

Chapter Twelve

Lily was jerked out of her doze by a lurch—and then, even before she could react, was thrown out of her seat altogether as the carriage swayed violently, tipped to the left, and stopped with a crash, floor slanting towards the ground at one corner.

'What in the name of—?' Denham was red in the face with shock and fury as he climbed across the tilted carriage and flung himself outside.

Lily, in the silence, struggled up from the floor in a tangle of skirts. She could hear him shouting at the driver, and then there was a solid thud as the carriage was kicked.

She opened the door and stuck her head out, to see the driver scratching his head in consternation and Denham, scarlet faced, demanding what was to be done.

'What is it?' she asked.

'The *wheel* has fallen off!' There was incredulity in his voice. 'Presumably because this *oaf*—' this punctuated with a swat to his driver's arm '—failed to check the carriage before we set out!'

'I swear, my lord, 'twas all in order!' the hapless man insisted, rubbing his arm.

'Well, you'd best get it fixed—and *quickly*!' Deham beckoned to Lily. 'Come out of there. It is not safe.'

'You care for my safety, my lord?' she could not help but say.

'Do not tax me further, Liliana!' He held out a hand to help her down, fingers beckoning impatiently. 'Come!'

Resigned, she let herself be escorted to the verge, past where the wheel lay on its side by the axle, which had made a furrow in the ground as the carriage lurched to a halt.

'My lord…' The driver appeared before them. 'I cannot fix this. Not by myself.'

Denham gave a strangled cry through gritted teeth. 'Then what do you suggest?'

'If I go for help…I could bring men, and tools. We can patch it up until we can get it somewhere for a more thorough repair.'

'And delay our progress?' Denham shook his head. 'No. Take one of the horses, ride back the way we came, and hire another carriage. This should suffice,' he added, tossing a purse of money at the driver. 'And for God's sake, man, do not tarry! The lady will get cold!'

'Yes, sir.'

Lily felt thoroughly sorry for the man as he left, and she strongly doubted that Denham's eagerness to be off had anything to do with her comfort. Still, this delay gave her the best chance for escape that she had so far encountered.

'Sit down, Liliana,' Denham commanded, as though reading her mind.

Reluctantly, she sat beside him on the grass, determined not to stay there for long.

He smiled at her. 'He will be back in no time.'

She merely stared ahead of her, expressionless.

He sighed. 'You know I do this for us, do you not? So that we can be together?'

She looked at him, surprised. So his conscience was bothering him. Because she was tired, and she did not wish to engage him in conversation, she nodded.

'Good.' His hand was on her arm now. 'Lily…?'

'What is it?' He was unnervingly close.

'We will be here for some time, I think. Perhaps we should think of ways to amuse ourselves.' His fingers walked all the way up her arm, until his hand was cupping her cheek.

'My lord,' she managed. 'Please…'

'You need not be modest, Liliana—there is no one to see.' He was even closer now, and anxious gooseflesh was beginning to break out all over her. She thought she felt another hand on her knee, stroking her over her skirts, and the realisation made her feel sick.

'Still…' she managed weakly, very aware that if he wished to kiss her there was little she could do to stop him.

'Come now.' He took her chin in his hand and brought his face close to hers, bearing down upon her, lips puckered.

'*No*, my lord!' She shoved him hard, so that he pitched sideways with an angry cry, his arms swinging out to save himself, releasing her.

Immediately, she was on her feet, kicking off her foolish high-heeled ballroom shoes and running as fast as she could, the stones in the road jabbing her feet through her fine stockings, causing her pain that she barely noticed, so desperate was she to escape the man she had once considered merely a harmless flirt. Her heart pounded in her chest and her breathing sounded loud to her own ears—but she kept running, not looking back.

Of course, he was faster.

She was grabbed roughly by her trailing skirts, jerked backwards and forced around to face him. He held her captive with one hand—and with the other slapped her hard across the face. Lily heard herself gasp as pain spread across her cheek.

Then, while she was still stunned, he pinned her arms to her sides in a tight, painful grip and, before she could evade him, covered her mouth with his—cold and slimy, so that she could not breathe. His kiss was painful—he held her still against his body now so that he could trap her head in position with his free hand. He was frighteningly, deceptively strong and Lily, panic blossoming, braced her hands against his chest to no avail, gasping for air and finding that she could not gather enough breath to scream for help. Not that anyone would hear her, or be able to help her, if he decided to act on the threat in his eyes.

'Stop!' she cried as soon as he came up for breath. 'For God's sake, stop!'

Her tone, it seemed, gave him pause. He fixed her with a cold blue gaze, then pushed her away.

She fell back in the grass, one hand pressed to her aching face, tears of shock and anger in her eyes. 'And you say I should marry you—a man who is so clearly not a gentleman?' she shrieked at him, fury making her bold.

A look of grudging guilt crossed his face as he stood before her, shoulders bowed. 'Forgive me. I was carried away. You are so beautiful… But you must not try to run like that, Liliana.' He raised his chin. 'If you only obey me—both now and when we are married—I will treat you with the utmost respect.'

Lily did not reply. She wondered now why she had never seen this ruthlessness in him, at all those balls and parties, why she had tolerated his presence at all. In humouring him she had never seen his true colours—when crossed, he was simply an over-privileged boy who had never been refused anything, who thought he could punish her as he would punish his dogs for disobedience. She could never spend her life with such a man. Not when she had lived with Daniel these past weeks, and grown used to something so different.

He sat beside her, close enough to prevent her from escape, though she feared to try to run again lest it spur him to assault her a second time.

They waited.

In the suffocating silence, Lily realised he was again playing with the necklace she had seen earlier. She looked down at the string of jewels in his hands. He was pulling it through his fingers, sending shafts of dancing sunlight glittering every which way.

'What is that?' she asked numbly.

Wordlessly, he passed it to her. It was the most exquisite necklace she had ever seen. Diamonds and emeralds caught and held the light as she lifted it closer to her face, its sheer beauty taking her out of herself, just for a moment.

'Where did you get this?' she asked.

'It was on the table in the drawing room at Oakridge,' he said matter of factly.

Her mouth dropped open. 'Then it belongs to Major Westhaven! How could you?'

''Tis only paste,' he assured her, as if that excused such a theft. 'He will not miss it. Most likely he was planning it to be gift to his mistress.'

Lily swung around to face him. 'He has a mistress?'

'Is the news so unexpected?' Denham's look told her she was being very naïve. 'All men of our class have a mistress, Liliana. He is no exception.'

Eyes wide, she stared at him.

'Do not worry—I will pay mine off before we marry,' he said soothingly.

Stunned by his revelation about the Major's private life, she drew her knees up to her chest and closed her eyes, head in a whirl. She had not slept after the ball, had barely eaten since…and now this… She was exhausted, physically and emotionally.

Unbidden, an image of Daniel's mistress rose up behind her lids. She could picture her now, all dark silken curls, large red lips and sumptuous breasts. Beautiful and sultry, she would know exactly how to please him and, no doubt, they would spend hours conversing on the state of the nation once they had finished… Blushing with shame, she laid her head on her knees. No wonder he had no interest in his young and foolish ward. No wonder he had looked at her with such pity when she had tried to kiss him.

'Do not despair,' Denham said cheerfully, beside her. 'Hopkins will be back with our carriage in no time, and then we can be on our way.'

'I am indebted to you, Jack,' said Daniel, as they drew rein outside the inn where the boy worked. 'You rode well.'

'Thank you, sir.' The boy's eyes gleamed with pride. 'They'll stick to the coach road all the way, I'll warrant, so if you ride on you shouldn't have too much trouble finding 'em.'

'Your payment.' Daniel handed over a handful of coins, and watched the boy's eyes widen.

'*Thank* you, sir!'

'You've earned it.' He smiled at the gangly youth. 'If you're ever tempted to seek a new position, come and ask for me at Oakridge.'

'I will.' With a grin, the boy leapt down from his horse, shook the hand Daniel proffered, and headed for the inn. 'I 'ope you find her, sir!' he called over his shoulder.

Daniel nodded, raising an arm in farewell. 'So do I,' he murmured.

Then, spurring his horse forward, he set off down the road in the direction of Scotland.

Lily, face pressed to the window of the new carriage, tried to make sense of where they were. The sun was well on its way to setting, and she was starting to wonder if they would ever stop. Opposite her Charlie's head lolled in deep sleep—should she wake him up? Surely it would not be safe to travel after dark, even if he did want to make up lost time for the two hours they had sat by the roadside?

Still, if she was abducted by brigands at least it would solve the problem of her imminent marriage, she thought with a wry twist of her lips.

Almost as if Fate had heard her thoughts and been sorely tempted, Lily suddenly became aware of another sound over the squeaking of the carriage wheels and the trotting of the horses. It sounded like another horse, the rhythm of the hooves different, faster, allowing it to be heard. Someone was following them.

Even as Lily realised this, there was a shout behind them. Because she could not resist, she pushed down the window and stuck her head out. Looking past her own tangled mess of curls, she saw a sight she had not dared herself to expect, so far from home.

Daniel Westhaven was behind them, riding as if death itself was at his heels—and he was gaining on the carriage. His face was grim, mouth set in a firm line of…what? Disapproval? Annoyance?

All this flashed through her mind in an instant, before he was alongside her, his chestnut gelding easily keeping pace. His hand, clad in a leather glove, gestured for them to halt. The coachman, confronted with a figure of such forbidding authority, did as he was ordered.

Beside Lily, Charlie sat up, jerked out of his doze. 'What the devil is going on? Is it the wheel again?'

'No, my lord.'

'Then why have we stopped?' A sudden fear crept across his aquiline features. 'Is it highwaymen?'

Lily raised a wry eyebrow. She would not wish to rely on this man to protect her had it been. 'Somewhat worse, I think.'

Before she could answer further there were footfalls outside and the door was jerked roughly open. Major Westhaven stood there in the gathering dark, looking at them.

Lily did not think she had ever seen such cold fury in the face of any man.

'Denham,' he said, murderously calm, 'would you care to explain to me exactly what you are doing with my ward?'

Charlie snorted. 'Your ward? You do not appear to be taking satisfactory care of her—or she would not be in a carriage on the way to Gretna with me, would she, *Lord* Westhaven?'

Lily could see by the tic in Daniel's jaw that the use of his title annoyed him. He regarded the younger man coldly for a further moment, then shrugged. 'That is easily remedied.'

Charlie frowned. 'How exactly—?'

But he got no further, for the Major had reached into the carriage, grabbed him roughly about the cravat, and pulled him bodily outside. Scrabbling to keep his balance, Charlie attempted to regain his dignity as Lily, hands clasped in her lap, her insides a churning mix of relief, excitement and foreboding, leaned out to watch what would happen now.

'How dare you lay your hands on me?' Brushing off his shirt front, the younger man squared up to Major Westhaven.

Even as he did so, there was a scrambling sound from around the front of the carriage, and Denham's driver appeared, face apprehensive, to discover the source of the commotion. 'My lord? Is everything...?' He trailed off as he took in the situation, looking guiltily at Lily, then quickly away.

'You!' The Major rounded on him. 'Did you not question why

your master wished to abscond in the middle of the night with a lady who is none of his concern?'

Hopkins, looking mortified, stared at his shoes. 'I do what I'm bid, my lord,' he said eventually, very quietly.

'Do you?' Her guardian looked disgusted. 'You had better trust, then, that you never need assistance from another as my ward did last night—for perhaps they, too, will do only as they are bid.'

Denham, watching with a scowl, stepped forward. 'What do you think gives you the right to speak so to my man?'

Ignoring him, eyes still fixed on the hapless driver, the Major jerked a thumb in the direction of the road behind them. 'Get out of my sight. And in future think about the orders you are given.'

Unable now to look anyone in the face, Hopkins slunk into the gathering darkness and disappeared.

Denham, puce in the face with rage now, watched him go. 'You had no right to send him away!' he spluttered. 'It is not for him to question the orders he is given, even if wrong had been done! I intend to marry your ward—yet you behave as if I have defiled her!'

The Major shook his head. 'This is the way you speak to me after I have ridden hard at your heels all day to prevent you making the biggest mistake of your life?'

Lily, wondering if it was she that was considered to be the mistake, let out an indignant huff, but the Major, eyes fixed on Charlie like a wolf considering an upstart fox, bore her no mind.

'I'll thank you to mind your own business.' Charlie was adjusting his cuffs now, trying to look nonchalant. But though his back was to her, Lily could see the tension in his shoulders. Thinking of his hands on her, she could not help but be glad that he was receiving his comeuppance.

'I am, as you know, responsible for Miss Pevensey,' the Major responded evenly, as if there had been no interruption. 'And I assure you that, in the event of your marriage to my ward, she will find herself swiftly penniless. There will be no dowry, and nowhere for you to go. Is that understood?'

'What?' Denham's hands balled into fists at his sides. 'How dare you suggest I marry her for money? *You* threw her out and gave us no choice but to marry this way! Are you hoping she will thank you for this interference, for trying to turn her against me?' He turned to look accusingly at Lily. 'Tell him, Liliana. Tell him how you came with me of your own free will!'

She could not speak, because it was a lie—but how could she admit that she had been tricked so easily when the Major must already think her a cotton-headed fool for requiring rescue? So she sat, merely looking back at Charlie and wondering what had happened to the arrogant but affable young man who had danced with her at so many balls. This man's face was twisted with temper, like a child stung by guilt into an elaborate anger he knew he truly had no right to. Scowling dismissively when he saw she had nothing to say, he turned back to the Major.

'She loves me. She told me so. She begged me to take her to Gretna—to help her escape life under your roof!'

'Did she now?' Daniel's tone was disbelieving, but when he looked again to Lily she could see the doubt in his eyes—and the flash of hurt in their depths—just for a moment.

Charlie saw it, too, and his eyes narrowed suddenly.

'It is not *me* you are so set against, is it?' A mocking smile twisted his face. 'You don't wish her to marry at all. Did you think to have her for yourself? Is this what it takes for you to secure yourself a bride?' His voice was warped with bitter mockery. 'She told me of her fears of being forced into a sham marriage to a lame old man—and I swore I would protect her!'

'No!' Lily cried aloud, shocked at the embittered lies spilling from Charlie's mouth, but her protest went unheeded as, with a thump that shook the carriage, Major Westhaven pinned Charlie to its side, one large hand spanning the younger man's lace-covered throat in an act that seemed to Lily to be of sweetly poetic justice. Their faces were very close together, the Major's a snarl of pure rage.

'*What* did you call me?'

'Unhand me!' Denham cried, voice constricted, hands moving use-lessly.

For a moment all they did was stare at each other, faces very close together; then Daniel let him go, the look of disgust on his handsome face unmistakable.

'My second will call on you upon our return to London,' he growled.

'You're challenging me to a duel?'

Daniel shook his head as if he could not believe such stupidity. 'You have conspired to marry my ward against my wishes, blackened her character with your damnable lies, and absconded with her into the bargain. You tried your utmost to ruin an innocent girl's reputation— I think the very least I can do is call you out.'

'How dare you!' Denham drew himself up. 'When my father gets to hear of this—'

'He has already heard of it,' Daniel said coolly. 'And from a source more reliable than his gambling wastrel of a son.'

'You told my father?' Denham's face was a picture of horror. Lily could not help feeling a small thrill of satisfaction.

'He was curious as to why I was looking for my ward at his house.'

'Then, sir…' Denham was quivering with rage '…you had better pray you are a better shot than I am.'

'I don't believe any prayers will be necessary.' Daniel gestured to the horse behind him. 'Now, if I were you, I would leave while I still could. You may take my horse—but mark my words, if you ride him too hard or he comes to any harm you will be sorry.'

'And what of my carriage?'

'Was that not your carriage I passed with its wheel off some miles ago?'

Denham did not reply save to grit his teeth.

Turning away, the Major raised a hand to his forehead, as if chas-tising himself for his forgetfulness. 'Oh, and one other thing. Lily, do you have the necklace that was on my desk at Oakridge?'

Startled, she stared at him. 'Me? No…I…'

'I suspected as much.' Turning back to Denham, he held out his hand.

'I have no idea what you are insinuating,' Charlie said haughtily.

Daniel took one menacing step towards him, the murderous look on his face frightening even Lily, who knew it must only be for show.

'Fine!' Shoving a hand into his pocket, Denham thrust the necklace at him. He shrugged petulantly. 'Such fuss over a mere paste bauble.'

'If you believed it to be paste, why take it?' Daniel pocketed the trinket. 'Now go, before I add theft to your lists of misdemeanours.'

He turned to bring his horse forward, momentarily facing away from the carriage—and in that instant Denham produced a pistol from his pocket and levelled it directly at his back.

'Major!'

Lily's heart-wrenching cry stopped Daniel short and stilled his heart in his chest. Turning, he saw the gun pointing at him—and his answering smile was no more than a bitter baring of teeth.

Did Denham think he would quail before him, just because he had stolen one of his father's duelling pistols and thought himself a man?

'What do you think to do, boy? Are you going to shoot me?'

Denham's eyes narrowed at the lack of fear in the face of the older man. 'I will do it,' he said. 'Do not test me!'

'Then do it, if you think your aim will prove good enough.'

Gritting his teeth, Denham hesitated for a moment, but he did not pull the trigger. 'Just go. Get on your horse and leave us.'

'I cannot leave her. You know that.' Daniel looked impassively at him.

'Wait.' Lily, face white, laid a hand on Denham's arm. 'I wish to go with you, Charlie.'

Daniel's eyes narrowed. What was she about? Even from this distance he could see the lines of ill use on her face—there was no way she would volunteer to go with Denham.

Also looking confused, Denham turned his head to look at her, taking his focus off Daniel. 'Truly?'

She nodded. 'I am sorry. I was afraid to go with you—afraid of what he would do. But you are right—he cannot stop us.'

A look of triumph appeared on the younger man's face. 'Of course I am right.'

Lily smiled sweetly at him. Then, so quickly Daniel almost missed it, she delivered a swift, hard kick to her captor's weight-bearing leg. Denham gave a shout of pain and fury as his knee buckled beneath him, the cry only audible for a second as his pistol discharged with an explosive bang, the force of the shot only serving to further unbalance him.

Daniel, twisting sideways to avoid the metal ball hurtling towards him, felt a white-hot pain in his arm. Disregarding it, he reached into his waistband for the weapon concealed there—and by the time Denham was on his feet again the tides had turned completely against him as he found himself looking down the cold metal chamber of a much superior pistol.

Daniel, coldly calm, gun steady in a hand that had fired countless times at countless enemies over the years, took aim squarely at Denham's chest, fixed the younger man in his sights—and adjusted his finger more snugly against the trigger. 'Give me an excuse to shoot you, boy,' he said softly.

Denham dropped his now useless weapon and drew himself up, aware of the tumble his dignity had just taken. 'I thought I just had,' he drawled, out of breath, but still defiant. 'Yet still you fear to act.'

Daniel's lip curled. Within his jacket he felt blood running down his arm, but the wound was not mortal. He would be hale for some time yet. 'Your father would have done well to buy you a commission,' he said. 'The army would have taught you that the skill is to wait until the need arises, not waste your powder on trifles. It would have been the making of you.'

'Do not patronise me!'

'Forgive me. I cannot think of a better way to deal with you.' Just for a moment, he allowed himself to look at his ward, shaking but still upright. 'Lily, pick up that pistol and come over here,' he said softly.

She did so, bending down to take the gun in both trembling hands.

But as she rose to cross to where her guardian stood, her path brought her, just for an instant, between Denham and the line of

Daniel's shot. Seizing his chance, Charlie grabbed her, pulling her backwards up against his body and pinning her there with one arm across her chest, shielding himself.

The cry she gave tore through Daniel, but he could not risk a shot—he would almost certainly hit Lily.

'Let her go,' he growled, voice full of a threat he knew he could not follow through.

Denham knew it, too, and he smiled cruelly. 'Perhaps, as you do not seem to care for your safety, I should try a different tactic.'

From nowhere he produced a dagger.

The blade, wickedly sharp, glinted menacingly as he held it, grasped firmly in one fist, under Lily's chin where the pulse pounded so fast it was visible. 'How would you feel,' he asked casually, 'if she was the one to die?'

Chapter Thirteen

Daniel felt ice in his belly as he beheld the sight of Denham's knife pressed against the smooth skin of Lily's throat. A paper-thin line of blood welled up to meet the metal, and Lily, who had become very still from the moment the blade touched her, drew in a ragged, pain-filled breath. Her eyes, staring desperately into his, were huge and very green, but she was trying to keep the fear from her face, he could see that.

Daniel, keeping his voice level, said, 'Your quarrel is not with Miss Pevensey, Denham. It is with me. Let her go, and we will settle this like men when we return to London.'

'Not with her?' asked the younger man, bile in his voice. 'Has she not just proved, once and for all, that she is a faithless—?'

'I had no choice but to mislead you, my lord. You were going to shoot him!' The tremor in her voice was like a fist in Daniel's guts.

'You don't have to justify yourself to him, Liliana,' he said firmly.

'Does she not?' Denham looked irritated by the look that passed between them.

'Not if the only way you can get her to agree with you is at the point of a dagger.'

Denham gritted his teeth. 'Perhaps you do not understand,' he grated. He shook her slightly, and Lily closed her eyes as the knife bit further into her flesh. 'You betrayed me, Liliana. I am the one who says what you must do now, not him.'

'I will not allow that.' Slowly, Daniel took a step forward. 'And a dowry is not worth ending your life over, believe me.'

'Perhaps not to you.' Denham snapped. 'But you have funds at your disposal—and your father is dead. He does not trouble you with prudish demands.'

Daniel fought down a flare of anger, taking care to let his face remain impassive.

'Besides,' Denham continued, 'my life is not the one that will end, unless you cease your chatter. She will be dead before you can pull that trigger, and you know it.'

'But if you kill her, what good is she to you?'

For a moment, frustration clouded Denham's face, and Daniel saw, just for an instant underneath his bravado, a boy who wanted to be given a way out.

He asked, 'Is it truly your wish to become a murderer?'

'I did not intend this to happen!' Petulance was clear in the younger man's tone. 'If you had not come…'

'Any man would follow you as I have. If you had the slightest sense of decorum, you would know that.' Meeting Lily's eyes, Daniel saw the determination there, despite her peril, to do what she could to assist him.

'Decorum?' Denham scoffed. 'Who are you to speak so to me? I am the son of an Earl! You are too lame and worthless to serve your country—you have no wife, no heirs—you have nothing!'

'You are right. I have nothing,' Daniel told him, and as he spoke the words he felt to his core how true they were. If Lily were to die, he would be as good as dead himself. 'But I know the meaning of honour.'

Lily's eyes were on his face, unblinking, watching.

'How dare you!' Denham's face was scarlet. 'It is honour that brought me here! Because I will not be slighted—because I will not be talked down to by the likes of you!'

'The likes of me?' Daniel kept his voice impassive and saw immediately that this only served to further enrage the younger man.

'Indeed! Who are you to dictate to me what I must do? You think your money gives you the right to behave so towards someone of my pedigree?' As he spoke, stiff with rage, he took the knife from Lily's neck and gestured wildly down the road with it. 'I should not have to accept such treatment—such a lack of respect! My name is revered throughout the country—and I will not—'

Seizing her chance, Lily, at a nod from Daniel, went completely limp. The dead weight pulled her captor's arm down, her body sagging in his weakened grip, her head falling forward, exposing one of Denham's shoulders and the corner of his chest.

Before the boy had time to grab her with the hand that held the knife and re-shield himself, Daniel fired.

The blast rang out, deafening, the impact jarring through his arm even as a jolt of helpless terror for Lily—so close…too close—flashed through him.

Time slowed down to a crawl as he waited, exquisitely alone, breath frozen in his lungs, to see where his shot had lodged.

Then Denham gave a strangled cry, releasing his hostage and staggering back—and Daniel saw from the ragged hole over his heart that his aim had been true.

He watched in a daze as the younger man clutched at himself in horror, hands covered in the blood flowing fast and warm from his chest. Grey-faced now, Denham took a step back, stumbled, then fell, crumpling to the ground as hard as Lily had, his body unmoving once it hit the road, splayed out beside hers.

And then—nothing. All was still.

For one long, dread-filled instant as he waited, Daniel knew beyond a doubt that all the hope he had was lost. He was convinced that she was gone—spirited away in a silence as loud as a gunshot and as thick as death—convinced he was alone as he stood on the road, every muscle tensed, watching her motionless form.

Then Lily raised her head, face streaked with tears, and his heart started to beat again. She said his name, very quietly, trying ineffectually to dry her cheeks.

Slowly, he walked towards her, weak-kneed.

'I thought I'd killed you.'

'So did I.' Very slowly she got to her feet and looked around, over her shoulder to the body beside her. 'Is he…?'

Daniel crossed to Denham's side and knelt, shaking his head as he searched for signs of life, though he knew already there were none to be found. 'He's dead.'

Lily covered her mouth with one hand, watching in a daze as her guardian reached down to close the young man's eyes. 'Oh, God.'

She felt the last of the colour drain from her face, fearing suddenly as she looked at the fallen body—at the blood staining his shirt—that she was going to faint.

Daniel, looking round and seeing her distress, crossed to her side. He took her arm, turning her away from the sight of their fallen foe, leading her gently around the other side of the carriage, giving her room to breathe.

'Stay here a moment,' he told her.

She braced herself against the carriage as he left, focusing on her breathing and nothing else, shutting out the world as the blackness at the corners of her vision gradually receded, leaving her conscious but fragile.

The first she knew of Daniel's return was when he said her name, very gently. Light-headed, Lily opened her eyes and looked up into his face. When she had thought of him—longed for him—this past day that had felt like a year, she had imagined she would throw herself into his arms if he came for her… Yet now she could not touch him for fear of her defences crumbling altogether.

'Where is he?' she asked, almost in a whisper.

'Inside the carriage. He will be safe there until we can reach a place where I can see to things.'

She pressed her lips together as a sob rose in her throat.

'Lily.' His voice was firm, forcing her to focus. 'We need to get you away from here. Can you walk?'

She nodded. But when she stepped away from the carriage her

knees buckled, and would have given way, had not strong arms taken hold of her.

'Are you hurt?'

He was very close, was all she could think, focusing on the buttons of his waistcoat. She shook her head, knowing that if she opened her mouth she would weep with shock and humiliation.

'Liliana?' He held her apart from him a little, looking into her face with its lids lowered like shutters.

'I…I'm—let me go!' She pulled herself away from him and promptly sat down hard in a flurry of skirts as her trembling legs gave way.

He followed her to the ground, crouching beside her. His formerly immaculate breeches were spattered with mud, she saw, his hair ruffled from pursuit. He was breathing heavily, as she was.

'Leave me—I'm quite all right!' she snapped, pulling her hands away from the large ones that grasped hers.

'Not until I am sure he did not hurt you.'

His tone was grim, and she looked up, startled, to find a concern she had not anticipated staring back at her. She had expected him to be angry at her for the way she had left, yet all she saw in his face was worry and strain—and it almost undid her.

'I'm sorry,' she said softly. 'Last night…'

'I don't want to talk about last night,' he said softly. 'I should never have spoken to you the way I did.'

'I was at fault,' she told him. 'And…to have you come all this way, despite…' She raised haunted eyes to his face. 'My lord—I did not want to leave with him. He drugged me, and when I woke up we were far from Oakridge.'

His face darkened 'He did *what*?'

'He offered me whisky… I don't know why I drank it, it was so foolish… I don't know what I was thinking. He said we had to be married. He said—'

'You don't have to explain,' he said, voice grim. She dared not look at him for fear of breaking down the reserve that she was so desperately holding together. 'You did the right thing, Lily. You let me know where you were.'

'But I…'

'This is not the place,' he said softly. 'Can you stand?'

'I think so.'

'Good.' With that he propelled himself to his feet, thrust a hand out for hers and said, 'Come, then.'

Lily took his hand and allowed herself to be hauled to her feet. What she did not expect, however, was how unsteady she still was. Lurching forward, she was mortified to find that the only thing to steady herself against was his broad chest.

He looked down at her hands, gripping the fabric of his waistcoat. Then he bent his head towards hers, and for all the world she could not keep her lips from tingling with the expectation of his kiss.

He stepped away.

'We're hours from home. We should find an inn for the night before it gets too dark to see.'

'What about…?'

'We will take him with us,' Daniel assured her. 'You will ride with me on the box, if you think you can.'

She nodded. 'I can.'

She waited while he secured his horse to the back of the carriage, so it could follow them. He helped her up, settling her on the hard wooden seat, then swinging himself up beside her, and Lily drew in her breath as he hooked an arm about her waist, steadying her against him.

'I won't fall,' she said softly.

'I'd like to be sure.' His face was impassive in the dying light as he took up the reins and clicked his tongue at the horses.

He drove with a light touch, urging the tired beasts forward, but not forcing them to over-exert themselves.

It was not more than an hour, heading back on the road that she had travelled earlier under such different circumstances, before the lights of an inn became visible, but to Lily—exhausted from forcing her spine to remain rigid, holding her away from Daniel's body—it seemed like ten times longer.

'This is where I sought help,' she said, squinting into the light that pooled in the road from within a cosy and very comfortable-looking establishment.

'I thought it an appropriate place to stop,' he replied, climbing down and reaching for her waist. She thanked him, trying not to dwell on the pressure of his hands, or the way her body slid past his on the way to the ground.

'My lord!' A skinny redheaded youth appeared in the doorway, excitement writ plain upon his face. Lily recognised the lad who had taken her letter, now beaming excitedly at the two of them.

'Surely it is past time for you to be abed?' the Major asked him.

The lad shrugged. 'I stayed up.' He tugged his forelock in Lily's direction by way of greeting, then turned bright eyes back to her guardian. 'You overtook them, then?'

'I did.' Daniel rested a hand on his shoulder. 'Jack, I need another favour.' He led the lad aside, spoke low and briefly to him, then turned back to Lily.

'Come. Let's go inside.'

The landlady, hovering in the doorway behind her son, led them through the main room with its low beams and open fire in which several men sat, tankards in hand, to a private parlour. The smells of beer and food all around made Lily immediately hungry.

Daniel spoke to the proprietress, then joined her before the fire. 'Food is being prepared for us,' he told her.

Lily nodded, thoughts trailing behind her on the road as she gazed into the flames.

He sat heavily on the bench beside her. 'Are you all right?'

'I am sorry he had to die,' she said softly. 'No one deserves such a punishment. And he was a friend of yours, after all.'

'Of *mine*?' His brows drew together in confusion.

She nodded. 'He told me of how you had known each other since childhood.'

Daniel made a sound that was halfway between a laugh and a snort of disbelief.

She looked up, frowning. 'What is it?'

'He lied to you,' he said baldly. 'We have barely ever had a conversation—we are members of the same club, but that is as far as it goes. Liliana.' He shook his head, as if he could not believe her naïvety. 'I know you have known him for a time. But Charlie Denham really was not the man you thought he was.'

She smiled slightly. 'I am not so green, my lord. I noticed how he changed towards me once I had a wealthy guardian.'

'Then why welcome his attentions?'

'I never have!' She shook her head regretfully. 'At the picnic, before Connor arrived—I was going to ask you to let him down on my behalf. But I never got the chance.'

'And then I told him he could visit.'

She nodded. 'I did not want to offend you by slighting your supposed childhood friend.'

He shook his head in disbelief. 'I was convinced you loved him.'

'Mere politeness, I assure you.' She frowned, trying to decipher his expression, and what that tone in his voice had been when he spoke of love. 'Why…why then did you refuse him?'

He smiled wryly. 'As I said last night—I could not allow you to marry such a man, whether you wished it or not. And I hoped…I hoped I was right in thinking that, if you knew what he was, you would not want such a marriage.'

'You were right.' Their eyes met for a moment, and held, and she was sure she saw relief in the depths of his gaze, and more. The moment stretched out, filled with awareness and things unsaid and unsayable, until she could bear it no longer. 'You told him he was a gambling wastrel,' she prompted.

He nodded. 'Lord Denham was a member of my club. Word is that he spent as good as the entirety of his allowance there every month and that his father regularly had to settle his additional gaming debts. There was constantly conflict between them because of it, and the old man would threaten to cut him out of his will him at least once a month.' He shrugged reflectively. 'Denham waited eagerly for his father's death so he could receive his inheritance and live as extravagantly as he liked. However, Lord Ashburton is far from his grave—so his son was left with a need for ready money.'

'Such as a dowry would bring,' she said thoughtfully. 'No wonder he was so interested to find out my exact circumstances.'

He nodded. 'If he was my son I would have acted on my threat and disinherited him. It would have done him good in the long run, I don't doubt.'

Lily frowned. 'You said you saw his father in your search for me?'

He nodded. 'I asked if he had seen his son—I did not say why. It isn't my place to tell Lord Ashburton what his son has been up to. I suppose it is kinder now if he does not know the full extent of what Denham was capable of.'

Something occurred to Lily. 'That means you were looking for me before you received my letter?'

'Of course.' His eyes were dark as he looked at her, flecked with amber shards of reflected firelight. 'At first I believed you had gone with him willingly. But as I thought about it, it did not seem right. Then Jo told me you had left your brother's letter—and it was obvious you had been taken against your will.'

'You did trust me, after all.'

His expression was sombre now. 'I should have trusted you from the start.'

'You came for me, that is all that matters.' She averted her eyes from his, lest he think her a fool.

The landlady entered, bearing a tray. 'The food'll be served shortly,' she said, smiling at them both. 'Your bandages, sir.'

'Thank you.' He smiled at her as she left the room.

'Bandages…?' Lily trailed off as he raised a hand to his left arm and she saw, for the first time, the rip in the upper sleeve of his jacket, bloodstain barely visible against the dark blue cloth. Her eyes widened. 'You're bleeding!'

A smile twitched up the corner of his mouth. 'Your concern is touching, if a little overdue.'

'My lord!' Guilt clawed at her. 'I thought he missed you!'

'I'm not as fast on my feet as I once was,' he said wryly.

'Take off your jacket,' she commanded, reaching for the tray on which a bowl of water and some salve and strips of linen were laid.

'I'm fine,' he protested. 'After a decade in the army one would assume I'd know how to dress a wound by now. If I can do it under fire, I can do it here.' But Lily, unheeding, was already helping him remove the garment. Daniel winced, pushing her gently away. 'It would be less painful, I think, if you allowed me to at least undress myself.'

'I'm sorry.' Lily, suffused with shame at her own thoughtlessness, sat back.

He removed the jacket to reveal a shirtsleeve soaked with blood, more of which began to ooze from the wound as he rolled up the torn sleeve.

'It's not deep,' he said, seeing her concern. 'The ball did not enter my arm—it merely grazed me on the way past.'

'It's deep enough.' She frowned at it, bandage at the ready. 'You'll have a scar to remind you of this day.'

'I have enough of those already as to make no difference,' he said grimly.

'Nevertheless—' Lily did not like the look in his eyes '—hold still.'

His skin was warm, firm against her fingertips. The wound was on the outside of his arm, a few inches above the elbow—not overly large, she was pleased to see. He allowed her to clean the gash and press a pad of linen to the bleeding area, holding his arm out as she wound a strip of bandage securely around the wound. She was aware of his eyes upon her as she worked, but she was not expecting what came next.

'You know,' he said softly, 'this is how my father met my mother.'

She smiled, eyes still on her task. 'He was wounded in the course of rescuing her from a brigand?'

'Almost,' he said. 'She shot him.'

Lily raised quizzical eyes to his. 'She…what?'

His smile turned ironic. 'My father was a highwayman when he met my mother. So I suppose he was the brigand, in that case.'

'A highwayman?' Fascinated, she let her hands drop from the now-tied bandages.

He nodded. Then, looking at the astonished expression she wore, the smile finally died. 'I do not tell just anyone that I am from criminal stock, Liliana.'

'You mistake me, my lord,' she said softly. 'Your father was a highly respected man, that much is clear. I do not believe he would take such a decision lightly. It is a trait he has passed on, I think.'

He dropped his eyes from hers. 'You don't know anything about it.'

'I think you are more like him than you believe,' she said, though the look on his face almost dissuaded her, 'and I think I would have liked your mother very much.'

'And she…' a wistful smile tipped his mouth upwards '…she would have greatly approved of your actions tonight.'

'I couldn't let him… Not when you were there because of me.' She stopped, suddenly shy. 'I didn't know whether you would come,' she confessed on a whisper.

'Of course I came.'

She raised her eyes to his, and in them she saw something new— something that gave her hope, that stoked the feeling of warmth she could not name when he looked at her.

He dropped his eyes. 'You are my ward,' he added gruffly. 'I'm responsible for your safety.'

'Oh…yes, of course.' A flush suffused her, one she hoped he could not see in the firelight. 'You…have a very good seat, my lord,' she said, desperate for a chance to regain her composure.

'Thank you. They tell me I ride well, also.'

Lily stared at him, eyes wide. Had he just made a joke?

Seeing her amazement, he gave a deep chuckle that curled itself quite distractingly around her insides. 'My father had me on a horse almost before I could walk, and nigh on every day after.

Then, of course, there was the army. Perfect preparation, all, for riding to the rescue of a lady in distress.'

'Yes, I can imagine…' Thoroughly disconcerted, Lily snaked a look at him from below her lashes, and found him still watching her.

'I should even thank you,' he said at last, 'for providing such exercise for my chestnut.'

She shrugged. 'I should thank you for rescuing me. Yet I have not. If you do not thank me, we will be even.'

He extended a hand and tipped her chin up, so that green eyes clashed with blue-grey once more, and for a moment she wondered what he was looking for. Then his gaze fell from hers, and his eyes narrowed. His fingers explored the long dagger-scratch on her neck, and she drew in a breath as he grazed the tender patch—there must be the beginnings of a bruise forming—where Denham had slapped her.

'What is this?' he asked, eyes murderous. 'Did he do this to you, as well?'

'I tried to escape.' She shuddered at the memory of Denham's cold, rubbery lips on hers. 'He…he was not impressed.'

'Then he is lucky he is already dead,' he muttered, face full of barely suppressed anger, still examining the mark. 'And yet, I would have liked to see him account for this in a courtroom.'

Lily, very still, tried not to think about how his fingers felt, calloused but gentle, trailing warmth across her skin. She swallowed hard, and his eyes followed the movement of her throat.

'Nothing hurts?' he asked again, as he had at the roadside.

And again, she shook her head.

'Only your pride was wounded, then,' he said, after a moment.

'And nothing, it seems, will ever dent yours!' she flashed back.

A crease of amusement betrayed itself at his mouth.

'My lord?'

He dropped his hand from her skin, looking round to where Jack hovered in the doorway.

'I've brought the constable as you instructed, sir.'

He inclined his head. 'Thank you. Tell him I'll be with him shortly.'

Turning to Lily, he said, 'I have business here—things will need to be arranged. Have something to eat and get some sleep, and I'll see you in the morning.'

Eyes wide, she nodded. 'Will there be trouble?'

'I shouldn't think so.'

She was not convinced, despite the certainty in his voice, but he beckoned to the landlady before she had a chance to voice her fears. 'I've engaged her two best rooms. She'll take you up.' Daniel smiled charmingly at the woman as she came to join them.

Lily nodded. She was exhausted, and could not wait to lie down. But as the landlady smiled encouragingly and gestured to the stairs, she still feared to leave him to explain events alone. 'My lord…'

'Lily. Get some rest.' His hand reached for hers, squeezing her fingers in his warm, coarse grip, providing comfort and reassurance.

Their eyes met, just for an instant. Then he was gone.

The landlady smiled kindly at Lily. 'Come, miss, I'll show you to your room.'

Lily followed her up a flight of narrow stairs, where she opened the door to a room under the eaves of the inn, small but clean, and pleasant enough. 'The gentleman'll be just next door. I'll have your food brought up directly.'

'Thank you.' Lily smiled at her, then went into her room and shut the door gently behind her.

It was only then, alone and unobserved, as she slumped on to her bed and the events of the day came rushing back to surround her, that she allowed herself to weep.

It was around midnight before Lily was woken by footsteps in the passage outside her room. Sitting up, still fully dressed, she blinked in the gloom. Her candle was guttering on the chair beside the bed. Hastily, she lit another, carrying it to the door and pressing her ear against the wood. She was rewarded with the sound of his door shutting, but nothing more.

She sighed, wanting nothing more than to go and ask him what had transpired. It was not proper, not at this time of night, but surely, in the circumstances…

A knock on the door inches from her ear made her jump.

One hand covering her pounding heart, Lily stood, frozen. Could it be Daniel? The thought was a ridiculous one, yet her pulse increased regardless.

'Miss?'

It was a maid. She shook her head at her own foolishness. Of course he would not come to her room—he knew, even if she seemed eager to forget, what was acceptable.

She unlocked and opened the door. A ruddy-faced maid stood there with a ewer covered by a muslin cloth. She bobbed a curtsy, murmured, 'Your water, miss,' and went past into the room, setting it down.

Confused, Lily opened her mouth to inform the girl that she had not asked for water—that it must be for the Major—but the maid had already vanished away down the passage. Sighing, she picked up the water, the heavy jug warm against her hands, and went next door herself.

His door was not quite closed, so, hands too full to allow her to knock, she pushed it with her foot until it swung open.

He was seated in a chair, left leg up on the bed beside him, busy rolling up the leg of his breeches. As she entered he broke off, swung his body around to face her, and froze.

'Lily.' Almost at once the surprise on his face turned to anger. 'For God's sake, did no one ever teach you to knock?'

Startled at such a reaction, she stopped where she was, still clutching the jug.

'Forgive me,' she said, dismayed. 'The maid brought your water to my room—your door was open…'

He swung his leg off the bed with a thud where his boot hit the floor and got to his feet. 'I don't care if there's no door there at all—you don't ever walk in on me without knocking,' he snapped. 'Do you understand?'

She nodded. 'Of course. Where shall I…?'

'Just put it over there and get out.' He gestured to the small table alongside the bed.

She crossed the room, face burning, and set down the jug. She could not think why he spoke to her so—could not understand what she had done. They had parted warmly for the night…he had held her hand… and now this. It had been some time since he had been so cold with her; she had thought they were past such things.

Then it occurred to her—he must be in pain. She had been thinking only of the new wound to his arm. But whatever old injury he nursed in his left leg, the journey to fetch her could not have been kind.

Steeling herself, she asked, 'Would you like some help to bathe your leg?'

He turned to her, gaze icy. 'What?'

She swallowed, suddenly timid before the force of the fury in his eyes. 'I was just thinking…if you need some assistance…'

'As I made clear to you before, I am perfectly capable of seeing to myself,' he said flatly.

'I know,' she said hastily. It seemed she was only making matters worse. 'But if I were to help perhaps it would be…easier…'

For a long moment his eyes met hers and she saw so many different emotions that she could not have named them all. But there was pain there, and pride—and shame—in equal measure. And, of course, that angry shield he threw up against the world—the defences she thought he had finally lowered, in her presence at least.

'You are skilled at nursing cripples?' he asked.

'No…' She did not know where to look now. 'But…'

'Then leave me in peace.'

She stood, wanting to weep—or strike him—but instead she turned and went to the door. It was only as she was leaving the room that something occurred to her.

She turned back.

'I didn't say those things Denham claimed I did,' she said quietly. 'You have been so kind to me, I would never—'

'Just get out,' he said from between his teeth. 'This is my private business, Liliana. It has nothing to do with you—I do not need your assistance, and I don't wish to discuss it. I would appreciate it if you would let me be.'

She closed her mouth with a snap. 'Of course. I am sorry. I was only trying to help. Good night.'

His eyes were on the floor as he waited wordlessly for her to leave.

In the hall again, with his door shut against her as securely as she had found herself shut out of his thoughts, Lily stood very still and tried to work out what had happened. She felt like a child who had been slapped very hard, and for no reason—too surprised even to cry.

Slowly, she went back into her own room, fell back on to the bed, and stared at the ceiling, feeling numb inside as she saw again the harsh, raw anger on his face, heard the vitriol in his words.

Deep down she knew that bitterness was not for her, that whatever he had been through around the time he was wounded had made deeper scars than she could see.

But how was she ever to know him if he would not let her?

And was she foolish even to try?

Chapter Fourteen

Lily rose with the sun, and washed her face in the ewer of cold water beside her bed, grateful for the freshness on her face. She had slept badly, her dealings with Daniel—and the notion of what might have happened to her at Denham's hands had he not appeared—playing on her mind.

She was just completing her *toilette* when there was a knock at the door.

She heard him hesitate on the other side of the wood. 'Liliana?'

'I'm awake.' She crossed to the door and opened it. He stood, very upright outside, and looking up into his face gave her no information, as usual. 'Good morning,' she said, determined to be civil. 'I trust you slept well, my lord?'

'Very.' He looked as if he had paced his room all night long. 'Yourself?'

'Like a log,' she told him, smiling tightly.

The lie complete for them both, he nodded curtly. 'I have hired a new carriage. We must get started on the road. I thought we should go back to Oakridge—keep you out of town for a couple of days so you can relax.'

She nodded coolly. 'I am ready.'

Head high, she swept past him, down the stairs and out to the carriage. He caught her up just as she was about to climb inside.

'I must apologise for the way I spoke to you last night.'

Lily shrugged extravagantly. 'I was wrong to involve myself with affairs that do not concern me. It is not a mistake I will make twice, I assure you.'

'I should not have been so rude to you.'

'I hardly noticed,' she assured him, still evading his attempts to catch her eye.

'Liliana.' He caught her by the arm and pulled her round to face him. 'You startled me. I'm...sensitive about my injuries. But I should never have snapped at you so.' He grimaced ruefully. 'I was not at my best yesterday.'

'I understand. I have devoted my life to embroidery and idle chit-chat, after all. I can be no help for practical things—binding wounds, for example,' she added, with a pointed look at his arm.

He sighed. 'Will you for ever make me rue the day I called you shallow?'

She tipped up her chin. 'Probably.'

A pause. Silent sparks flew between them as neither gave ground. Then, suddenly, he grinned—and it was so unexpected and so infectious that she could not help smiling wryly back, until embarrassment overcame her and she dropped her eyes.

'I just wished to help,' she murmured.

'I know that. Do you forgive me?'

She nodded. 'As you ask so prettily. Now, should we not get started on the road? I am eager to be home.'

He nodded, his smile enigmatic. 'Of course.'

With words of thanks they took their leave of Jack and his family, Lily settling herself ready for the journey. It was only some hours later that she realised what that smile had been for. She had called Oakridge 'home', without even thinking about it. It seemed she had come a long way from the girl who had refused to live under his roof under any circumstances.

Lily opened her eyes to find her head resting on something warm and hard—and realised almost immediately that it was her guardian's shoulder. Moving slightly, she became aware that the pressure she felt was his cheek, resting in her hair. The rhythmic breathing in her ear told her that he was deeply asleep.

Lily smiled. The rocking motion of the carriage was very soothing, as was the early afternoon sun slanting in upon them—it had been hard for her to stay awake and it seemed the Major had had the same problem.

He smelled very good indeed, like cigar smoke and cologne. And something else—his own musky masculine scent, remembered from the night of Lady Asterley's ball, the last time she had been so close to him. Surrounded by his familiar fragrance, for a moment she was perfectly happy—in a place she would have been quite content to remain for the longest while. But the very knowledge of this unnerved her.

Gently, she sat up.

Immediately he was awake, blinking once, eyes scanning the carriage as he ran a hand through his hair.

'Forgive me,' she said softly. 'I had not meant to wake you.'

'I was not asleep,' he said gruffly.

She bit back a smile. 'Would it be such a sin if you were? You must have had little sleep these last couple of nights, my lord.'

'Some things are more important,' was the quiet reply.

She looked at him, hair ruffled, jawline rough with a day's worth of stubble and felt something odd in her chest. It was not either of the usual feelings he inspired in her—not that teeth-clenching anger, nor shamefully melting desire—but something else entirely. Something softer.

She said, 'Thank you for coming after me.'

'I thought you said you were not going to thank me.'

She smiled. 'I could not help it.'

He looked at her for a long moment, unblinking, his eyes fathoms deep, his defences lowered for once—worn down, as hers were, by recent wakefulness.

Lily, unnerved, dropped her gaze before she lost herself and said—or did—something foolish.

She said, 'Tell me about your father the highwayman.'

He considered this request. Then, as if he could not think of a reason to refuse, he shrugged. 'It was his brother's idea. Debt forced them to it—and a need to support themselves after their father died and left them only debts. His main concern, he said, was to keep from having to sell Oakridge, but I think he enjoyed the life, though he would never admit it.'

'And he stopped your mother?'

He nodded. 'She was out in her carriage one night, alone—'

'Alone?' Lily, interest piqued, forgot she had been speaking of this merely to change the subject.

He shrugged. 'She was fleeing the country. To avoid a husband, ironically—but that is another story. He stopped her. She did not take lightly to being threatened—she carried a pistol, as all enlightened young ladies should, and the rest, as they say, is history.'

She shook her head, amazed that the painted couple she had so admired had been brought together in such a dramatic fashion. 'I thought you said he married her for her money.'

He nodded. 'Once he had renounced his nights on the road.'

'It must have made a fascinating bedtime tale when you were a child.'

'He never told us,' he said. 'Until that is, I heard him reminiscing one night in the library with John, when I was about ten.'

'You were eavesdropping?'

'I was reading,' he clarified, responding to her teasing tone. 'Absorbed in a book. It was no fault of mine that they did not notice me.'

'Where were you?' she asked.

He shrugged, eyes twinkling 'Under the table.'

She suppressed a smile. 'Small wonder, then, that you were not detected. What happened?'

'I was…at pains to conceal my surprise,' he said. 'He was not pleased at first to discover me. But eventually he allowed himself to be persuaded to part with the tale.'

'And?'

'And…' his smile was wistful '…I could not believe that this romantic, adventurous figure was my father. And yet, at the same time, such a role suited him exactly.'

'You were never tempted to follow in his footsteps?'

He shook his head. 'His younger brother, my uncle, was hanged for the crime of highway robbery.'

'Oh, God.' Lily's hand crept unwittingly to her neck.

'It was before they were married. My brother James is named for him.' He paused, eyes far away. 'I never saw such sorrow in any man's eyes as when my father told me of his brother's death.' He paused. 'At least, not until my mother died. It was enough to convince me that such a life is not play.' He smiled slightly. 'I think that is why he never told us before then.'

'And then you found yourself pursuing a carriage through the night, as he did,' she said.

He nodded. 'Though for an entirely different reason.'

Lily returned the smile he gave her, warm from reminiscence. 'I didn't say those things about you to Charlie,' she said suddenly, repeating her words of last night. 'Truly.'

Something changed in his face, so that now his eyes were impenetrable. 'It doesn't matter,' he said softly.

'It matters to me. I need you to believe I would never say such things!'

'Why is it important to you what I believe?'

It was not the first time he had posed such a question—and once more, she had no answer, only the swirling, confusing mess of emotions his closeness evoked in her. So she chose the safe reply. 'You have been so kind, and...' She looked away, embarrassed. 'I know that is not why you refused Charlie—you did not plan to keep me for yourself—to marry me, as he suggested.'

'I would not ask such a thing of any woman.' His voice was almost a growl.

Lily was horrified at the look of self-disgust on his face and her mouth dropped open.

'No, forgive me, I did not mean to imply...' She felt herself turning scarlet. 'I meant only...I know you had only the most honourable of intentions when you took me in. And in refusing Charlie...you were trying to protect me. I just meant you would never...' Mortified, and aware she was babbling, Lily stopped, closing her eyes. 'My Lord, any woman would be fortunate indeed to be your wife.'

He did not reply. When she opened her eyes he was looking away from her, out of the window. 'We are almost home.'

'My lord—'

He cut her off with a raised hand. 'Enough. I am not a child. I do not need to be pacified.'

And, just like that, the lazy warmth of moments ago was lost.

Lily sighed and turned her face away.

They arrived at Oakridge to find John awaiting them at the front door.

'He's been in that spot every time I've come home for my entire life,' Daniel said softly as the carriage crunched over gravel towards the house and drew up alongside the steps. Before Lily had a chance to reply he was outside, holding up a hand to help her down.

'Lord Westhaven.' John was all smiles. 'You found her.'

'That I did.' He clapped the old man on the back in a way Lily feared might send him sprawling, but apparently he was tougher than he appeared.

'Miss Lily.' Thin, dry hands grasped hers. 'It is good to see you home safely.'

'Thank you, John.' She smiled at him. 'And thank you for your part in recovering me.'

He bowed. 'I will ring for some tea—and you must be hungry.'

'None for me,' the Major said. 'I must go to London to speak with the Earl of Ashburton.'

Lily turned to him. 'You're going now? Will you not rest a while?'

He shook his head. 'He should not have to wait for news such as I have to give.'

She nodded. 'Of course.'

'I'll have a horse brought round,' John told them, and seemed about to say more before he was interrupted by the arrival of Connor, at speed.

'Westhaven—I can't believe you went chasing off to Scotland without me!'

'We did not get anywhere near Gretna, Captain,' said the Major.

'But you engaged the enemy, did you not?'

Daniel sighed. 'Later. I will tell you all you wish to know, but now I have business in London.'

His tone chased the playful look from the Irishman's face. 'D'you want me to ride with you?'

The Major shook his head. 'I'd rather do this alone—but I'd go easier knowing someone was with Liliana.'

'I will be fine—' Lily began, but he held up a hand to silence her. 'Indulge me.'

Silenced by the earnest look in his eyes, she nodded.

'Right.' Connor gave her a supportive wink. 'I'll sort your horse out then, save the grooms a job.'

Daniel turned to Lily as Connor strode off. 'Have your tea. I will be back by nightfall.'

'Take care, my lord,' she said softly. 'If the Earl is anything like his son…'

'He is entirely different.' He managed a smile, though he was obviously distracted by the task that lay ahead. 'Do not worry.'

She wanted to tell him that she could not help it, but could not quite make her tongue move to the words. 'John is allowed to call you Lord Westhaven now?' she asked lightly.

He shrugged. 'He keeps pointing out that it is my title. It is better than arguing.'

'And you are a…'

'A viscount,' he said wearily.

She nodded. 'Why, then, do you not use your title?'

A cloud passed over his handsome features. 'My father was Lord Westhaven. I do not pretend to be half the man he was.'

'No one is asking you to.' She laid a brief hand on his arm. 'Besides, pretence would not be necessary.'

He looked at her for a long moment. 'Thank you. You did not know my father, but I appreciate the sentiment.'

'I know his son,' was all she said in reply.

He shook his head at her insistence upon having the last word, a smile playing about his lips. 'I will see you upon my return.'

She turned and watched him head away, towards where Connor was coming around the side of the house leading his horse.

'May I call you Lord Westhaven?' she called after him.

'No,' he said firmly. Then he stopped, looking back at her. 'But you might try calling me Daniel once in a while.'

She nodded slowly. 'Perhaps I could.'

He smiled, exasperated, and pulled himself up into the saddle, wheeling his horse around and raising a hand to her as he set off at an easy canter.

Lily waved back, slowly. She did not envy him the news he had to give, and she could not quite suppress the fear that he would be blamed somehow, punished—even imprisoned. It had not been his fault, not at all. But Denham had been the most unreasonable of men—what if it was a trait he had inherited from his sire? Despite the Major's words of reassurance, she could not quite chase the spectre of doubt—or that of Denham—from her mind.

'C'mon.' Connor gave her an irrepressible grin and offered her his arm. 'Let's have that tea before John thinks we've abandoned him.'

She found a smile for him, and took his arm. But though her feet went up the steps of Oakridge, her thoughts went with the Major, riding his second-best horse to London, to tell an old man that his son was dead.

'Poor bastard,' said Connor succinctly.

Daniel, dusty and downhearted upon his return from speaking to the Earl of Ashburton, had summoned his friend to the study to relate the events of the past two days. 'No man needs a son like that,' he remarked grimly now, downing the whisky he had been longing for the whole ride home.

'How did he take it?'

'He was very dignified.' With a sigh, Daniel remembered the old man, ashen faced but upright as he received the news. 'He offered his apologies for Denham's conduct. He asked if there was anything he could do to make amends.' He refilled his glass. 'Obviously, I told him there was not.' He sighed. 'This has hit him hard—yet I got the impression he had been waiting, sooner or later, for his son to send trouble to his door. It is a shame it came so dramatically.'

'What will he tell people?'

'An accident,' said Daniel quietly. 'I will not say otherwise.' When Connor looked up in surprise, he frowned. 'What good will the truth do? It will only further crush an old man already weighed down by grief and shame. He will tell people that his son fell from his horse while riding. That is all. No one knows any different except Jack's family at the inn, and I think I can trust them to be discreet.' He sipped his whisky. 'Besides, it would damage Lily's reputation, though she was not to blame. Even if it did not, I will not have her exposed to speculation.'

The Captain reached over and squeezed his shoulder. 'You did her proud.'

Daniel shrugged. 'She is my ward. It is my duty to protect her from harm. Besides…' he frowned '…what makes you think I did this for her? My reputation as her protector was at risk also, you know.'

'My mistake,' said his friend, but there was no mistaking the teasing tone in his voice. 'I do apologise.'

Daniel shook his head. 'Enough. It has been the longest of days. I want my bed.'

'That's all you want, is it? Your bed, you alone?'

Daniel lifted a wry eyebrow. 'Are you offering to join me? How your unit will talk when they hear.'

Connor snorted. 'I was just thinking…you and Lily have spent a lot of time together these last couple of days.'

His friend pointed a stern finger at him. 'One more comment like that and I'm calling you out. I haven't spent all day safeguarding her reputation so you can ruin it with a few flippant remarks.'

'Guilty conscience, is it?' Connor relented somewhat at the murderous look his friend threw at him, holding up his hands. 'All I'm sayin' is that I see the way you look at her.' He held up a hand. 'Don't try to deny it.'

Daniel clenched his teeth, began to do just that, then stopped with a sigh. 'It's merely lust, Connor—the lust any man would feel for any beautiful woman.' He looked down at the drink in his hand, amber in the firelight. 'But I'm not any man. And she is not just any beautiful woman. My promise to Robbie—' He stopped, frustrated. 'I shouldn't have to spell this out to you.'

Connor regarded him levelly. 'You're not spelling it out. You're talking yourself out of it.'

'I don't need you to tell me what I feel.'

'While she's under your roof the least you can do is be honest with yourself.'

'Well...' Daniel reached behind him and pulled the bell cord '...that's something I've been giving serious thought to since we arrived home.'

'Being honest with yourself?' Connor looked pleased.

Daniel scowled at him. 'Having her under my roof.' He looked up as a maid entered.

'Sir?'

He mustered a smile. 'Tell Miss Liliana I'd like to see her, please.'

'Yes, sir.'

As she left, he raised his glass to his friend. 'You're right, Connor.'

'Am I now?' The Irishman looked distinctly suspicious at this declaration.

'Mmm.' Daniel sipped his drink. 'It's time to take things in hand.'

Lily arrived in the hall just as Connor emerged from the study. He said nothing, just gave her his usual wink. She smiled at him, distracted, as he passed.

One of the maids had sought her out and told her Daniel wished to see her, so—distinctly perplexed and despite the advanced hour—she had come downstairs. He had returned from town and closeted himself away with Connor and only now, when she had been about to get undressed for bed, did he summon her.

The hall was dim, only one lamp lit. The maids, too, were probably preparing for bed. Lily paused in the shadows as the door to the study opened and her guardian emerged, slowly, lingering in the doorway. In the half-light, shadows played across the sculpted contours of his face, making him appear so unapproachable that for a moment she feared to go forward. But then she saw the signs of fatigue in his face and how, tonight, the limp in his gait seemed more pronounced. He was, it seemed, as tired as she was. Lily stepped out from her shadowy hiding place.

'Daniel?'

He stopped, turned towards her—and something in his face brought to her attention that this was the first time she had called him aloud by his Christian name.

'I was told you wanted to see me.'

He nodded. 'Come in.'

The room was dim, and two glasses remained on the desk, beside a decanter that was substantially depleted. She wondered what he and Connor had discussed in the hour or so they had been alone. Had they spoken of Denham? Had they spoken of her?

She perched in a chair in front of the desk and watched him as he moved slowly to his own seat.

'How was Denham's father?'

He shrugged, the lines of strain around his mouth deepening. 'It is not news any father should have to hear of his son.'

'I know you would have done it kindly.'

He dropped his eyes from hers. 'Nevertheless.'

'What did he say?'

'He does not blame me. He knew, I think, what his son was capable of. Years of debts ignored and trouble avoided by a whisker have led up to this.' He sighed. 'He is a good man. A man who hoped for more from his eldest son and now has nothing at all to show for it.'

'I am sorry for him.' Lily bit her lip.

He nodded. 'And I am deeply sorry for my part in it.'

'It was not your fault.'

'I would do it again, and more, if it meant you were safe.'

She felt the colour rise in her face. 'My lord...'

He glanced down at his desk, as if checking himself—and when he looked back up at her his eyes were distinctly cooler. 'I wanted to discuss our living arrangements.'

She frowned. 'Now?'

'You are busy?' His tone was distant.

She shook her head, sensing something volatile in his mood. 'No.'

'Very well.' He cleared his throat. 'As my ward you need not feel that you are expected to live where I live.'

'I do not,' she told him softly. 'I love it here, at Oakridge. And Brook Street, also. I have told you before, I feel at home here. That is no small thing for me.'

He nodded, expressionless, though she had spoken with feeling. Then he straightened his spine, a gesture she knew he was unaware of—but it told her what he was about to impart was significant.

'I wanted to ask you what you would think to a few months in Ireland with my brother.'

'Ireland?' Frowning slightly, she considered. 'Well…I have never been there, of course, but I have heard it is lovely. Why—do you have business there?'

He hesitated only for the slightest instant. 'I meant you, alone.'

'Oh.' For a minute she was so hurt she could not reply. 'I…I realise I have caused you much trouble over these past few days…but sending me away—'

'I am not sending you away. Ireland is not a punishment.' His mouth twisted wryly. 'If my mother could hear you say such a thing…' He stopped, jaw tight as he met her eyes. 'With one of my sisters, then, if you do not wish to go so far—in Bristol, or with the other in the country?'

'It sounds as though you want me anywhere but here.'

He did not reply, but she saw the truth of it in his eyes, and knew that she was right. She regarded him, trying to swallow away the sudden tightness in her throat.

'My lord…I do not understand.'

He sighed. 'Liliana…I have been a less than effective guardian. I think a change of scene would do you good, help you forget recent events.'

She stared at him, confused and wounded. 'You think there will be a scandal? That people will find out what occurred?'

He shook his head. 'Denham's father was as keen as I that no one should know.'

'Then…why…? You have been the best guardian I could wish for! You have—'

'I just…I do not think this is an appropriate environment for you.' He turned away. 'That is all there is to it. Please do not keep asking me why.'

'But…' She could not help herself. 'If you could just explain…'

'It is late,' he said flatly.

She frowned, refusing to be dismissed. 'Please.'

'Very well.' He gritted his teeth. 'I tire of being surrounded by a household who are here because it is their duty to be.'

'What?' She regarded him, dumbfounded.

'Is it not the truth?'

'I am *not* here because I have to be!' she retorted, hackles rising. 'And John…he's so patient with you and you're just so…'

'So what?' he growled.

'So…*unpleasant* to him. He holds you in such regard—'

'No.' Daniel raised a hand, cutting her off. 'He gave his whole life in my father's service. He stays because I am my father's son and for no other reason.'

Lily shook her head. 'You're wrong. And you will not frighten him away by shouting at him—so you might as well stop trying.'

He opened his mouth, then shut it again, frowning in what seemed to be genuine surprise. 'You think that is what I am doing?'

'Why else, then, do you behave in such a fashion?' She was too angry now to stop. 'Why are you so determined not to be worthy of your father's name? Who has ever held you up against him for judgement—apart from yourself?'

'I do not appreciate being spoken to this way,' he said, jaw tight.

'Well, I do not appreciate you summoning me when you are… drunk and…maudlin!' she snapped, unable to hold her tongue.

He glared at her, jaw tight. 'I am not drunk. Kindly show me some respect.'

'*You* show some respect!' she shot back. 'Show some respect for your father's memory and stop blaming him for something he has nothing to do with!'

His fist made contact with his desk, making her jump. 'Do you think he would have dealt with this by shutting himself away, as I have?'

Lily blinked. 'Dealt with what?'

He froze. For a moment there was perfect, unbroken silence between them, not even sullied by either taking a breath.

He drew back, closing his eyes briefly. 'Nothing.'

'My lord…'

'No.' He turned away for a moment, running a hand through his dark hair. 'My father's exalted reputation is not the reason I wished to speak to you.'

Sighing inwardly, she nodded, bringing her temper under control with an effort. 'You wished to tell me I am being sent to Ireland.'

He fixed her with a stony gaze. 'I wished to put the idea to you, yes.'

'And you do not believe I stay with you because I want to?' Because she did, she realised suddenly, anger melting into sorrow. She could not imagine life alone now—and it was not just that she loved Oakridge.

'Either way, it is better that you do not stay.'

'Please,' she managed. 'You know I did not leave with Denham of my own accord, I—'

'I know,' he said quietly. 'But…quite honestly, I would rather you were no longer under my roof.' He turned and headed for the door. Lily followed, reaching out a hand to grab his arm.

'No—Daniel—do not just send me away without at least telling me the true reason why!'

He stopped, gaze focused resolutely above her head. 'Let go of me.'

'Not until you *tell me*.'

At last his eyes fixed upon her, and she saw with a jolt the unrest that went far back into their stormy depths. 'I am sending you away,' he said tightly, 'because I am finding it increasingly difficult to keep my hands off you.'

Lily stared at him, speechless. It was the last thing in the world she had expected him to say—and it seemed to have taken him by surprise also.

'Forgive me,' he murmured, voice laced with longing as he looked at her. 'I should never have said that.'

Lily, unable to speak, could do nothing but look back at him, her lips parting as if under the command of his will as the moment of exquisite, breathless yearning stretched between them.

Then something in his face changed, giving her just enough warning so that when he lowered his head to hers she did not flinch.

The nature of his kiss was no softer this time than the other, so many years ago now, it seemed; he drew her to him with both his hands at her waist, her head tipping back to allow her lips to meet his more fully. Her eyes closed as her senses came alive: the scent of him surrounding her, the trace of whisky on his lips, the roughness of his cheek against her questing hand; the way his kiss grew deeper as he felt her response, a reaction from so deep inside her rapidly melting core that she could not control it, even had she wanted to.

Their mouths moved effortlessly, exploring, tasting, sharing fears and longings that neither knew how to voice. Lily thought she might faint from the desire pulling from deep within, so strong was it, so wantonly wonderful. She hooked one hand about the base of his neck, desperate for him to remain kissing her for just a little longer, so when she woke up tomorrow and realised that this was all a dream, she would have something to remember, something to—

The door behind them opened.

'Lord Westhaven?'

Lily sprang back, one hand to her mouth, to find John standing there, evidently mortified, his eyes averted. 'Do forgive me, sir. I did knock…'

'What is it, John?'

Daniel's voice seemed deeper than usual, it seemed to Lily. Blushing scarlet at being caught in his embrace, she dropped her eyes and made a half-hearted pretence of smoothing her skirts.

'I just wished to inform you…Captain O'Flaherty is staying another night.'

'Good. Please see he has all he needs.' His voice was completely calm, as if he had been doing nothing more extraordinary than taking a midnight stroll.

'Of course.'

'Thank you, John.'

John bowed, eyes still firmly on the floor, where they had been during this entire exchange. 'Good night, sir.' He disappeared soundlessly, clearly eager to be away.

'Poor John,' Lily whispered shakily.

Daniel said nothing, his hand resting lightly in the hollow of her collarbone, fingers playing with a curl of golden hair that had escaped its confines. But his eyes, when they met hers, held such wistful sorrow that for a moment she forgot about how intensely she longed for him to kiss her again.

'Daniel…' she said softly, 'is this so impossible?'

Again his lips sought hers, but this time gently, in a kiss so fleetingly gossamer soft that it sent a rush of dizzying sensation straight to her brain. Then, slowly, as if saying goodbye, he tucked the wayward curl behind her ear.

'I think,' he said, voice like black velvet, stirring her insides even as his fingers brushed her cheek, 'that it would be best for both of us if you went to Ireland.'

Then he released her hand and strode away, leaving her with his kiss still burning the tender flesh of her lips and her insides hollowed out.

And Lily, speechless, could do nothing but watch him go.

Chapter Fifteen

Lying in her bed in the early hours of the morning, sleep evading her as it had all night, Lily clasped her cold hands on her stomach and tried not to think about Daniel seeing her off as she boarded a ship to Ireland.

She could not leave him, not now. Why had he survived that horrible war as so many had not—as her own brother had not—if it was only to waste his life as he was doing, shut away with his own bitterness, rejecting all offers of friendship as he had rejected hers?

She sat up, long braid falling over her shoulder. Perhaps she should have told him how she felt when she had the chance. But what good would that do? He would think her foolish, a green girl. He would not feel the same for her.

She thought of the necklace Denham had stolen—the jewels that had shattered her illusions—all sparkling sophistication, taunting her with everything she was not. No doubt it was hanging about the shapely neck of Daniel's mistress this very moment, a testament to what he looked for in a woman. Everything Lily could not offer. Everything that was not associated with duty—and a promise kept but bitterly regretted.

It was too late now, at any rate, she told herself, falling back. She had not told him—she probably never would. As soon as he could procure her passage on a ship she would be heading away over the sea—and he would be back in the arms of his mistress.

Lily knew it was foolish to dwell on this other woman that she had never met. But ever since Charlie had told her of the existence of Daniel's mystery companion, her mind had returned to the subject again and again.

She must try to sleep, she told herself.

She must resign herself to the way things were.

Daniel stood on the terrace dressed only in his shirtsleeves, the cool morning air swirling about him. The taste of Lily was still on his lips— he had not slept last night for the dull ache of desire that throbbed through every muscle in his body.

God knows what she thought, after he had accused her of staying only for duty and then kissed her because he could not do otherwise. She had looked, in the aftermath of their passion, as confused as he felt.

And, God help him, she had kissed him back.

Daniel's hands clenched into fists where they lay on the stone.

The things she had said…no one had spoken to him that way in a long time. She had chastised him as one would a wayward child— *maudlin*, was that not the term she had used? He did not expect her to understand; but she had dismissed his worries as though they were foolish—as though he was being ridiculous.

His frown deepened. Her offence at being told she remained out of duty had been genuine, he would stake his life on it. Perhaps she truly had come to feel at home here—had come to *be fond* of him, as Connor had so memorably put it. The knowledge eased his mind but little—fondness would never be enough to fill the yawning ache within whenever he thought of her, no matter how well she thought she understood his plight. And if he judged himself too harshly, it was because there was no one else to judge—there had not been since he had returned from America.

Except John, of course.

The old man had always been there, had seen the twisting, bitter change that Daniel had felt all too keenly, but been powerless to prevent. But in speaking merely for herself, Lily had been wrong about the old man. No matter what she said, Daniel knew there was at least one other person under this roof comparing Kit Westhaven to his son and finding much lacking.

He exhaled forcefully, mind churning with the guilt of years and this other, new uncertainty.

He would see if Connor was awake. He needed to ride out—to get some exercise, to work off this frustration. He wanted to shoot something.

Anything to take his mind off her until she was safely away.

Until he was alone again with nothing to tempt him into dreaming of a life he could not have.

The house was quiet when Lily awoke. Once Jo had dressed her she went down the stairs, softly, as though treading any harder would disturb the silence that hung heavily over the house.

The dining room was deserted, one place only laid out for breakfast.

John appeared in the doorway as Lily sat down, with his usual ready smile for her as she bid him good morning. It was, she thought with a flicker of amusement, as though he had seen nothing amiss last night.

'What shall I have Cook prepare for you, Miss Lily?' he asked.

Lily swallowed. The thought of food did nothing for her—it would take more than Cook's excellent eggs to fill the emptiness inside today. She shook her head. 'Just some tea.'

He inclined his head, but it was clear that he did not approve of her decision.

Lily looked about her at the silent room. 'Where is the Major?'

'He has taken the Captain out shooting,' said John, placing a cup of tea before her. 'They left early—they should be back shortly.'

Even as he spoke, hoofbeats and then voices became audible through the open window, Daniel's deep tones as unmistakable as Connor's gentle lilt—and much more unsettling to Lily's already churning stomach.

Rising, she threw a smile at John and went outside, where, leaning on one of the large stone acorns that topped the great balustrade, she watched them approach, laughter on their faces.

Daniel reached her first, drawing up his horse alongside the terrace where she stood so they were almost on a level.

'You are up early, Miss Pevensey,' he said, lightly enough, but the warmth in his eyes had died as soon as they lit on her face. There was no sign of merriment now.

'I couldn't sleep,' she managed, holding his gaze.

Connor grinned at her, though she was sure he could not be as oblivious to the tension as he pretended. 'Making sure we're both back in one piece? Which is more'n you can say for these poor beasts.' He held up a brace of pheasant. 'Never had a chance.'

'Only two?' Lily asked, smiling at him.

Connor shrugged. 'The Major's been out of the army for too long. His aim's not what it once was.'

'Well, they'll do well enough,' Lily said, avoiding Daniel's eye. 'Come inside. I'll get the kitchen to work making breakfast.'

She looked tired, Daniel thought, sitting very upright on his horse and watching as his ward took the pheasants from Connor and tried to pretend that nothing was wrong—drawn, as if she had been weeping.

Yet still, all he had thought, as he reined in before her like a knight errant returning to his lady from some far-flung battle, was how very beautiful she was. The sunlight on her honey-blonde hair picked out highlights that shone like gold, and though her marvellous green eyes were dulled with hurt...there had been something else there when she looked at him, but briefly. Something he had seen there before, and tried to ignore. Something he could not name for fear of finding an answering emotion nestling within his own breast.

She was his ward. She was not for him.

He threw his right leg over the back of his horse to dismount and slid to the ground—but even before his feet hit the gravel he knew something was wrong.

Daniel froze, all thoughts of Lily chased from his mind. He had felt something give, one of the straps that encircled his left thigh. Had a buckle broken? Had the leather snapped? His weight still felt fairly secure. Perhaps he could risk it…

He took a couple of paces towards the steps that led up to the front door of his home—and there was a definite extra movement, pushing him off balance, making him unsteady. He stopped, brows drawing together.

'Daniel?' Lily was looking at him. 'Are you all right?'

He looked up at her and nodded. 'Mmm.'

'Are you coming?'

'You go on ahead,' he told her. 'Make sure my eggs are as I like them.'

She looked a little confused, but seemed to accept this. 'Very well.'

Connor came to his side as she turned to go back inside. 'What is it?'

Daniel shook his head. 'I don't know. It's loose somehow. This has never happened before.'

'Do you want to take my arm?'

He shook his head. 'I'll be fine. Just…go in and distract her a while. I need to go upstairs and re-attach it.'

Connor nodded and headed off up the steps.

Daniel, bracing himself for unsteadiness, lifted his prosthetic leg first, and managed the first step. But as he stepped with the other leg, transferring his weight, lifting his wooden foot off the ground, he felt his flesh come loose from the cup, lost his balance and found himself pitching forward.

Then several things seemed to happen all at once.

His knees hit the edge of the stone step hard, his hands coming out to break his fall even as Lily appeared again at the top, saying something about eggs. Her expression changed immediately to one of horrified concern. Connor was behind her, with John at his heels—and they both followed her down.

'Daniel!'

Weeks of calling him Major, he thought wryly, eyes closed, and now she had started calling him Daniel she could not stop. Even here, in this most humiliating of all situations, he loved the way his name sounded on her lips.

She was at his side now, in a swirl of skirts, trying to look into his face. 'What is wrong? Were you hurt while shooting?'

'I'm fine,' he told her gruffly, conscious of the odd angle his left leg was at, not wanting to move in case he made it worse—praying only that she did not notice. 'Go into the house, Lily.'

'What?' Confusion stood out in her green eyes. 'Why?'

'Just, please, do as I say.'

'I don't understand…' There was more than a little anxiety in her voice now.

'Connor!' Desperately, he looked up as his friend and his butler joined their pathetic huddle at the base of his family home. 'John!'

'Miss Lily.' John's hands were on her shoulders. 'Why not come inside? Connor will see to his lordship.'

She looked thoroughly baffled now, and not a little frightened. 'What is going on? Daniel—are you ill?'

'Lily—for pity's sake, *go into the house*!' Shame made him harsh, lent a cruel note to his voice.

She sat back, shocked into silence. Her eyes were huge and hurt, as though he had struck her. He made himself face her down, scowling until, very quietly, she said, 'Very well.'

With immense dignity she rose, back straight, and swept up the stairs.

'Connor,' snarled Daniel, turning to his friend, 'which part of "distract her" did you find hard to understand?'

'Apparently you've never tried distracting her!' Shaking his head, the Irishman took him by the arm. 'Come, let's get you upstairs.'

'I will make sure the lady is not too upset, my lord,' John said softly.

Daniel wanted to protest, wanted to go himself—but he knew it was for the best, so he merely nodded. He felt drained, as if he had lived a whole day in these last few minutes, and every moment of it had been full of degradation. 'Thank you.'

Lily, ordered back inside like a naughty child who was not old enough to understand, slammed the door of the dining room behind her and flung herself into a chair.

He *was* hurt, that much was obvious. He had received some new wound, or opened an old one—and he had gone to great pains to conceal it from her, as if it did not concern her! Just as last time she was pushed out—when he had apologised before, and she had been so certain they were building bridges…

She put her elbows on the polished dining table and her head in her hands, trying to force down the nagging worry for him that pushed at her from all sides. If he would not allow her to be concerned, then she would not be!

But it was one thing to wish for and quite another to feel…

'Miss Lily?'

She looked up into John's kind brown eyes. So deep in thought had she been that she had not even realised he had entered the room.

'John.' She took a deep breath. 'Is he hurt?'

'Just a little unsteady. He will be fine in a minute.'

'I don't understand!' she wailed, pressing her forehead to the cool mahogany of the table. '*Why* will he not let me help him?'

He sat in the chair beside her. 'Because he does not know how to.'

'What do you mean?' That brought her head up.

'No one has been close to him for some time, Miss Lily. You must give him a chance to trust you.'

'Last night… He said I am only here because I have to be. Because I am bound by law to him.'

'It is easier for him to think that.'

'He said the same of you—he credits neither of us with the wit to choose!'

'Did he, indeed?' John was silent for a time, a small smile playing about his lips, eyes distant.

Lily shook her head plaintively. 'How can I understand what he is going through if he will not tell me even the simplest things? I have no idea what happened outside.'

'He will tell you, if you allow him time. Be patient.'

'Sometimes I wonder if he wants me here at all. I was sure that he did, even after how we began. But now…I don't know any more.' Lips trembling, she pushed her hair out of her face.

'What is it?' he said, so gently that, for an aching moment, she missed her parents so acutely she could almost taste the loss.

Lily sighed. 'I'm in love with him.'

The confession slipped unaided from her lips, and the pain of saying the words aloud, words she had never even admitted to herself, was so exquisite that she closed her eyes. 'What am I going to do, John?'

John put a hand over hers. 'I think you are exactly what he requires, Miss Lily. And you need not do anything at all.'

But tears were running down her cheeks now, for she knew he only meant to make her feel better. 'How can you say that?'

He shrugged lightly. 'I held him when he was a baby. I know him now he is a man.'

She gave him a watery smile. 'I wish I had your confidence.'

He patted her hand, then stood with a creaking of his knees. 'I have enough for both of us. Now come, let us get you your breakfast.'

The leg did not take much fixing. A strap had given where it was attached to a buckle—the strain of the past few days' wear showing. Daniel, accustomed to repairing his own clothes in the army, had soon made sure it would be secure in the future.

Connor had left him to it—and from his friend's face it was obvious he thought Daniel had reacted badly.

But what else had there been to do? More than anything he had ever experienced in his life, he hated the feeling of helplessness and shame when Lily saw him as she had seen him today. He would rather never see her again than have to bear that look in her eyes.

Sitting by his window, his leg re-attached, he wondered what to do now. Facing her again today was the last thing he felt like doing. She would want to know what had happened, would ask all her questions with that look on her face that he so despised.

He was supposed to protect her.

He had let his guard down last night. He should never have touched her so, as though he was free to do so and she was just any woman.

She was not for him—how many times must he tell himself that before it filtered into his brain?

Sighing, he rang for John.

It took the butler some minutes to reach him, and when he did so he was noticeably out of breath. 'My lord?'

Daniel frowned at him from his seat in the window, momentarily forgetting why it was he had called. 'Have you never considered retiring, John?'

The old man looked confused. 'Is this why you have summoned me?'

Daniel shook his head. 'I would like a bath, please. And tell Lily I will be indisposed for the remainder of the day. Tell her I am resting…or…' He shrugged. 'Think of something to tell her.'

John nodded. 'Is that all?'

'No.' Daniel rose, steadying himself on the wall, Lily's words from the previous evening surrounding him. 'You have served my family your whole life, but you need feel no compunction to carry on doing so.'

For a moment, hurt flickered on the butler's face. 'If you feel I can no longer perform my duties…if you would rather employ a younger staff—'

'I am not trying to rid myself of you, old man,' his master assured him brusquely. 'I am merely saying you will continue to receive your salary and have a place here for the rest of your days—whether you fulfil your duties as butler or…simply sit by the fire all day. Do you understand?'

There was a pause. Then the old man nodded. 'Thank you. But I cannot have many days left to me, and I would prefer to spend them as I always have.'

It was exactly what Daniel had known he would say. 'I just wished you to know you do not have to work for me.' He looked away briefly. 'I know your loyalty was to my father.'

Deep within the weatherbeaten face, brown eyes regarded him seriously. 'My loyalty is to you, Lord Westhaven.'

Daniel frowned. 'To…me?'

John nodded with great dignity. 'I loved your father—he was my greatest friend. But I do not serve you merely because you are his son. I am not here because I have to be, any more than Miss Lily is.'

Daniel closed his eyes. 'She had no right to tell you what I said to her.'

'She thought I should know what was in your mind.' A somewhat mischievous smile passed across John's lips—a gesture so reminiscent of his father that Daniel felt his chest tighten. 'But Kit allowed very generously for me in his will, Daniel. I have never worked here because I had to. I thought you knew that.'

His master maintained eye contact with difficulty. 'Thank you,' he managed, moved by such candour. 'I had no idea.' He paused for a moment, remembering the period after his return, while he was learning to walk and after, when there had been no one to vent his anger on but the man before him. The man who had picked up his crutches, brought his meals—he had stayed specifically so he would not be alone, it suddenly appeared. 'I have behaved badly, and often, since my return from America. Forgive me, John.'

'Things have changed,' said the older man. 'You are no longer the man you were when you returned from the war.'

'I hope you are right.' Daniel remembered the constant, blinding anger that had stalked him every day. At losing his leg and his future in the army he loved—at losing his father.

'I will see to your bath.'

'Thank you.' Daniel sank back into his seat as the butler turned away. 'Lord Westhaven?'

He looked up. 'Yes?'

'If you tell her the truth, there is a chance she will leave, of course. But if you do not, it is a certainty.'

Daniel looked down at his leg. 'I know. Yet…it is better if she leaves.'

'Better for whom?'

'For her, of course. She deserves more.'

John pursed his lips. 'And you? You do not deserve happiness?'

'There are more important things,' was all he said, very quietly.

'Besides,' he added, frowning. 'She is my ward, that is all. I do not feel anything more.'

His butler inclined his head, blank faced but, Daniel knew, unconvinced by such an obvious lie. 'I will see to your bath,' he said again.

When he was gone, Daniel ran a hand through his hair, tired of the thoughts that battered him from all sides.

John was right—she would leave if he continued to shut her out. But it *was* for the best. She did not need a cripple for a husband. She did deserve more—and he was determined to ensure she would get it.

Chapter Sixteen

'Daniel?' Outside his door, Lily steeled herself and knocked again.

There was no answer, but she thought she could hear movement within, footsteps. She called his name again, knocked once more.

She had come to a decision, following her talk with John, and it was this: if Daniel would not trust her to know his past, then she could not stay, hoping foolishly for something to happen between them. He was not ready to let another close to him. She would live wherever he was not, therefore, until she thought of a more permanent alternative. This very afternoon, she planned to set out for Brook Street, leaving him here, at Oakridge—reclusive and solitary as he had been before they met. If he was determined that she should go to Ireland, then she would go—it would be better, perhaps, if she did not have to see him always. But until then she wished to be as far away as possible.

She had her own heart to protect now.

Teeth gritted, she knocked one more time, harder than necessary, needing to say what she had to say so she could put some distance between herself and his ever-changing moods.

'My *lord*!'

Finally, after another pause, the door opened and he stood before her.

Lily's eyes opened wide at the sight of him, clad in only his boots and breeches. Bare chested, hair ruffled, he looked every inch the rough-mannered soldier she had always suspected him to be, underneath it all.

The lines of his torso were firmly sculpted, muscles beautifully defined and with a criss-crossing of scars, some tiny, some significantly larger. It was a body honed in combat, unmistakably—and he had not, it seemed, allowed himself to get out of condition since leaving the army.

'What is it?' he asked. 'I'm about to have a bath.'

Lily swallowed and tipped her gaze away from the smooth skin of his chest. 'I'm leaving,' she said succinctly. 'You don't have to wait until I'm in Ireland to be rid of me. I'm going back to town now.'

He looked at her for a moment, jaw tight. Then he nodded. 'Fine.'

Lily, about to launch into the speech she had prepared, found his door swinging shut in her face.

'Wait!'

He paused, opened the door once more. 'What is it, Liliana?'

'I…just…thought I should tell you, as you seem to wish to know my movements.'

'Thank you.'

She paused, brows drawing together. 'You do not wish to know why?'

He shook his head. 'It is for the best. You do not want to miss the rest of the Season. The social life in Ireland is somewhat limited, you should—'

'I don't care about the Season,' she told him flatly.

'I see.' He looked exhausted, suddenly.

'I cannot live here,' she told him calmly, as she had rehearsed in her mind all day. 'Not even for another few days. Everyone seems to know something I do not. I am tired of being kept from the truth.'

'What is it you want, Liliana?' His voice was emotionless.

She gritted her teeth. 'I want to know what John means when he says few lost what you did in the war. Why Connor says you saved his life at your own expense. Why, when you fall, I am not allowed to help you up…and *what* your father would have coped with better than you think you have.' She stopped, shrugging helplessly. 'I wish you thought enough of me to trust me.'

'You imagine you know what I think of you?'

She almost laughed. 'I have absolutely no idea! Sometimes I think you feel only a sense of duty towards me…but…' She paused for a moment. 'You kiss me as if duty is the furthest thing from your mind.'

'Liliana…' He looked away.

Irritation flared, despite her resolve. 'Must I not speak of you kissing me?'

'What good is such talk?'

'Because I can no longer pretend there is nothing between us,' she said vehemently. 'You have not been honest with me, Daniel! You make me doubt myself!'

'*I* make *you* doubt yourself?' He turned away, into his room, though he left the door open now. 'Dear God, I should have married you to Denham when I had the chance.'

'How can you say such a thing? I never cared anything for Charles Denham!' she cried to his retreating back. 'I love *you*!'

He froze.

Lily, throwing both hands up to her cheeks, bit down hard on her lower lip. What had possessed her to say it? She knew he did not return the sentiment—it would ruin their fledgling friendship for ever. What had she been thinking?

Very softly, back still to her like a wall of iron, he said, 'You don't know what you're saying.'

'What?' Stung out of her doubt, she marched over the threshold and up to him. 'How dare you tell me I don't know what I'm saying! Do you not trust me to know my own mind?'

He turned, very slowly. 'More than any woman I have ever known.'

'Then how can you presume to say—?'

He held up a hand, abruptly silencing her. 'What do you know of my injuries?' he asked bitterly.

'Nothing!' she cried, voice cracking. 'Except that I do not care about them!'

'Then you do not know what you are talking about.'

'That is unfair!' Lily protested as he turned to leave. 'I know nothing because you will tell me nothing!'

'It is for your own good.'

'I am not a child,' she protested. 'Daniel, please—what do you think will happen if you show me?'

He did not reply. But in his eyes, the colour of the sea, she saw such a look of haunted grief that she knew, suddenly, why he had never wished to speak of his injuries.

'You think I will be disgusted?' she asked softly. 'You think I will pity you?'

'Lily…' He turned his face away.

'Do you not know me better?' He did not move. 'Please,' she implored him, 'trust me! We cannot live like this!'

'*We* cannot?' Slowly, he looked at her, and now there was anger in the hard lines of his face. 'What do you know of how I have lived this past year?'

Lily flushed. 'I did not mean to imply…'

'You truly want to see my wounds?'

'Do not make it sound as if I have paid a penny at the carnival,' she protested. 'I just want to know—'

Eyes blazing, he silenced her with a gesture. 'No. Enough.' He crossed the room and shut his bedroom door so hard it startled her. 'If you wish to see then, by God, you shall. Come.' Taking her by the arm, he propelled her across the room and shoved her down into a chair. 'Sit. I would not want you to miss anything.'

'But—' She tried to rise and found herself pushed firmly back down.

'Sit, Liliana. Enjoy the show.'

'No—not like this!'

'Then how? Would you like to invite some friends?'

Tears sprang to Lily's eyes. 'Why are you being so cruel?'

'I am being honest.' He sat in the chair opposite her and started to roll up the left leg of his breeches, just as he had been the night she had walked in on him at the inn. 'That is what you wanted, is it not? Honesty?'

There were straps and buckles about his upper leg. Lily frowned, confused, distracted into silence and stillness as he began to undo them.

'And then,' he was saying, fingers working the buckles, 'you can tell me *honestly* how you feel about professing to love a man like me. Does that not sound appealing?'

'Daniel...'

She trailed off, however, for he was unfurling leather flaps from around his thigh. She could see the flesh beneath now, the long scar that ran along his thigh, intersected by smaller lines and pockmarks.

He looked at her one more time, dark hair falling over his forehead, that unfamiliar hostility carving deep lines around his mouth. 'Ready?'

Then he took his left calf in strong fingers, tugged lightly—and his entire lower leg, boot and all, came away in his hand.

Lily heard herself gasp. Her fingers bit into the arms of her chair and she was immediately grateful that she was sitting down, for the shock would surely have felled her.

He dropped what she now realised was a false leg with a thud, and pulled himself upright. Braced against the chair, he stood looking down at her with a fury born of anguish in his eyes.

'Are you satisfied now?'

She stared at the malformed, uneven stump below his knee, covered in angry, ugly, shiny red scar tissue, and tears came to her eyes. No wonder he had not wanted her to see... She could only imagine how painful it had been to lose his leg, in every sense of the word. She could not believe he had picked himself up and learned to walk again.

Love welled anew in her, and pride, for this man who had borne such a burden and borne it alone.

It was horrible to behold, he was right—she could not imagine how he had felt the first time he had seen himself, and her heart ached with sympathy. But at the same time it was a badge of honour, of bravery and survival beyond the ordinary. Lily wanted to stroke the shattered flesh, to soothe the aches that must lie beneath such tightly stretched skin, to kiss away the horror of the memories that went with it.

She realised that tears were running down her face, and that he was no longer angry. He stood, head bowed, eyes covered with the hand that was not holding him up, exposed and exquisitely vulnerable.

He said, 'I think I would like you to leave now.'

Shakily, she rose to her feet.

She went to him, took his large hand in both her own, and pulled it away from his face so she could see the moisture in his eyes.

Then, raising herself up on the tips of her toes, she raised her mouth to his, like a rosebud unfurled in sweet offering.

He did not move at once—just held himself very still, as if deciding whether to cast her off and flee. She did not give him the chance. Locking her arms about his neck, she pulled his head down to her. Their lips met with a jolt, her body pressed to his, both supporting him and letting him hold her up. She kissed him as she had wanted to a hundred times over the past month or so, firmly, passionately, as unlike a lady as she knew how to be, her mouth seeking his, coaxing a response, telling him all that she felt and soothing the pain he had faced, yet again, in showing her this most private part of himself.

And then his arm wound around her waist and he pulled her body close into his, so close there was almost no room to breathe. He kissed her back fiercely, his mouth unyielding, as if testing her strength.

She did not fail him. She matched his kiss, pressed hard up against him, his bare flesh against her chest, her fingers splayed across his warm, broad back. For a moment there was nothing in the world but this sensation, her teeth nipping at his lips, his tongue exploring her mouth, her mind melting slowly into pure ripples of pleasure that spread throughout her body, until her skin tingled all over.

Then, just as she was sure she was about to faint with ecstasy, he pulled away with a guttural groan and stood, breathing hard, looking down at her.

'Tell me I feel sorry for you,' she said, before he could speak. He said nothing, eyes drawn to her mouth, tender from his kisses. 'You cannot,' she said triumphantly, 'because you know it would be a lie. You know what I feel for you, and you know I do not care about anything else.'

'Lily…' There was an old pain in his face now when he looked at her. 'I am half a man…'

'Do you truly believe that?' she protested, incredulous. 'You are more of a man than any I have ever met!'

'Yet this is as fit as I will ever be. My leg will not improve—I will never change.'

'Yes, you will,' she said with conviction, for change was the one thing that she did know.

He sighed. 'Lily…'

'You will change, Daniel,' she insisted. 'You will grow old, and stiff—your hair will fall out, and perhaps you will get fat. And I will still love you.'

He was motionless, just watching her. 'You will still…?'

'Love you,' she said again. 'See? You grow deaf already.'

But he did not smile. 'Don't play with me, Lily. Don't say such a thing to me again unless you are sure.'

'And I,' she continued as if he had not spoken, 'I will lose what looks I have, and probably my teeth, and I will have to wear a truss. But you will still love me.'

He said nothing to this, just let go of the chair that held him up, took her by the chin with both hands and kissed her again, body perfectly balanced against hers.

This time there was no interruption. He kissed her until she could not breathe, his fingers loosening her hair so that it fell down about her shoulders, and then he moved his lips slowly down her neck, his face in her hair, his hands unlacing the back of her gown.

'Come.' He took a walking stick that leaned against the wall and captured her hand with the other. Slowly, because she seemed to be suddenly unable to move very far without seeking his lips once more, they moved to where his large bed awaited them, Daniel drawing her down beside him, her gown half-undone, golden ringlets falling about her flushed face. She pulled him towards her, kissing the line of his jaw, her fingers deep in his dark, luxurious hair, holding him captive.

'My hair is not going to fall out,' he muttered, eyes closed. 'My father had a full head of hair until the day he died.'

She smiled, mouth seeking his once more. 'We shall see.'

He helped her shed her dress, kneeling on the bed, her back to him. She dropped her head back against his shoulder as he removed the outer garments, leaving only her petticoats and her stays, confining breasts that seemed suddenly exquisitely tender under his touch, even through the fine-boned fabric that covered them.

He kicked off his remaining boot and, naked but for his breeches, pulled her down on top of him. She could feel him, hard and insistent, through the layers of cloth between them, and the answering sensation, a velvety throbbing deep within, made her feel light-headed.

His long fingers were at her waist now, plucking at the laces of her petticoat. When it was undone she wriggled out of it and into his waiting arms, his lips now on the upper curves of her breasts, shaped and uplifted by whalebone. He inserted one finger down the front of her stays, teasing her nipples into hard peaks that chafed against their confinement, even as her gasp in his ear begged for release. He unlaced her once more, flung the stays across the room, and turned back to behold her upon his bed, naked apart from her stockings.

'Lily,' he whispered softly, hands and eyes everywhere, caressing the rounded undersides of her breasts, skimming her hips and the gentle curve of her belly.

'What is it?' she asked as his lips followed the trail his fingers made, but he did not reply and she did not care—could not think—for the tongues of flame that licked at her all over. Her back arched of its own accord when his tongue, too gentle, circled each of her nipples in turn. Aching with frustrated pleasure, she grabbed a handful of his hair, only to cry out as he drew the tender nubs of flesh between his teeth, one by one, sending silvery shards of pure joy in all directions within her.

He was on top of her now, braced on his knees and one elbow so as not to crush her, the other arm pulling her bodily off the mattress into a deep, deep kiss.

Lily pushed at him with what strength she had left, and he raised his head.

'Are you all right?'

She nodded, wondering at the smoky blue of his eyes, the way his pupils were so wide she could see herself in their dark depths. 'I was…just wondering why I am the only one…who is naked…'

His laugh was deep, reverberating through her skin, serving only to further awaken her. 'That can be remedied.'

Then, rolling off her, he removed his breeches and unmentionables in one swift movement—and she became immediately distracted by the body laid out before her.

He was magnificent without his clothes, firmly sculpted, his thighs muscular, his waist smooth, defined by ridges of muscle that led to his flat stomach. He was hard in all the places she was soft, but the skin covering his torso was warm to the touch. And the place between his legs...the place he was hardest of all... Lily stared at it in fascination. She had never seen such a thing; the statues in museums looked nothing like this. Carefully, knowing he was watching her, she ran a finger along it, enjoying the hissed gasp of air that he drew in between his teeth, the way his breathing altered.

'It hurts?'

His eyes twinkled. 'No. It doesn't hurt. I will show you how to—'

'In a moment,' she told him, exploring his chest with her hands the way he had hers, then going lower, as he reclined like a marble masterpiece, eyes never leaving her face. As soon as her fingers touched the scars of his left thigh, however, he pushed himself up on his elbows.

'Lily, don't.'

Her eyes met his. 'Why?'

'I don't want you... You shouldn't have to look at it.' The pain was back in his voice.

She frowned, ever so slightly, to tell him what she thought of this. Then she lowered her lips to the puckered flesh, exploring the smooth scar tissue and the strange shapes it made, about that long central gash.

'Lily...' His protest lasted only a moment, before his elbows gave way.

She went lower, past his knee, tracing the patterns that led down to the abrupt end of his leg, kissing the place where metal gunshot had twisted him, where the surgeons had worked. All she could hear was his breathing, ragged and shallow, and, when she looked to check that he was not upset, she found him lying back, eyes closed, the oddest expression on his face, a mix of pleasure and confusion, as though he was enjoying her touch, but not sure that he should be.

She smiled. Then, starting at the toes of his whole right leg, she kissed him all the way up to his thigh, finding little scars all the way, moulded into the firm flesh, allowing her hair to trail behind her, tickling his warm skin.

He was even harder now.

Creeping past, she laid a gentle kiss on his mouth. His eyes opened, hazy with desire. Then he pulled her to him, crushing his lips against hers once more, taking her hand even as he kissed her and moving it downwards, curling it about the rigid length of him, showing her how to touch him even as she broke the kiss to watch the effects of her efforts on his face.

'Enough,' he murmured, pulling her hand away. 'I cannot take much more.'

Rolling over, covering her body with his, he kissed the fire within her back into raging life, until she was making small gasps against his lips, her most secret places throbbing with anticipation, every part of her body tender to the touch.

'You are ready,' he whispered, breath fanning her ear, holding her tight to him. She nodded desperately, although she did not quite know what it was that she was ready for. His thigh was between her legs now, nudging them apart, his fingers following swiftly, caressing her where none but she had ever laid a hand, stoking her to ever greater heights of ecstasy.

'Oh, Daniel,' she whispered into his neck, damp with perspiration, the heightened scent of him surrounding her like a heady drug. 'Please…'

At her urging, he guided himself into her, gently at first, so that her eyes opened wide with surprise and—just for a moment—a sharp pain that was swept away by the sweetest, newest feeling as she surrounded him, arching against him, drawing him deeper inside. After a moment in which they simply enjoyed the closeness of this coupling, he began to move, slowly at first, with ever-deepening strokes. She did not miss the way his breathing hitched every time she moved her lower body against him, the deep moan that he uttered when she tried this a little harder, a little faster.

Moving together, rhythmic and breathless, they clung to each other, his face in her hair, her head back against the bed, lost together in a desire that built, gradually, until Lily did not know how her pounding heart would take it.

Eyes squeezed closed, she curled her fingers into his broad back and hung on for dear life as her insides began to contract, sending fast, hard waves of pleasure through her body and limbs, building ever more until—without warning—something deep within her exploded, shattering her senses, a convulsive release that made her cry out, stars forming behind her eyelids. Even as she heard her own voice, above her Daniel gave a guttural sigh, body tensing in a shuddering, forceful climax of his own.

Bodies fused, they soared and fell, deep down into a silken blackness that reached out and enveloped them both, together as one.

Much later, the evening sun slanted its rays in through Daniel's window and found them lying together in his huge bed, limbs entwined, Lily's head on his chest. Both of them were half-asleep, reclining in the warmth of the evening and each other.

'After they took my leg, I almost died from fever,' he said softly, fingers in her hair. 'I used to see your face, in my dreams—sometimes before my very eyes.'

Lily turned her head so that her lips brushed the warm skin beneath her cheek. 'You should have come to me sooner,' she told him.

He sighed. 'When I returned from the war I had resigned myself to forgetting my promise. I did not think I was capable of safeguarding another when I was barely able to care for myself.'

'What changed your mind?'

He smiled wryly. 'John. He kept putting your brother's letter where I could see it. Very subtle, but it was enough. I realised I could not go back on my word. So, as I learned to walk, I gathered news of you. I started to send money when I realised it was needed. Eventually I could ignore my responsibilities no longer.' He smiled enigmatically. 'Plus I wanted to see you in the flesh.'

'You would have kept your word, even without John,' she told him.

'You sound so sure.'

'I am.' She lifted her head off his chest and looked at him earnestly. 'And Robbie knew that when he asked you to take care of me.' She smiled suddenly, tracing the lines of his chest with a fingertip: the silver tracks of scars and the firm ridges of muscle. 'Do you think he meant for this to happen? He knew you as well as he knew me. Surely he would have known we would meet and...'

'Despise each other on sight?' he supplied.

She grinned. 'Not exactly what I was going to say.'

'I think he has been somewhere laughing at us all along,' he told her softly.

'And congratulating himself, also,' Lily added. 'Watching you foil Denham, he must have known he had chosen wisely.'

Daniel snorted. 'I have faced far worthier adversaries in my time. However, that reminds me...' Leaning across her supine body, he reached into a drawer in the mahogany table that stood by his bed, and pulled something out that caught and held the light as it moved. 'I think it's about time this found its proper home,' he said softly, lowering it, link by link, into her hands.

Lily looked in confusion at the thing sparkling between her palms. The necklace. 'It is real, then?'

He nodded. 'Not paste, as our fanciful friend would have it. Emeralds. And diamonds. Yours.'

She sat up, covering herself with a hastily gathered sheet, brows drawing together, the thing she had put out of her mind so successfully until now returning in a rush. 'I do not want a second-hand present, sir,' she said coolly. 'No matter how beautiful, or costly. I insist that you give it to the lady for whom it was bought.'

He raised himself up on his elbows, face impassive. 'And whom, may I ask, do you imagine it was bought for?'

'I do not need to imagine, my lord.' She felt herself flushing even at discussing such a topic. 'I know this is a present for your mistress.'

His eyebrows shot up. 'For my…?'

Scarlet now, she dropped her eyes, trying not to let him see how the knowledge upset her. This was something she would have to live with, after all, as all women must. 'Yes, I know you have a mistress. I am told all gentlemen do.'

'Are you, indeed?'

'Yes,' she whispered, starting to feel uncomfortably like she was being mocked. 'I am.'

'Liliana.' He tipped her chin up so that their eyes clashed. 'Do I look like I am interested in keeping a mistress?'

Almost immediately, she was lost in his gaze, swimming in a hazy sea of longing so that her lips parted, ever so slightly. 'I…'

'Who told you such a thing?'

'Lord Denham,' she murmured, wishing he would kiss her.

'Hmm.' His brows drew together, and his gaze abruptly went cold. 'If I never hear his name in my entire life again, it will be too soon.' He crossed his arms and scowled at her. 'So you are telling me that, although every other syllable the boy uttered to you was a damned lie, you believe this tale completely?'

'You…you do not have a mistress, then?' Hope sprang to life in Lily even as the image of the buxom, winsome brunette evaporated in a puff of jasmine-scented smoke.

'Not since my twenties.' He smiled wryly. 'These days I have too much trouble with one woman in my life, Liliana, to go and get myself another.'

'So…' She looked down at the necklace, glittering with truth and promise. 'You bought this for *me*?'

He nodded. 'I was going to give it to you on the night of the ball, but you seemed so attached to your brother's pearls… And it did not really seem an appropriate gift for a guardian to give his ward.'

'Yet you give it to me now?' she asked quizzically.

'Now I am a man, giving it to the woman I love,' he told her softly. 'There is nothing inappropriate about that.'

She stared at him, wondering if she was imagining what he had just said. 'To the woman you love?'

He nodded. 'That is you, before you invent some fictional lady to take your place.' He sighed. 'I have been lying to you, Lily. Every time I told you I saw you as just my ward I was trying to convince myself, but it has not worked for weeks. And now… Now that you have seen me as I am… I have not felt whole in a long time, but I feel it now. I knew I loved you before you kissed my scars—though, of course, I would not admit it—but that confirmed it.'

'I knew it—I knew you loved me,' she whispered, amazed. 'I knew there had to be a reason you kept kissing me.'

He gave a deep chuckle, the one that always reached down into the depths of her and plucked at her soul—and more. Then, while she was still recovering from the vibrating thrill it gave to her insides, he growled, 'I want you to marry me.'

'I should hope so, too,' she told him. 'First you teach me the waltz, and now this. You have thoroughly compromised my honour, my lord.'

'Was that an acceptance?'

She nodded, smile radiant. He pulled her to him and kissed her, then held her for a long moment, against his chest, his face in her hair.

'You understand,' he said at last, 'that my entire family will descend upon us as soon as they hear the news of a wedding? Sarah and Emma will be beside themselves to learn that their brother has finally per-suaded a woman to be his wife—and my youngest brother John is never so absorbed in his studies that he cannot come down to satisfy his curiosity.' He sighed dramatically. 'I dare say even Jamie will bring his enormous brood over from Ireland for the occasion.'

He could not conceal the affection in his voice, however, and the thought of his siblings and their children filling the rooms of Oakridge was not at all an unpleasant one for Lily.

'I think I would like to have a family again,' she said softly.

His face softened as he looked at her, and now there was no sign of the joking tone in his voice as he said, 'Then you shall. We shall invite them all, if you wish it, every last one of the Westhaven clan.

And then, God willing, we shall have our own, as many as we can manage.' A smile curved his lips. 'If I am to live up to my father's legacy I must have a whole litter of sons.' There was no bitterness in his tone now, Lily noticed, only affection. It seemed that, finally, he was stepping out of the shadows.

But she could not dwell on such serious thoughts for long, when he lay beside her in all his glory, watching her.

A wicked smile crossed her lips. 'Then we should begin straight away.'

'Indeed.' With an answering grin, he whipped the bedclothes away. 'And then I must beg an audience with your guardian to ask permission to marry you.'

'He is quite the ogre,' Lily warned. 'What do you think he will say?'

He shrugged, lips already on hers, offering himself now without shame, claiming her as his own after all this time. 'I think I can persuade him,' he said.

* * * * *

HISTORICAL

Novels coming in May 2010

THE EARL'S RUNAWAY BRIDE
Sarah Mallory

Five years ago, Felicity's dashing husband disappeared into war-torn Spain. Discovering a dark secret, she had fled to England. Still haunted by memories of their passionate wedding night, Felicity is just about to come face to face with her commanding husband – back to claim his runaway bride!

THE WAYWARD DEBUTANTE
Sarah Elliott

Eleanor Sinclair loathes stuffy ballrooms packed with fretful mothers and husband-hunting girls. Craving escape, she dons a wig and disappears – *unchaperoned!* – to the theatre. There she catches the eye of James Bentley, a handsome devil. His game of seduction imperils Eleanor's disguise – and tempts her to forsake all honour…

THE LAIRD'S CAPTIVE WIFE
Joanna Fulford

Taken prisoner by Norman invaders, Lady Ashlynn's salvation takes an unexpected form. Scottish warlord Black Iain may be fierce, yet Ashlynn feels strangely safe in his arms… Iain wants only to be free of the rebellious, enticing Ashlynn. But then a decree from the King commands Iain to make his beautiful captive his *wife*!

HISTORICAL

**Another exciting novel available
this month:**

PRACTICAL WIDOW TO PASSIONATE MISTRESS
Louise Allen

From servants' quarters to master's bedroom!

Stranded in France, and desperate to reunite with her sisters,
Meg finds passage to England with injured soldier Major Ross
Brandon. Dangerously irresistible, Ross's dark, searching eyes are
those of a man with the weight of the world on his shoulders…

It would be wrong to fall for Ross. But when he offers her
a job as his temporary housekeeper she can't refuse – and
soon sensible Meg is scandalously tempted to move from
servants' quarters to the master's bedroom!

**The Transformation of the Shelley Sisters
Three sisters, three escapades, three very different destinies!**

HISTORICAL

Another exciting novel available this month:

HER BANISHED LORD
Carol Townend

Claimed by the Norman Count

Hugh Duclair, Count de Freyncourt, has been accused of sedition, stripped of his title and banished from all of King William's land. Proud and determined, Hugh vows to clear his name!

Childhood friend Lady Aude de Crèvecoeur offers her help – but how far will she go? Should she risk her reputation and her life, or save her reputation and become Hugh's wife? Turbulent times call for passionate measures…

Wessex Weddings
Normans and Saxons, conflict and desire